SHAFTED

Devil's Blaze Motorcycle Club

Jordan Marie

SHAFTED

Cover Art by LJ Anderson of Mayhem Cover Creations
Models: Alfie Gordillo & Colleen McMahon
Photographer: RLS Images Randy Sewell

WARNING: This book contains sexual situations, violence and other adult themes. Recommended for 18 and above.

Dedication

I've been so blessed with an amazing group of ladies and I'm thankful for each of them. #BB4L I hope you all grow to love Shaft as much as I did. This book was supposed to be a novella and it didn't work out that way. I had a picture purchased and then I met this amazing model at a book signing and I just had to make sure he was on this cover.

I'd like to thank Aubree Elizabeth Brown and Roxanne Smith for letting me use their names. Aubree was so sweet. I got to meet her in Florida and her name just clicked and I knew that I wanted a heroine with that name. Roxanne… dear…you name made me sing the Police song over and over and well like any good ear worm…I had to kill it. BUT I love you.

I hope you guys like this book. It's completely independent you can read it without reading the rest of the series, though enjoyment might be better if you read all because you will see familiar faces all through the book.

This year will be busy for me. Beast's book (Learning to Breathe) will finally be released (he's next!), and then I'm returning to my bestselling Romantic Comedy books with Happy Trail and Black Lucas's book (Title coming soon). I'm also working on a new series that I'm very, VERY excited about and I hope you will be too.

I will have links to my pages at the back of the book. Feel free to contact me, I love hearing from you guys!

Love you all!
xoxo
Jordan

Table of Contents

Chapter 1

Shaft

"FUCK MAN," I groan, all but falling down in the chair.

"Rough day old man?" Briar asks, and I flip him off. Bastard has a right to laugh. He and his old lady, Stephanie *conveniently* picked today to spend at Cumberland Falls. Conveniently, because today is the day the rest of the brothers and myself worked like fucking dogs, fixing up the outside of the club for BB and Diego's birthdays. BB is a nickname for Torch and Katie's little boy, and Diego is the president, Skull and his old lady Beth's son. The two women are sisters and somehow managed to have kids on the exact same day just minutes apart. The Pres is going all out to make sure there's a huge celebration for the boys' second birthday.

It sure as hell don't feel like they should be two already. Time flies fast, and *damn* if my body ain't living proof of that today. I feel old all the way down to my bones. I've been a sworn in member of the Devil's Blaze for the last two years, getting the nod from the other members during all that shit with Beth, Katie and the *fucking* Donahues.

It's what I wanted, what I worked for, not even minding that I was serving as a pledge with men ten or more years younger than me. Now at forty, I'm probably one of the oldest members. It didn't used to bother me, but lately I'm feeling like I missed out on something. Especially when men my age, or close to it have all settled down with old ladies, and here I am alone.

It's not like I haven't had relationships, I have. It's just none of them are even slightly memorable. More often than not, I wish to hell I could forget them. I look through the room and it's mostly quiet. The new prospects are partying with a few of the club girls. Even that—easy pussy, doesn't interest me tonight and that is just fucking depressing. The club needs new women or something. Hell, maybe I need to get off my ass and get out and find a woman, a woman of my own. That just seems like too much fucking effort right now. Especially when I've been breaking up cement and shit all day to make way for the new patio that's being poured tomorrow. My back hurts like a motherfucker.

"I think I'm crashing for the night brother," I tell Briar, taking the last swig of my beer.

"*Damn,* you are getting old," he says with a chuckle as he shakes his head.

"Nothing here seems to be holding my interest tonight. Club needs some new talent."

"You need to settle down brother. Find you a good woman like my Steph," he boasts.

"I think all the good ones are probably gone."

"Nah, they're still out there. Just hard to find," Briar says.

I look around the room one last time. Just as I'm about to write the night off as a loss, *she walks in.*

"Who's that?"

He looks around the room. "Who?"

"The chick that just walked through the door," I tell him without taking my eyes off her. She's fucking beautiful, and I don't mean that in a normal way. *Hell no*, this chick could have just walked off the pages of a magazine. She's got hair that you can't really call blonde. It's like multiple colors, blonde on top then slowly shifting to darker locks on the bottom, and every now and then there's a strand of almost white. It's cut so it curves toward a perfect face reaching below her shoulders. She's got red lips that could make any man beg—including me. She's wearing a black jacket, not leather, it's more polished, expensive, though the look is similar. Under that she has a white shirt that clings to tight, perky breasts that are easily a 'C' cup. *Perfect size to fill my large hands.* Tight blue jean shorts that cling to her curvy ass and show off long fucking legs, that'd I'd give my eye teeth to feel wrapped around me. She's wearing flip flops and fuck, even her toes are sexy, painted clear with bright white tips. There's a silver ring around one of her toes and even that looks sexy. She looks around like she's searching for someone. *Me baby. You're definitely searching for me.*

Almost as if she can hear me, she looks at me. Those sweet red lips give into a smile, and I need her closer, so I can tell exactly what color those eyes are. I can feel my dick hardening. I reach down under the table to adjust him. I'll be letting him play tonight, that's for *damn* sure. I stare straight at the woman of my dreams. Is it coincidence that her tongue comes out to brush against her top lip, or is she trying to drive me in-fucking-sane?

"Down boy." Briar puts his hand on my chest as if to hold me back. "That's not for you."

"Why the fuck not?" I shove his hand away. "She been claimed by one of the other brothers?" *Please say no.* Briar laughs, and as much as I hate it, I pull my eyes away from my dream woman and look at him. "What the fuck do you find so funny?"

"The fact that you're setting yourself up for a whole hell of a lot of trouble."

"Quit talking in circles, Briar. I got more important shit to do." *Like her.*

"Not with her you don't."

"You're starting to piss me off man."

"That girl is off limits." His tone is hard and matter of fact.

"Says who?"

His eyes harden. "Her family."

"Give me a break. Do I look like I give a fuck?" *What the fuck has he been moking?*

"You might on this one."

"I doubt it."

"It's your funeral."

Standing up, I ignore the son of a bitch. My dick is so hard I could lay fucking bricks. I've got a much softer place in mind for him though.

"Something else might talk you out of it though."

"I doubt it," I repeat, walking toward my future.

"She's jailbait," he calls out after me.

Motherfucker. I stop mid-step, and I swear my dick would cry if he could.

Chapter 2

Aubree

I'M EARLY, AND I was supposed to wait outside, but I couldn't resist coming in. I've heard all the talk about the Devil's Blaze men and it sure worked out for Beth and Katie. They've got good men who love them. I couldn't resist seeing how the other side lives. Pops will have a fit, but I don't really care. Maybe if I'm lucky he'll never find out. I'll just tell Katie I misunderstood. I can sell that, surely.

It takes me a minute after my eyes adjust to the change of light before I can focus. At first, I'm let down. I've never been inside the Blaze's compound before. That's something Pops has completely forbidden. I don't know what I was expecting, but it wasn't this. This seems like any bar on any night of the week…well not really, maybe every night except Friday and Saturday, because this sure isn't lively.

There's some seventies rock playing over the speakers. There's men at the bar and though a couple of them are cute, they aren't anywhere close to the idea I had in my head of a biker. Maybe Beth and Katie just got lucky and got the only two hot bikers in existence. I should have learned from Pops, but a girl has to hope. I read these books and they make it sound…*totally different,* exciting even, and God knows I could use a little excitement in my life. Of course, if I had it, I'd need to keep Pops completely clueless. Glancing around the room, I feel several sets of eyes on me, but then again that's nothing new. I don't mean to sound conceited, I'm not. Not really. But, I do know I'm not unattractive—at least with some effort. I even use it to my advantage at times. I look around scanning their faces in search of my....

My thought stops completely when I look up and my eyes lock with those of a man across the room. That may sound crazy, but it's true. His eyes literally bore into mine, so powerfully I can feel the heat from them all the way over here. He stands up and parts of me that have never taken notice of a man before all come to life at once. It's as if electricity runs through my veins. The sensation is so strong that I squeak, barely containing a cry of victory when he takes a step toward me wearing a determined expression on his handsome face...and then...*he stops.* I don't do it out loud, but inside I'm crying, "*But, why!?*"

"Who are you looking for?" a man at the bar asks me, pulling my attention from where I want it the most. Before I can answer him, I hear a high pitched squeal that pierces my ears. I turn around, seeing Katie and Beth, and I can't help but laugh as I run to them.

"Aubree! You're early!"

"Yeah, they closed school down early for a bomb threat, so I was able to get Pops settled and stuff done around the house early. Figured I'd just come on over here tonight instead of meeting you at the house in the morning."

Beth holds a hand over her mouth. "Oh my God! Are you okay?"

"I'm fine Aunt Beth. It was a hoax. A couple of the football jocks were bragging about it. It was all a bad prank, but hey, I get to start our weekend together early, so I'm not complaining."

"I'm so glad. It's great that Pops agreed to let you come. We wondered if he would. Him and Skull are getting better with each other, but…"

"Yeah, I know. But, Pops doesn't want to do anything that might upset you two now that you've started letting him see his grandchildren again regularly." I'm told that there was a time when Skull and Pops got along. Pops even lived in a house next to them for a while. Then something happened between the clubs and relationships were strained. Pops found out about me and moved into my father's house back at the Chrome Saint's compound. I've been hinting to both him and Skull that I'd like to live close to Aunt Beth and Katie, but so far it seems to fall on deaf ears.

Beth and Katie are twin sisters, identical really, but they do have some slight differences. The main being their hair color. Beth has white blonde hair where Katie has darker brunette hair.

"Like we could stop them. He has them spoiled rotten." Katie sighs.

"They're so cute, you can't hardly stop from it," I tell her.

"You say cute now, wait until this weekend is over," Aunt Beth says.

"I'm excited about it."

"Come on, let's get you out of here before the boys start partying a little too much."

"Aunt Beth, I am eighteen. I'm not exactly innocent," I tell her a little annoyed. For over two years, people have been sheltering me from real life, and before that I didn't get to have a life. It's frustrating as hell. You would think when your grandfather is the President of one of the biggest motorcycle clubs around I'd be able to spread my wings—*at least a little.*

"Sweetheart, trust me. Some things you don't need to see," she says. I sigh, looking at Katie. She shrugs, as if to say whatever, and I guess that's all I can say. I follow them out of the room. I look over my shoulder at the man from earlier. He's sitting now, but he's looking right at me. Butterflies are fluttering in my stomach, and I bite my lower lip, wishing I could stay…

Near him.

Chapter 3

Shaft

"WHO IS SHE?"

"She's Viper's offspring," Briar informs me.

"Viper's? You're fucking shitting me." Isn't that the fucking luck I'd have?

"Nope. The old man Tucker has raised her the last couple years. She's gotten pretty close to Katie and Beth. She's here for the birthday party."

"Tucker let a sweet young thing like that loose in the Devil's Blaze compound?" I can't believe it.

"She's under Skull's protection." He knocks his bottle back downing the rest of his beer.

"*Fuck*," I say, feeling like I'm repeating myself, but that's about as much as my brain can process—probably because all the fucking blood is pounding in my cock. *Damn*, she's a looker, and when her eyes met mine, I just got this feeling. I can't explain it, but the way she looked back at me told me she felt it too.

"Yeah, and if that's not enough reason to stay away from her, *you know, just in case you needed it*." I flip him off, but he's not wrong I do *need* it. *Hell*, I'm still debating whether to hunt her down now. "She's still in high school."

"You're shitting me." I feel like a broken record here, repeating the same lines.

Briar holds his left hand up. "Hand to God."

"Thought you were an atheist?"

"On some days. Facts don't change though. That girl is off limits as they come."

"Yeah, guess so." I shrug.

He holds his empty bottle up, signaling for another. "Denise is eyeing you. Go get your rocks off there. She's a good girl."

My eyes go to the blonde at the bar. Briar's right. She's a decent girl. I like her, and when I decide to use a club girl, she's the one I always seek out. I even think about it right now, but she's not who I want. Not even close. My mind and my cock are concentrating on a beautiful girl with cherry red lips and wondering if that juicy mouth tastes as sweet as it appears.

"Nah, man, I think I'm done for the night. I'm going to go shower and hit the bed. My dick's too tired to party tonight anyways," I lie. The fucker feels like he could go for days right now.

"*Damn.* I hope I never get that old."

I don't respond. Instead, I head to my room feeling older with each step. My brothers don't know how lucky they've got it. Coming home to one woman and not having to deal with bullshit. Well, maybe they do. Skull and Torch, hell even Sabre and Latch seem pussy whipped and happy to be that way. The bastards were lucky. In my forty years, I can't say there's been one woman who stands out. It's fucking sad. The women I've had, are just that. *Women I've had.* A sea of faces, and I can't recall one clearly. *Not a damn one.*

Kicking off my boots, I crash back on the bed, clothes and all. I reach over on the bedside table and grab a half bottle of Jack, downing a couple drinks before I put it back. I let the burn settle and close my eyes. I'll shower tomorrow. Maybe tomorrow I'll feel better.

It doesn't surprise me that when I close my eyes the first thing I see is the girl from before. It does surprise me that I don't even try to fight it. Instead, I let myself dream of fucking her hard all night long. *Hell*, instead of feeling guilt, in one part of the dream I'm pretty sure I'm fucking her up against a school bus. Her perfect 'C' cup breasts are pressing against my chest, and her legs are wrapped around me as I pound into her, filling her completely. *Jesus Christ, I'm a bastard.*

Chapter 4

Aubree

I'M RUNNING LATE. The Aunt Beth's babies were cranky this morning. I took care of them and little Hunter this morning. I can't make myself call Hunter, Bart or BB like everyone else does. That's why I'm here. I mean I'm going to the party tomorrow for sure. I love Beth and Katie, and they've been really decent to me considering what my sperm donor did to put them through hell. But, the real reason I'm here is to help with the kids while they organize everything for the birthday party.

It's just today is the day I have to take my SAT's. It's probably a waste of my time. I have zero interest in going to college. I don't know what I want out of life, but I know that's not it—another four plus years of school, no thanks. Sounds corny I guess, but I'd be happy with my life if it turned out like my aunts'. Married to a man I love and spending all my time with him sounds like a dream come true. I've never had big aspirations of a career or going abroad like some of my other friends. I like it here. However, to keep Pops from having an aneurism I agreed to get ready for college and to keep the peace, I am.

Pops has been good to me. Before him I didn't have crap. I pretty much raised myself. I cooked my own dinners from the time I was nine years old. It was that or starve. Before that I made a lot of peanut butter sandwiches. I used to be mad at Pops and everyone in the Chrome Saints, until I realized very few people knew I existed. Viper, my sperm donor, kept me in a house away from the club and only one or two people knew I was even alive.

When Pops found me, he cried for days. I did too, but for different reasons. His tears were from the shame he felt that his granddaughter was forced to live the way I did. Mine were from the relief I felt when I was rescued. I fought hard to go to public school. I had been homeschooled by one of the club whores, and I wanted out. I wanted to breathe fresh air and meet other kids…be normal. Pops did everything he could to give me the normal life I craved and he continues to give me a lot more. The addition of my aunts only helps me to feel…*ordinary*. Say what you want, but being *ordinary* is amazing.

But, right now I'm running late for my SAT's. I finally got the kids happy. It took my singing along with their favorite cartoon and building a big tower of blocks and pretending I was a monster knocking it over, but I got them settled enough to get in the car. I left Beth's and brought them here to the club. An older woman that the girls trust, Mattah, is going to take care of them while I take my test. So, before I was late, now I'm *really* late. Added to that, I rush back to my car, only to find that for some reason it won't start. I was only in there three minutes, tops! The car was fine before!

"Shit! Shit! Shit!" I mutter, slamming my car door shut.

"Problems?" a deep voice asks.

I look up and it's him. The man from yesterday. The one who made every feminine part in me stand up and take notice, even from a distance. The man I dreamed of last night. His voice is deeper than I imagined—*huskier*. I can feel shivers of awareness run all through me.

"Uh…yeah," I say stupidly. I'm having trouble thinking, all I can do is stare at him. He's taller than I noticed last night. I stand 5'7" and he makes me feel small. He towers over me. A fact that is clearer when he walks closer to me, and I have to keep looking up to find those dark brown eyes. *Brown.* His eyes are chocolate brown, dark and mysterious. His dark hair has touches of silver peppered throughout and somehow that makes him even sexier. It gives him an edge. His hair is cut short on the neck, but the top is shaggy with waves appearing unkempt…like someone has been running their fingers through it. *I wish it had been me. Is it as soft as it looks?* He's got a beard that's trimmed and neat, but looks sexy. I've never liked men with hair on their face, but he could make me change my mind. He's broad, and big, but somehow skinny at the same time. He has an air of danger about him, but yet I don't sense darkness in him. *Believe me, after living with my sperm donor I've seen darkness and evil.*

"You okay?"

"Okay?"

His lips move into a smile, and I catch a glimpse of perfect white teeth before he shakes his head. He moves around me and goes to my car, getting in and popping the hood. I don't do anything to stop him. I'm too busy concentrating on the way those jeans stretch over his ass. How that faded gray t-shirt gives me just a peek of his skin under it, and how said skin is tanned a beautiful golden bronze color, just like the rest of his body. That quiver in my lower belly just got more intense.

"Get in and try to start your car," he says, and I shake myself out of the mini-trance he has me in. I do as he says. It doesn't even enter my mind to argue with him. There's something about him that makes me want to obey everything he tells me. *Dangerous, for sure.* I turn the key and the motor turns and cranks, but nothing happens. I get out disappointed.

"It's okay. I'll see if I can get Katie or Beth to take me. I'll just have to have Pops look at it later."

"Pops? He asks, walking around me and getting inside my car. "Is that your old man?"

"My grandfather. I don't have an old man," I tell him, my face heating for some unexplainable reason. His being close to me seems to warm me up.

"Figured," he says and gets out of the car, with an almost disgusted look on his face.

I frown. "What does that mean?"

"Two things," he says, slipping his sunglasses back on. They're mirrored and reflect back at me, and I instantly hate them. I want to see his eyes again. So bad that it's all I can do not to physically reach over and rip them off his face.

"Which are?"

"One you're too damn young to have an old man," he starts and that bothers me. Mostly because I don't want *him* to view me as young—and definitely not off limits.

Sticking my chest out, I tell him, "I'm old enough."

"You're jailbait."

"I haven't been that for a while," I tell him stretching the truth. "Besides, if that's how you felt, why did you ask who Pops was?"

"Curiosity."

"Curiosity killed the cat," I mutter, annoyed with him. He's making me feel bad, and I don't like it. I'm used to boys trying to compliment me and throwing themselves at me. For the first time in my life, I actually want one to, and he's making me feel... *stupid.*

"So did messing with the wrong girl. Especially the wrong *underage* girl," he stresses.

"I'm not underage," I tell him, wondering what exactly *messing with* means.

"How old are you?" he asks, and even though his eyes are

hidden, I get the feeling they're boring into me. I can feel the heat from them.

"Eighteen."

"Fuck," he rumbles rubbing his fingers through his hair, and I'm instantly jealous of those fingers.

"What? I didn't lie. That's the legal age of consent. Anyways, I gotta go. I'm already late. I'll just try and get one of my…"

He cuts me off asking, "Where are you going?"

"I have a test."

"A test?"

"Yeah."

"It's Saturday," he states as if I don't know what day it is.

"I know. It's my SAT test for college. I can't miss it or Pops will have a shit-fit."

"Jesus Christ. Briar was right, you are in high school." He shakes his head, but he doesn't walk away.

"Well, yeah. For a little longer."

"How much longer?"

"I don't see why this is important. I really need to get going." I sigh, stepping forward to walk around him.

He matches my step, cutting me off. "How much longer?" his deep voice rumbles, even deeper than normal, and it scrapes across my nerve endings making my stomach clench. Or it could be the way he reaches out and grabs my hand, keeping me from leaving. There's so much heat coming from his touch, it envelopes me, and I swear I feel my knees grow weak.

"Four weeks," I whisper, and it *is* a hoarse whisper, worse, I'm pretty sure he can feel the way my body just shook with a tremble. His thumb brushes back and forth on my arm. I watch it, because for some reason I can't make myself look up at those mirrored glasses again. I'm afraid I'd reveal too much about how he is affecting me—especially since I can't see his expression.

"It'll have to work." He sighs vaguely, confusing me. Before I can ask him, he's pulling me across the parking lot. "Let's go," he says.

I do my best to stop, though it takes me a minute to realize I need to. "Go where?"

"I'll take you to your test," he says coolly as if him taking me somewhere is natural.

"Oh. Are you sure? I could get my aunts to…" I trail off intrigued by his offer.

"I'm sure," he says, walking me over to a parked bike. He gets on and looks at me expectantly. "Get on."

I have a moment of indecision, before I decide to go with it. I brace my hand on his shoulder, more of that electricity passes between us, though to be honest, I'm starting to enjoy it. I swing on behind him and settle in. He reaches around me with a helmet placing it on my head. It has to be his, because it's a little big. He adjusts it as much as he can before turning back around, he pulls his sunglasses down to look at me. I can feel the heat of his gaze like the flames of a thousand candles. I hear an almost soundless sigh come from him, and then he faces to the front powering the bike to life.

"Hold on," he orders, and I gladly wrap my arms around him, leaning into his back. It's like wrapping around the sun and all the heat settles between my legs.

Finally, I think I know what they meant when the other girls in my class used to say their boyfriends set them on fire. I'm feeling that way, and the only thing I know about him is he thinks I'm *too* young. I didn't even look at his name on his cut. I was too busy checking the rest of him out.

Dang it.

Chapter 5

Shaft

IF THERE'S A sweeter Hell on Earth than feeling her legs tightening against my thighs, having her body lean into me, her arms wrapped around me, as I'm driving her down the road on my bike, I don't know what it is.

Fuck, it feels so good.

No.

She feels so good.

She fits.

She belongs to me.

Christ. That sounds so fucking stupid and it's impossible, but that's exactly how I feel—*like she's mine.* Which is crazy. Completely and utterly stupid, in fact. She can't be *mine.* She's too damn young, she's *property* of another club. A club that the Blaze have just recently buried a hatchet with. *Hell*, Skull, our President, and Tucker still barely like each other. I fuck around with Tucker's granddaughter—*his eighteen-year-old, still in high school granddaughter*? I'll probably blow the truce, have my cut taken, be left without a club, and wind up six feet underground. It would be a toss-up as to if Skull or Tucker would put me there.

I have to be completely insane to even be thinking about her. But…I am. She's awoken something inside of me, I've never had any idea existed. I have a suspicion it's what has been leaving me so unsatisfied with life. What I can't fucking understand is how an eighteen-year-old girl could be the answer to what I've been searching for, for years. *Fuck*, I've probably been searching longer than she's been alive. That thought alone should be enough to freeze my fucking balls into ice cubes and yet, it doesn't.

Instead, my cock is as hard as it was yesterday, as hard as it was last night, and as hard as it was even after I jacked off in the shower this morning, while I thought about the dirty things I'd do to her if given the chance. I'm in deep shit, and instead of getting space, here I am giving the woman a ride on my bike. A bike that has never had another woman on it. My bike is sacred, putting a bitch on the back implies something, something I haven't wanted...*until now*.

I had her give me directions, but I don't think I was prepared to pull into the parking lot of the local high school. *Goddamn*. Seeing the damn buses parked in a nearby lot reminds me of my dream. I pull up to the front door, ignoring the looks the people that are scattered around are giving us. I'm used to looks, it's just I'm pretty sure these are calling me a dirty old man. A pervert and *fuck* I am. I'm both of those because it wouldn't take me too much to lean her over my bike and fuck the hell out of her right now. I wouldn't even give a fuck who is watching. Part of me wants them to see it. See me claim her. Watch as I sink my cock deep inside her branding her as mine. All mine.

She gets off my bike when we park, and I instantly miss her arms around me. She takes a step to stand in front of me, her soft hair is windblown, wild around her face, her cheeks are blushed from the sting of the wind and the exhilaration of the ride. The 'V' cut in her shirt gives me just a peek of her ample breasts, and it's not too much to imagine this is exactly the look she would have after a healthy work out in the bed, or on the floor, shower…against a fucking wall…over the seat of my bike.

"Uh…thank you, I'm sorry I don't know your name," she says, interrupting my list of all the places I want to fuck her.

"Ajax."

"Ajax? Like the cleaner?"

"There's nothing clean about me, sweets," I tell her and that's more true than ever since I met her. Her nose curls in disgust and it's damn cute. Jesus, even that makes me want her.

"Don't call me that. I don't like it," she sasses.

"What?"

"Sweets. My name is Aubree."

"What's wrong with sweets?"

"That's what you call a woman when you know you aren't going to expend the effort to learn her name. I have a name. I like my name. Call me by it," she demands, even as her blush is deepening. Baby girl has a kick to her, and *fuck* if that don't just turn me on more. I like a woman who speaks up for herself. I like her even more when she knows to do as she's told, and I'm thinking Aubree knows that for sure.

"I doubt we'll know each other long enough for me to use your name much."

"That would make me sad, Shaft," she says, her voice soft, using the name on my cut. I look down at my name and wish it hadn't been there. Her calling me by that name is wrong.

"Don't call me that," I all but growl at her.

"It's your club name, isn't that what your friends and family call you?"

"That's not you. Don't call me that," I tell her again.

"Oh. Okay, right. Thanks for the ride. I'm sorry to bother you," she says, the hurt in her voice is clear, making me feel like a real asshole. I'm biting my tongue to keep from explaining—especially when she starts to walk away with her head down.

"Aubree! You're late. I been waiting for you, babe." *Babe.*

I watch as some jock with a jacket on like football players wear comes running towards her and just like that my will for pushing her away is gone.

"Bree," I growl, and it is a growl. A fuckin deep growl, and it's the only thing that's keeping me from cutting off the high school Casanova's hand when he dares to put it on her shoulder. Heat bubbles in my chest, it's a raw feeling, one I'm not used to. It isn't quite anger, but I don't want to say I'm jealous either. She stops, her feet stumbling a little, and then she turns around. My chest constricts.

"Everyone calls me Aubree," she says, her eyes, a mixture of brown and green looking at me confused.

"I'm not everyone. Especially not to you."

Her head tilts to the side just a little and she studies me. "I get it. You're special," she says, and those cherry lips once again lift into a smile.

I nod, my lip twitches wanting to say something smart. However, I respond, "Something like that."

"Okay, *Jax*," she says, and I find myself laughing, something I never do.

"Everyone calls me Shaft."

"I'm not everyone. Especially to you," she throws my words back at me.

"That's it baby girl. That's it exactly," I tell her because I can't stop myself.

"We better go," football jock, mutters, putting his hand on Bree's back.

"I'll be here to pick you up when you get out, Bree," I tell her, and I don't think it's my imagination that happiness vibrates from her at my announcement.

"It's over in three hours," she confirms with the hint of a

smile.

"But we have a date, remember? A bunch of us are going to meet up at the diner and go to—"

"I'll be here," I tell her interrupting the asshole who doesn't have a shot with her. He'd bore her to tears. She needs a man. *A man like me.*

"Okay Jax." She smiles and then walks away.

I don't know what the fuck I've got myself into, but I'm not sure I give a damn either.

Chapter 6

Bree

"WHERE'S YOUR BIKE?"

"The sun's going down, you're not dressed to ride," Jax explains as he helps me in his truck. I settle in and I reach up to grab the seatbelt, but I'm too late. Jax already has it and he clicks me in. The snap of the seatbelt seems overly loud in the cab of the truck. I look at him and his face as he tests the seatbelt.

"I could have done that."

"I wanted to," he says and for a minute our eyes hold. An electric hum vibrates in the air between us.

"Okay," I tell him, I'm not about to object. If he's going to touch me, I'm more than okay with it. He closes the door, and a minute later he's behind the wheel starting up the truck.

"I do like your bike, though," I tell him.

"I don't normally let others ride on it," he says and immediately I worry that's why he's in the truck now. I shrug it off. Something passed between us before I went into my test. *I know it did.* I couldn't have imagined the connection we had. I hold onto that, until we've been riding for at least five minutes, and he still hasn't spoken.

"I really like your name. It's unique," I tell him lamely, trying to jumpstart the conversation.

Silence.

"What did you do today?" I try again.

"Work. Like most other adults," he grumbles.

"Is something wrong, Jax?" I question. I watch as he shifts his hands on the steering wheel and the skin goes a pale white as he tightens on it. I swallow, definitely sensing a difference in the Jax now and the Jax from before.

"No," he barks. *Yeah, definitely something has changed.* It makes me sad. I don't know what I hoped for, but I definitely wanted to continue getting to know him. Now, instead of waking up parts of me I hadn't felt before, he seems to be freezing me out.

"Okay. Could you take a right at the next light, please?"

"What for?"

"I want to meet my friends at the diner."

"Why?"

Rolling my eyes, I repeat his question, "Why?"

"That's what I said," he says in a flat tone.

"Because I'm hungry. I haven't eaten all day and suddenly, I'm starting to think riding home with you, isn't the fun I thought it would be."

"I'm supposed to take you home. Skull wouldn't exactly like it if I dropped you off without someone watching over you."

"I'm eighteen, not eight. I don't need someone watching over me. Besides, my friends are there. I won't be alone."

"I'm not leaving you alone with that *jock*." His voice raises on the word jock. Is he jealous?

"Jeff? He's sweet."

"He wants in your pants," Jax growls, for a moment robbing me of my breath.

"We don't know each other, right?" I don't wait for a response. "Is there some reason you think you can act like my father? Because, I had one of those, and I don't really want another one."

"I'm trying to look out for you," he says deflecting my question.

"Thanks, but no thanks." I shake my head before leaning it against the window. He's so frustrating. His hot and cold is giving me whiplash.

"Are you kidding me right now?"

"I have enough people looking out for me. We're basically strangers. I don't need someone else *helping* me."

"That's sure a different tune from earlier," he observes. I can feel his eyes on me, but I won't give him the satisfaction of my looking at him.

"I was just thinking the same thing," I snap, as the truck pulls up to a red light.

"What are you talking about?"

"I thought…never mind. It's not important," I say, because as I start to form the sentence in my mind I realize it does sound stupid. I thought what? That this man I don't know liked me? That he might want to date me? I doubt Jax has ever dated anyone in his life. Besides, I may have been sheltered from the Chrome Saints, but I'm not stupid, and I have seen *enough*. He's got plenty of club women. He wouldn't want someone like me, who doesn't even know….

I've never been one for self-pity, and I'm not someone who accepts anything that makes me feel unsure of myself. My father spent his whole life making me feel less because I was a girl. I won't have that now from anyone. Even if I'm jumping the gun with Jax—no, *Shaft*, even if I am being overly sensitive, it's best if I just walk away. With that thought, I open my door with one hand while I undo my seatbelt with the other.

"Where the hell are you going?" Jax growls, grabbing my free arm before I can hop out.

"I'm going to walk to the diner," I inform him, trying to jerk away from his firm grip. My skin flames under his touch.

"Close that fucking door."

"Take a flying leap," I scoff.

"Close that fucking door, Bree. I'm warning you, I won't tell you again," he grits through his clenched teeth.

I raise my brow at him. "Gee, Jax, what are you going to do? Tell Skull on me?"

"Spank your ass."

My mouth falls open but closes quickly. "You did not just say that."

"I did. Obviously, Tucker has let you run too damn wild," he growls and maybe he would continue, but the cars blowing their horns behind us takes his attention away. The light has turned green. "Close the fucking door, Bree," he says, and this time his voice is deadly cold. I do it out of reflex as he lets go of my arm. I let my small token of rebellion be that, and I slam the door hard enough to vibrate the whole truck. Folding my arms at my chest, I turn straight ahead, while silently vowing not to say another word to him, even though I miss his possessive touch.

"Buckle up," he demands and though I don't want to, I find myself obeying his command.

Chapter 7

Jax

"WHAT ARE WE doing here?" Bree asks, which incidentally are the first words she's uttered in over fifteen minutes. I understand why, I was kind of a bastard. This morning held promise and getting her to smile was like I won a fucking war. But, all day I kept going over all the reasons I shouldn't—*couldn't* touch her. When I picked her up this evening, I promised myself I would be distant, do nothing to encourage that smile, nor the stars twinkling in her eyes. That was my goal and sure as I'm sitting here, I'm about to fuck up. I can't help it though, because I want her, and even if I can't have her, I still want to see her smile. Her smile warmed something inside of me that I thought had been dead for a long time.

"You said you were hungry," I tell her shutting off the truck.

"This is the wrong diner," she grumbles.

"This is the one you're getting." I jump out of the truck, walk around and open her door. She hasn't moved. She's looking straight ahead at the restaurant, then back at me. When she doesn't make a move, I reach in and unbuckle her seatbelt. It's an operation in torture being this close to her tits and not diving in head first, or maybe dick first. Fuck, those babies would wrap around my cock so fucking good. I have to shake my head and file away the image of my cum dripping down her neck, running down her breast, sliding around the nipple…

Son of a bitch, I jacked off twice this morning, and I already know when I leave Bree with Beth and Katie, I'm going to be spanking the monkey again. *Christ*, the woman is like walking Viagra.

Her hand comes down and clasps mine at her waist, stopping me from making sure the belt goes back without hitting her. I look up and those deep hazel eyes capture me. I watch as flakes of green sink into the brown, her pupils large and dilated. It's then I notice her breathing has jumped. I even catch a glimpse of that pink tongue between those lips I've been fantasizing about.

"Jax..." she whispers, confused. I want to kiss her. Her lips are right *there,* ripe for the taking. My body literally shakes with the need, but I lock the urge down and contain it. I might not be able to freeze her out, but I can't go there. I can't...even if she wasn't the granddaughter of the Chrome Saints, she's in high school for Christ's sake. *Hell*, it's a wonder I don't have a daughter her age walking around. That thought helps douse the hard-on a little. Enough so I can walk without my balls protesting at least.

"Come eat with me Bree," I tell her, hoping I made sense, because in my head it's her I want to eat. She nods once in agreement, and I help her down from the truck. If my hand accidentally brushes against the curve of her ass a little too long, I can't be blamed. I'm only fucking human here.

We make it inside, and I slide in next to her at the booth. It's nothing fancy, but their food is good. I don't eat here often, it's why I picked this place. Hoping no one I know sees us. Not because I'm embarrassed, I just don't want anyone getting the wrong idea.

The waitress takes our drink order and hands us a menu. Bree's quiet for a bit, at least until she gets her drink. That's when I feel her eyes narrow on me.

"You confuse me, Jax."

"I'm pretty much a what you see is what you get kinda man," I tell her and it's not a lie. I always have been, at least until she walked into my world and twisted me up in knots.

"If you say so. I'll just take chicken strips," she says. I order her chicken and me a burger. Then I sit back and wait. I throw my hand over the back of our booth and stare straight ahead, wondering what the fuck to do now. When I hear Bree sigh I look over at her.

"If you were just going to ignore me, you could've just driven me straight to Beth's. I would've found food there."

"I'm not ignoring you." I don't offer any further explanation. Glancing around the dining room, I look at the rustic décor. A picture of John Wayne hangs on the wall under a longhorn skull.

"It sure feels like it. If you don't like me why are you picking me up? I'm sure one of the others would have." She fidgets with the red and white checkered napkin, unfolding the silverware.

"I told you I'd pick you up and I did. I keep my word." My word is the one thing I have.

"Well, you shouldn't have bothered if it's gonna be a struggle to talk to me."

"I can talk," I offer. "What do you want to talk about?" I angle my body towards her, and she turns into me. The sweet smell of her hair hits me. Sitting beside her was a bad choice, but what can I say, I'm a glutton for punishment.

"Okay then. How'd you get the name Shaft?"

I go tense. "About anything but that."

"What? Why?" she scoffs.

"You're too young," I answer her honestly, knowing she'll be insulted by my choice of words.

"You heard the part where I'm eighteen right? I'm pretty

sure that's adulthood in most countries." She rolls her eyes, and I want to bend her over my knee right here and spank her ass.

I deadpan, "I think you're confusing that with twenty-one."

"The right to drink has nothing to do with being an adult. I'd say I'm more adult than any twenty-one-year-old I know," she counters smirking those thick lips at me, lips I'd love to have wrapped around my cock. I've got to stop thinking about her like this. Nothing good can come from it.

"You do? Tell me *sweets*, how many twenty-one-year-olds do you hang around with?"

"I told you, I hate that name, Jax. If you insist on using it, then I will call you Shaft. Well, that or *asshole*. Right now, *asshole* seems a better fit."

"*Damn,* you can be mouthy for a kid." The girl has sass and it makes my dick practically weep with want.

"I'm ignoring you now." Those tempting lips screw into a pout, serving as a reminder of how old she is.

"What? Did I hurt your feelings? Pouting is not what an adult would do."

"You really are an *ass*. I happen to think that your experiences, and the things that life throws at you can age you as much, if not more than years, *Shaft*. I grew up with Viper as my father for most of my life. That's it, unless you count a club whore, who took *pity* on me. I had no one other than them, until my grandfather rescued me. So, I figure in the grand scheme of things I'm more adult than most people I know. Especially asinine bikers who think they can talk down to people and get away with it."

"Viper was a fucking prick, I give you that. But, at least you had him. You had someone to look out for you. You have no idea how cruel the real world is. Be thankful for the hand you got dealt," I tell her. I admit I shouldn't say that to her. It's a dick move, but she touched a wound I haven't revisited in way too many years to count.

I expected her to spring back at me. If there's one thing I've learned about Bree, she's quick to come back at me. She doesn't take crap, and I have to admit I like that about her. I like it more than I should. *Fuck*. I like every damn thing about this girl—except her age and her relatives. I could get lost in her, and I can't. I'm *too* fucking old for her. She's beauty. The real kind. The kind that goes to the very depth of the bone. The kind a man protects and feeds. The kind that makes a man sell out his own brothers to touch. *Too* fucking precious for a son of a bitch like me. She doesn't come back at me though. She goes quiet, too quiet, and I'm too fucked up in the head to push it, so I let the words lie between us. I let the silence stand as a wall between us.

The waitress brings our food and Bree offers a quiet, polite thank you to the waitress. She pushes her fries around on her plate. I try to concentrate on my burger, knowing I've hurt her, but it's for the best. *Really*...it is.

"Can you let me out? I need to go to the restroom?" she asks, her voice and face strained, making me feel like even more of an asshole. *Shit*, she's gonna go in there and cry, and I have to let her. I clear my throat as I get up. I stand there watching her walk to the back where the half-broken neon sign flashes the word restrooms. When she disappears out of sight, I finally sit back down. I rub my chest where a slight pain has started. *Shit*, maybe I'm having a heart attack.

Chapter 8

Bree

I HATE HIM. How I ever thought he could be someone *special* I don't know. I hate him with a passion. Leaning against the restroom door, I try to stop myself from letting the anger take over. Because, I know what will follow the anger…my tears. Tears I haven't shed since Pops found me. Tears that I swore I would never give into again. That is what makes me hate Jax even more. I could have taken it if he was an asshole. I could have. I could have accepted it and moved on. But…he was an asshole who made me think he might be *more,* and that makes me want to cry. *That shit hurts.*

He wants me to be thankful I had my sperm donor? He has no idea the abuse and life I had with that man. It's a story I don't want to share with Jax. He doesn't get that from me—*not now.* I have to get away from him. I can't go back out there and let him tear me down. That's out of the question. Tears are burning in my eyes, threatening to run down my face, and if I'm not able to fight them down, I sure as hell ain't letting him see them. Letting people see your tears exposes your weakness. Viper used to love to see me cry. No one. Not *one* more person will ever get my tears again.

There's a small, sketchy looking window over by the toilet. It's tiny, but I think with some work I can maneuver through it. I go straight to it, turning the trashcan over for a makeshift stepstool, and I don't stop pushing and wiggling till I break free. I fall, letting the pavement below catch me. Now, there's a rip on the knee of my favorite jeans and that is all Jax's—*no Shaft's* fault. I guess I should be thankful I didn't land in the dumpster judging by the smell out here.

I take the long way around the diner, avoiding the windows. I don't want to take the chance that the asshole will see me. Once I get back along the main road, I breathe easier. I'm not too far from Aunt Beth and Skull's house. I'll have Mattah bring the kids to me and figure out how to get through the party tomorrow without seeing *Shaft again.* It's a great plan. I look at my scraped palms where I caught myself when I fell, it stings, and I hope he chokes on his food.

Chapter 9

Jax

BREE'S NOT COMING out. It's been nearly fifteen minutes, and I don't care who the woman is, it doesn't take that long to use the restroom. I should have expected a childish temper tantrum. It's just further proof that she's too damn young. I stalk back towards the restroom, my anger growing with each step. I pound on the door, it's a wonder the thing doesn't collapse.

"Alright you've had long enough in there. It's time to get out," I yell, thinking I should paddle her ass for acting like a child. Then, getting even madder when my dick jerks in my pants at the thought of spanking Bree. "Damn it! Get out here now, or I'm coming in to get you!" I bark. Maybe I should shove her up against the wall and show her what happens when she makes a man mad. "Either you get out here right now, or I'll show you exactly how I deal with temper tantrums."

Silence.

"Damn it woman. I know you're in there. I can hear you moving around. Get your ass out here right now, or so help me I'll come in there and paddle it until it's blood red. That's what you need anyways. The men in your life have let you run too free. It's time you find out what happens when you piss off a real man."

"Sir, really, you're disrupting the diner. If you could just go back…" a waitress says appearing in front of me. Ignoring her, I pound on the door again. "Sir I mean it. Don't make me call the police!" the waitress warns.

"Fuck off, this isn't your concern," I growl, being an epic jackass, and not even giving a damn. This is all Bree's fault. The waitress gasps and she might have said something more, but the door opens up, interrupting our exchange. *Thank God.*

I'm about to shove Bree right back in and take out my frustrations when this little old lady, probably in her eighties, looks up at me and slaps my face. My hand goes to my jaw, rubbing it. She might be old, but damn she can hit. She doesn't say anything, but she leans on her cane and her eyes shoot knives at me. *Shit.*

"Fuck lady, I…I mean I'm sorry, Ma'am. I didn't know…I thought you were the girl I was with. I mean I thought she was in the restroom and not you—"

"I hope she got smart and left you then, asshole," the old lady says. The waitress looks at me with pity as she helps the woman leave.

"I think you should leave now and don't come back," the waitress snaps at me, and I just stand there with my head down and my hands shoved in my pockets.

I don't know what's worse. That I made an old woman cuss, or that I've been thrown out of a diner.

Chapter 10

Bree

I'M MAKING PRETTY good time. I really am. I figure another twenty minutes walking along the road, and I'll be home free. There isn't much traffic and it's the edge of twilight. The temperature has only dropped a few degrees, but a chill in the air, has me rubbing my arms. I sing and hum along to myself to pass the time. I'm trying not to think about anything creepy that could be lurking in the woods, or some random weirdo stopping to offer me a ride. So far, I haven't run into either. However, when I hear the sound of a vehicle coming up behind me and look over my shoulder, I know my run of good luck is over. *Shaft.* Not Jax. Shaft. That's all he is now.

Shit. Shit. Shit.

I hear him pull up to a stop behind me, and I walk faster, only wanting to get away from him. When I hear the slamming of the door, I almost run. Before I can contemplate my next move, he wraps his thick, strong arm around my stomach, picking me up. I let out a scream and beat on his arm, but it doesn't help. Shaft isn't letting go, and there isn't anyone around to make him. He hauls me back against his hard chest. The heat of his body instantly surrounds me, and I'd enjoy it, if I didn't hate him so much right now.

I try to kick back at him, wishing I had on heels instead of damn tennis shoes. He pulls me further back and then spins me so I'm pressed against the side of his truck, sandwiched tight between the metal bedside and his hard body. I try to kick again, aiming for his shin, and that's when I feel the stubble from his beard tickle against my neck.

Despite how pissed I am, I'd be dead not to admit the friction that results from his facial scruff scraping along my sensitive skin sends shivers down my spine.

"Keep it up, and I'll make your ass so sore you won't be able to sit for days, Bree," he threatens.

"You wouldn't dare! My grandfather would have your head!"

"You don't know me well enough, but I've never been afraid of any man. I'm not about to start now," his voice is calm and smooth, he means every word.

"Skull will kill you," I growl trying to kick him again, but he maneuvers his leg so it pens mine and I can't move.

"You're probably right. But, you know what, sweet Bree? I think it'd be worth it. Now, hold still," he snarls.

I try with everything I am to fight, but in the end I give in, because I can't move anyway. He has me pinned against the truck. The weight of his body and his hold on me keeps me gathered in so tight that there's no hope for freedom. I give in with a heavy, exerted breath.

"Fine," I grate.

"Are you done now?" he asks. I don't answer, but he must take my lack of movement as agreement. "Why did you run out on me?"

"Because you're an asshole," I growl.

"I told you to behave," he whispers in my ear, the tone of his voice much softer than it was moments ago, and I can't deny the chills that run through my body, nor the fact that they have everything to do with excitement and not fear. I'm so lost in the sensation; I don't expect what happens next.

His hand moves down my back, slowly. So slowly I can't concentrate. So slowly it's getting scrambled in my mind as to whether this is torture or pleasure. *I think both.* My breath stills in my throat as I feel his large hand spread and cup my ass.

"Jesus," he mutters and my heartbeat goes crazy. I can feel a hunger inside me. I've never felt it before, but I know that's what it is. My body feels heated, my breasts feel like there's a current of power running through them. My nipples tighten aching to be touched, but I'm pretty sure only one touch will do. The magnetic pull I've felt toward Jax from the first minute I saw him has suddenly exploded. Wiggling my ass against him, wanting more of his touch, I can feel the hard ridge of his cock.

It should scare me. For all my talk about being an adult at eighteen, I've never had sex. I've never wanted to. I thought there was something wrong with me honestly. Until I laid eyes on Jax, I had never felt a pull towards a man. I've never felt such desire. So, these new feelings? I'm not scared. *Not at all.* Mostly, I just want more. *More of whatever he will give me.*

"You feel me don't you, sweet Bree. Feel how hard I am? I told you it was dangerous to tease a grown man."

"Fuck you," I taunt, pissed that he chooses this moment, this moment when I finally feel like a *woman* to make me feel like a *little girl* again. He's taking something beautiful and earthshattering and *ruining* it for me.

His hand leaves, and I wait for him to let me turn around so we can fight and get it out there—*so I can finally get away from him.* That doesn't happen. Instead his hand connects hard with my ass.

I am barely able to register what just happened before he's speaking again. "Little girls shouldn't use such language," his dark, sexy voice rumbles low in my ear just as he's spanking me hard again, just below where his first one hit. With the initial shock gone, the sting and the pain are almost instant. I try to twist away, but he doesn't let me, he just lands another slap against my ass.

"Fuck you," I hiss, using language no other person, not even my father has driven me to. Jax's response is another well placed slap against my ass. The sting vibrates through my body, burning me like fire, but something strange happens. The heat seems to settle between my legs. I can feel myself growing wet and shock now wars with need. I grow perfectly still, confused and unsure of what is happening. When he spanks me again my pussy actually contracts. *What's wrong with me?*

"Watch the language, Bree. You might not like what I wash your mouth out with," he warns and maybe it's because I'm already aroused. Maybe it's because Jax's voice is hoarse and he's in control of my body. It could be because I can still feel the hard line of his cock pushing against my ass. Whatever it is, at his words the vision of me on my knees in front of him, taking his cock into my mouth zips through my mind. My entire body does a full shudder. I know he can feel it. There's no way I can hide it. Just like there's no way I can stop the soft moan that's full of need escaping from my lips.

I want him.

I need him.

Chapter 11

Jax

MOTHERFUCKER.

I feel her body shake and there's no way to deny that she's excited. The knowledge cements in my brain so much that when my hand lands on her ass, it clenches against the soft juicy bottom in reflex. Her moan is the last straw.

"Jesus Christ, are you wet right now, Bree?" I have to know.

"Jax…" my name on her tongue is the sweetest, hottest motherfucking sound.

"Answer me. Are you wet?" I demand once more. The anticipation of her answer is driving me mad.

"Yes," she whispers like it's a dirty little secret and it is. *Jesus*, it is, but it's *ours*.

"I could make you cum like this couldn't I Bree? Spank you until that sweet pussy explodes from my touch."

"Jax…" Fuck me, there's my name again.

"Answer me, Bree." I'm about to lose it, we're playing a dangerous game.

"I don't know," she stalls.

"Not the answer I wanted," I admit, and I could say the Devil made me do it, but the truth is I'm doing it because I fucking can't stop. I spank her ass again, and again…and finally, again.

"Oh God, Jax," she cries, and her cry is my reward. A cry

full of hunger and need, and it's *my* name she calls out. What man could resist? *Any?* Certainly a better man than I am.

I back up a step, giving her a little freedom—*very little.* Then I spin her around to face me. I need to see her eyes. I want to know if they are as hungry as my own.

"Do you see what happens when you tempt a man, Bree? Do you see what you invite? Is this what you wanted?" I demand, angry at her, at myself, at the situation, and so *fucking hard* it hurts.

"No…yes…Oh God Jax, I don't know," she cries. Her beautiful eyes wound me. They're begging me, wanting to make her come, but at the same time I see the confusion—*the innocence* there. Christ. Is this completely new to her? That thought alone should be enough to make me stop, but it doesn't. *I'm a bastard.* I shove my leg between hers and pull her up to me. Her thighs are strong and they immediately hold onto me, clamping down hard and pressing my thigh right where she wants me the most.

"That feel good, sweet Bree?"

"Jax?" she whispers.

I shouldn't touch her. I know I shouldn't, but nothing could stop me now. I push her body closer. One hand sliding under her shirt and shoving her bra up out of the way, so I can palm her tit. Heat, electricity, need, all zap me at once. Her large nipple presses into my palm. I move my hand down so I can capture her tender bud in my fingers. I tease the plump little morsel while wishing we weren't beside the road so I could suck it…The minute I start teasing her, her hips move erratically, rocking on my leg, searching.

"That's it, ride my leg. Find what you need," I whisper in her ear, still stroking her nipple.

"I need more, Jax," she says breathless, her nails biting into my sides so deep, she's scoring the skin.

"Then take it, take what you need," I urge her, barely holding onto control. Sanity is gone. It left the minute I allowed myself to touch her, but the last thing I need to do is bend her over the truck and fuck her. If her grandfather found us like that, he'd have my head, and if he didn't Skull would.

"I'm not sure," she whispers breathlessly, ending with a moan as I twist her nipple and pinch it. Her body lurches forward hard, her head going back in passion. "I don't know how," she gasps, frustration thick in her voice. I'm not sure what she means it can't be what I'm thinking. She's young, but *she is eighteen.*

"Bree have you ever had an orgasm before?"

"Jax, please."

"Answer me."

"No," she whispers and it's right then my fate is sealed. To be fair it probably was before, but now there's no going back. If I'm going to be the first to make this sweet body come, I'm going to teach her everything. It will be my mission in life.

My hands go to her hips and I help navigate her body, showing her a steady rhythm. It just takes a moment of her following my lead before she takes control, riding my leg like a rodeo queen. Not being able to stand it any longer, I tilt her so her back is leaning on the truck. I begin unbuttoning her shirt, ignoring the way my hands are shaking. By the time I get the third button down, I'm tired of messing with it and just pull the shirt until the buttons give and the shirt pops open.

"Jax," she whispers, looking around, as if just now realizing we're outside.

"No one will see, Bree, I got you," I lie. Anyone could see, and right now I don't care. I'm not stopping.

Her nipples were already hard with excitement. The cool air seems to make them harder. I suspected she was gorgeous, seeing her now with the glow of the moon against her pale skin...*Fuck*, she robs me of words. I lean down to run my tongue along the outline of her nipple, before moving to the swollen bud and taking it in my mouth. I use my tongue to push it against the roof of my mouth, sucking it deep and then slowly releasing.

"Oh...Oh...Wow..." Bree gasps, bearing down on my leg and taking what she needs. I let my fingers tease her nipple, with what my tongue is doing to her other one. I can tell the way her breathing picks up that she's close to coming. She's riding my leg harder and harder. Any second she's going to come...for me...*for the first time*...

I'll own this. I'll be the first one to give her body pleasure. It's mine. No one else will ever have this from her.

"Come for me Bree. Don't be afraid baby. Give in to what your body wants. If you're a good girl, I'll give you even more later," I whisper in her ear. Even as I say it, I know it's wrong. I also know that I'm going to turn this good girl into a very bad girl, one who knows exactly how to give me what I want. One who will crave exactly what I can give her.

"I'm trying, Jax," she gasps my name when I bite into her nipple. Her body jerks and trembles, I could almost smile at how responsive she is. I kiss up the valley of her neck, finding her ear again, letting my teeth tease along the lobe.

"If you come for me, sweetheart, I'll let you watch me come later," I promise.

"Yes," she whispers, her whole body trembling.

"Would you like that, sweet Bree? Watching me stroke my cock for you and only you, until I can't hold back any longer, and I shoot cum all over you?"

Her chest heaves as she pants, "Oh God."

"You want it don't you Bree? You want covered in my cum.

It's all yours, sweetness. All you have to do is come for me. Come for me, and I'll show you all the naughty things I want to do to that sweet young body of yours." I move my hand between her uncharted pussy and my thigh, cupping her crotch, teasing my thumb along the seam of her pants.

"Oh, God. Jax, I'm coming! I'm coming!" she cries out and the joy and sense of victory I have is something I have never felt before. This was her first orgasm, and it's mine, but I'm a big enough bastard to admit I want all of her fucking orgasms. *Every last fucking one.*

Chapter 12

Bree

I FEEL AMAZING—exhausted and yet strangely unsatisfied all at the same time. I think I might slide to the ground because my feet feel like rubber, but Jax takes me in his arms holding me close. His hands rake softly through my hair. His lips are pressed against my temple, giving me small kisses. It feels like praise. It feels like he *cares*. Maybe I'm fooling myself, but I don't care.

"Let's get you fixed up, sweetness," he whispers, pressing me close to his side, and I have to force my legs to walk so I can follow his lead to the truck door. Helping me inside, he's taking such care with me that I feel like I'm fragile and precious to him.

"*Shit*," he growls quietly, and I look up at him confused. He's buttoning my shirt, at least the buttons that are left.

"What?"

"I made a mess of your top, Bree. There's no way you can wear this back without everyone knowing that you just…"

"Got off?" I ask boldly. My blush is intense, but inside I am so happy I could scream it to the world.

"Yeah," he says. He looks at me and though there is still kindness and caring, I see something else. Something I don't like. *Regret.*

"Don't do that, Jax," I say, stroking my finger down his arm.

He pulls away slowly. "Do what?"

"Regret what we just did. Please?" There's so much more I

want to say. Don't push me away. Like me. Let me know this will happen again. That more will happen between us. Give me more. *Give me more of you…*

I don't say any of that. I'm afraid. All I can ask is that he doesn't take what we shared away from me. That he doesn't ruin it.

"Bree, we're beside the road, almost to Skull's house. What if one of the brothers had seen us? What if your grandfather had?"

"They didn't," I remind him.

"Only because we were damn lucky. This can't happen again."

I should've known the moment wouldn't last.

"Why not?"

"I'm too fucking old for you, for one thing. I'm forty years old. You're eighteen. *Hell*, I could have kids out there older than you."

"Do you?"

"Not that I know of," he barks, raking his hand down the side of his face.

"Then what's the problem? I don't understand. I like you. I like what we just did together. I want more," I tell him, hoping he will think I'm just talking about the sex.

"Sweetness, you deserve more than an old, worn-out, broken biker. Someone like that kid who was hanging around you this morning."

"Jeff? Please don't tell me that you think he'd be the better choice for what we just did here. And you are not old! When you're a hundred, I'll be knocking on eighty. I don't see a big problem at all." I shrug.

"Let's fight about this later. I'd rather not be caught arguing with you beside the road with your shirt ripped open. Skull or Torch could come driving by at any time and… *What in the fuck happened to your pants?*" he yells, so loud my head jerks up.

I look down at my knee. There's a little blood where I scraped it against the pavement earlier. The tear in my pants is wide enough it shows the damage.

"I fell getting out of the window at the diner."

"Christ." He throws his hand up and brings it down pinching the bridge of his nose.

"Just take me to Beth's. I'll clean up there," I tell him, suddenly feeling tired.

"I take you to Beth and Skull's like this, and I'm a dead man. I'll take you to my apartment, clean you up, and find you something to wear."

"I thought you lived at the club?" I ask confused. His place is the last place I expect him to take me.

"I do mostly. I rent a crap apartment for when I want to be alone," he explains.

He finishes putting my seatbelt on and then slams the door walking around to his side.

I could have told him that no one was home at Beth's, or even reminded him of my forgotten jacket laying between us on the seat, but I don't. I want to go to his place. I want more time with him. So, I say absolutely nothing.

But inside, I'm dancing.

Chapter 13

Jax

I'VE LOST MY *damn mind.* I shouldn't have done that. I shouldn't have…but, *fuck* I want to do it again. *Hell*, I want to do more. Bringing her back to my shit apartment is the last thing I should be doing. Maybe she'll take one look at it and realize that a forty-year-old man who has nothing isn't someone she should ever give herself to? I don't fucking get how two days and one episode of dry humping can have me in knots over a woman, but it's true. She's got me all tore up inside.

I open the door, the smell of musty carpets and dust assaults my senses at once. I reach over and flip the light. I haven't been here in weeks. Dishes are still piled in the sink and empty pizza boxes decorate the room which doubles as a kitchen and living area combined. There's a small hall on the left, that always serves to make me feel claustrophobic that leads to a bedroom, which is just big enough for my bed, a small chest, and a bathroom. My place is definitely nothing to write home about. Being here depresses me. *Fuck*, I'm a loser. This wasn't how I saw my life playing out by the time I hit forty.

"Sit on the couch. I'll go get some things to clean you up with," I order, letting go of her hand now that we're inside. *I shouldn't have been holding her hand in the first fucking place.* I lock the door and walk out of the room, all without sparing her a glance. I'm not sure if it's because if I look at her right now I'll take her up against the wall, or if I don't want to see the look on her face—*just in case she feels sorry for me now that she sees the place I call home.*

It's not a home. I haven't really had one of those. *Ever. Hell,* the Devil's Blaze is the first time I ever felt like I had a place where I belonged, but even with that, I don't feel like the rest of the brothers. Maybe I'm always destined to be alone.

I come back in the room and Bree is on the sofa, looking around. I don't know what she's thinking, it's not showing on her face. When I get close to her she jumps slightly, before giving me a smile. There's no pity, no judgment. *Just Bree.* Christ Almighty, I'm in trouble. I clear my throat trying to choke down need, wants, dreams, and the hopelessness of wishing I was twenty years younger.

"Let's check those knees out," I tell her, sending up a small prayer of thanks I didn't say tits, cause they're straining against her bra—*her red silk bra*, and all I want to do is face-plant right here.

"Okay," she whispers, with a gentle smile. Why does it feel like everything about Bree is gentle, unless I push her? *And I bet I could push her.* How much would it take before I have her clawing into me, screaming my name? My balls are blue and my damn dick is killing me.

I lean down in front of her, getting on my knees. I move my thumb around the outside of the deepest scratches. There's blood and dirt there that will need cleaning.

"You should be more careful, sweetness. Something like this could scar," I warn her. Scarring her body would be a fucking sin. She's perfection. Bree leans in closer to look at her knee. It's probably not on purpose, but *fuck* her tits are so close, I could reach out and run my tongue along the valley of them.

I grab the ragged ends of the tear on her jeans on each side and rip the hole so it's wider. I'm taking my frustration out on them, so they tear clear down to the bottom of the leg. I hear Bree's breathy gasp. *Hell*, I can even feel her warmth brush softly against my hair. Before Bree, I never realized I enjoyed self-torture.

"I liked these jeans," she says.

"I wasn't the one jumping out of windows," I tease.

"You drove me to it," she confides, and when I look up at her, it feels like my fucking heart freezes. *She's smiling. Her eyes are filled with pleasure and it's all aimed at me.* Her lips are just a couple inches away. The urge to kiss her is so strong, I fucking shake from it.

"You need to learn to control your impulses. That will come with age," I tell her like a jackass as I put a bandage over her scrapped knee. I have to put distance between us somehow. Immediately, I regret it however, when the light in her eyes dims to a dull twinkle, then nothing.

"I should be getting back. I told Beth and Katie I'd be back this evening to help with the kids while they work on last minute party things," she says, looking across the room at a bare wall, instead of at me.

"Don't be like that, Bree." I take the seat next to her.

"Like what?"

"Close up on me," I tell her, at the same time kicking myself, because this was what I wanted. I just can't stand to see that light gone. "I'm only telling you the truth, here."

"What was *that* about then?"

"That?"

Her hand waves toward the door. "What we did together? If you're so hell bent on telling me all the reasons you shouldn't touch me then what just happened on the side of the road?"

I frown. "Something that shouldn't have."

"But it did. I didn't see you reminding me how young I was then. I didn't see you calling a halt to it then." She's calling me on my shit, but I can't change the way things are.

"I lost my head. When you toy with a man, there are consequences."

"You're a liar. I might be young, but at least I'm honest. You want me. Maybe as much as I want you," she challenges me to tell her she's wrong.

"You're jailbait."

She counters, "I'm eighteen."

"You're a world of trouble, Bree. Even if I ignored your age, being who you are makes anything impossible. Besides, I'm not the kind of man you want."

"Why impossible? Skull and Torch are family? They're your brothers."

"Exactly. If they even thought I was thinking of staking a claim on you they'd cut off my dick and feed it to the buzzards. And baby girl, no offense, but I ain't risking my dick for any pussy, doesn't matter how sweet it promises to be."

"How do you know what kind of man I want?"

"You're young. Still a dreamer. You want a man with a regular job, a house with a picket fence, and kids. Which is fine, but none of those things are who I am."

"I bet Skull thought the same thing before Aunt Beth."

I shake my head. "And that proves I know exactly what you want."

"Fine. Then how about a deal?"

"A deal?"

"What if you give me more of what we just shared together?"

"I told you just a few of the many reasons why that can't happen."

"It can if we obey rules." She's seriously thinking hard about this.

"Rules?" I repeat, needing a moment to think.

She winks at me growing bolder. "No one knows but us."

"You're awful sure of yourself. What makes you think I'd even agree to this?"

"I might be young and innocent, but even I know when a man is looking at me like he wants to eat me alive."

"Bree, you're young. What do you want with me? You could have anyone your own age. *Hell*, even a bastard my age with better prospects," I tell her, giving up all pretenses. She wants to talk plain—*I'll give it to her plain.*

"I don't want them. I want you."

"You don't know me."

"I know how you make me feel." She leans closer to me, tempting me to taste those lips.

"That's just sex. Any man can give you that, sweetness," I tell her, hating the very idea of it, even as I say it.

"I've never wanted it before. Not until I saw you across the room."

I cup the back of my neck and clear my throat. "And if that doesn't sound like a dreamer right there."

"You looked at me too. I know you did. I saw you stand up. Go ahead, Jax. Deny that you want me. I'll stop if you can tell me that you aren't dying for more of what we do to each other."

"What if I do? I'm a man. I'm just saying you could have that with a man more suitable and get all those dreams that pretty little head of yours is entertaining."

"I'm a virgin."

My breath catches in my throat. I know she is. "I gathered that already. You pretty much gave that away when you said you hadn't come before."

"I want you to be my first. I want you to teach me about sex, Jax. I want you to *own* all of my *firsts.*"

Motherfucker.

Chapter 14

Bree

OH GOD, OH *God, oh God! What did I just do?*

Oh, I know! I just told Jax I wanted him to be my first…*at everything!* I can't let him see that I'm really freaking. I'm doing my best to appear like I'm in control here. If he knew how nervous and scared I was, there would be no way he would agree. Especially, if he knew that he's right.

I may have only known him for two days, but I definitely want him *forever.* I know that's crazy. I know most people would call it stupid, and I *definitely* know that there's no way that Jax is looking for any of that, especially with someone he just met. *Especially with me.* That means I'm going to try and get all I can from him. I may get my heart broken, but at least I can say I tried. And who knows? Maybe he will decide he wants to keep me. Stranger things have happened…right? *Please God, let him want to keep me. If he doesn't I may not survive.*

"Christ Almighty, Bree. What in the hell are you thinking?" he says getting up and walking to the window.

"Never mind," I tell him, feeling stupid. I stand up, intent on nothing else other than to leave. I make it to the door before his hand slams over top of my head, caging me in and fixing it so that there's no way I can pry the door open. "You don't get to drop a bombshell like that and leave, sweet Bree."

"Why are you always calling me sweet? I asked you to stop."

"You asked me to stop calling you sweets. I did."

"They're all the same. I have a name, Jax."

"You do, and trust me, I'm not about to forget it. It's just that I know beyond a shadow of a doubt that those lips will be the sweetest drink I've ever had in my life."

His words reverberate through me, but it's the look in his eyes that freezes the very breath in my lungs. It's that look that gives me courage.

"Then maybe you should kiss me." I lean up on my toes.

"Bree..."

"Kiss me, Jax," I urge him, wondering if he can hear the beating of my heart. It seems so loud it echoes in my ears.

"Fuck," he groans, "I'm going to regret this." His fingers tangle into my hair to the point of pain.

"I won't," I tell him truthfully. No matter what happens, nothing that I do with Jax will ever be a regret. He pulls my lips to him and crushes them with his own.

Heaven.

His tongue sweeps against mine, tasting and exploring. My tongue brushes against his in a counter motion. I can't breathe as his mouth owns mine, claiming me, ruining me from ever being kissed by another.

Chapter 15

Jax

THERE COMES A moment in every man's life where he meets his downfall, with this kiss I'm sure mine is Aubree Davis. I don't have one doubt. The moment my tongue plunges into that sweet mouth, I'm gone. She tastes of sex and the sweetest candy known to man. With one kiss she's promising pleasure worth dying for. Which is probably apt, since I know touching her practically ensures my death.

My fingers tighten in her hair, moving her exactly where I want her. My other hand is at her neck, feeling her pulse beat, and holding her so that she can do nothing but accept what I give her. Her tongue tentatively comes out to dance with mine and I wage a war with it, overpowering, fighting with it, and demanding submission. Her moan is swallowed down with victory as her body trembles against me.

When we break apart she takes deep breaths, her body vibrating with hunger and a need I'm not sure she understands. *Hell*, at forty, I've never felt anything like it, so I don't completely understand either. This small, slip of a girl has managed to bring me to my knees. She's going to destroy me.

"Can we do that again," she whispers, her delicate fingers touching her lips, her eyes looking at me like I hold all the answers to the mysteries of the universe. *I don't.* I'm completely clueless for the first time in my fucking life. However, when a woman looks at you like that, there's pride that grows deep inside. Pride that makes you want to go out and capture the world for her. Unravel every single question, gather the answers, and give her anything she could possibly want.

"We'll be doing more than just that."

"Does this mean what I think it means?" she asks, and I swear it looks like she might laugh. There's so much happiness on her face right now, it makes me feel…*young*.

"Maybe. We need to discuss more terms."

A little bit of the light dies down in her eyes, and I regret it, but I need to try and minimalize damage here. Touching Bree quite literally is signing my death warrant. I'm not sure I give a fuck, but I think the rules need to be out there, because I don't have doubt in my mind that somewhere along the line she's going to realize that I'm not worth her time of day. She has a bright future ahead of her and she doesn't need to be saddled down to a broken-down, rusty, old biker.

"Okay," she says, and I take a step away from her, leading her to the sofa. Her big eyes look up at me, anxiously waiting.

"First, you were right. No one absolutely can ever know what happens between the two of us."

She nods eagerly. "Got it."

"I mean it. No talking about it with your friends. No writing in diaries, no chatting with your girls about this shit. What goes down between us, stays *between us*." I motion between the two of us.

"I already agreed to that, Jax and I don't write in diaries or journals. I don't think that's done anymore. The only people that do that shit are idiots in Washington. Don't you watch the news?"

I rake my hand through my hair and hold my head down so she can't see my smile. This girl has no idea the effect she has on me, and I'm not even talking about sexually. She's like fresh air to a man that's been dying in a dungeon for years.

"While we do this, there will be no other men in your life. I catch you with someone else and it's over. That's it."

"What about other women?" Her words hold a hint of jealousy and it warms me to know she feels so strongly.

"You swing both ways?" I tease her.

"No, idiot. If I'm supposed to save myself for only you, are you going to return the favor? I'm not stupid. I know the Blaze have women, and I know more about bikers in general and club life than I ever wanted to."

"While I'm with you, sweetness, you can guarantee I don't want any other women. You'll be it," I tell her, and I watch as the light slowly comes back on in her eyes. Then, those beautiful red lips slide into a long smile, and *fuck* if that pain in my heart doesn't start again. I bring my hand to rub it idly, imagining all the things I want to do to that mouth. "Next, when I want you, I want you. You don't argue, you don't fight it. You give yourself to me, where I want, how I want, and most importantly *when* I want."

Bree swallows nervously. I watch the movement of her throat. I see her tongue come out and dance across her lip. She bites into her bottom lip, and I stare intently as the color gently bleeds away to a pale white before she releases the skin, nodding her head in agreement.

I want to leave it there. I want to take the victories I have and move on. I don't. I need to push her. Half of me is hoping she'll walk away and save me from myself, and the other half of me is praying she doesn't. She has me that wrapped in knots.

"And last, when I say it's over. It's over."

"Jax…"

"That's non-negotiable Bree. You need to understand going

into this what's happening. I'll give your body pleasure. I'll teach you everything I know and hopefully, together we'll discover new ways of reaching satisfaction. Exploring every avenue of gratification and need, but when it's over…it's over. This isn't forever. I'm not a knight in shining armor. I'm a bastard that's taking what you're offering because I want it. I'm just going to make sure you get all the pleasure out of it you can find. If you can't agree to that now you need to walk away."

She's silent for a few minutes. Her face is downcast and she's staring at the floor. I'm waiting, and it feels like I'm standing on glass, waiting for her answer, wanting her to say yes, but *needing* her to say no.

"Okay, Jax. I agree to your demands," she whispers, finally looking up at me.

The blood is pounding in my head and it sounds like nails in my fucking coffin. It's done. Bree will be mine. There's no way to walk away now.

I don't think I could if I tried.

Chapter 16

Bree

THE PARTY IS going great. Pops doesn't let me around the Saint's parties very often, but the few I've gone to, there's a sense of brotherhood for sure, but this is different. The Devil's Blaze aren't just a brotherhood. They feel like a family. All the old ladies and members alike are treated the same. There are kids running around. And everyone's laughing. *Even Jax.*

He has me so confused. I thought once we made our agreement, that we would continue what we started beside the road. *We didn't.* Instead, he gave me his shirt to wear and a pair of jogging pants. Then he snuck me back, making sure Skull's house was empty before he let me get out of the truck. *He didn't even kiss me goodbye.* All he did was tell me he would see me later. Now it's later. It's much later. In fact, it's a day later.

The party is in full swing and everyone is having fun. Katie and Torch are playing Red Rover with the kids. It's hilarious watching Torch play with them. He looks like the ultimate biker, but he's just a giant kid himself. Nothing explains that more than the T-shirt he's wearing. It's black with large white writing that says: *Be kind to my wife, she's pregnant.* Of course, when he turns around, there's a picture of a squirrel that's dressed like Darth Vader—except for its bushy tail. The shirt says: *Yes, I am the father. The power of the nut juice is strong in me young Jedi.* Katie apparently doesn't mind because her matching black shirt says:

Baby on board. Then in parentheses it says: *I refused to swallow so he knocked me up.*

Their relationship is both hilarious and beautiful. I love watching them together. Skull and Beth are different. Their relationship is intense. They share this connection that anyone can see. It's crystal clear. Like right now they're across the yard from each other. Beth is laughing and talking with some of the other old ladies, while Skull is drinking a beer, standing around some of his men, but every so often he'll look over at Beth, as if he's just making sure she's okay. She immediately looks up at him, as if she can feel the heat in his gaze. Maybe she can, it's palpable.

"What are you doing over here by yourself?"

My head jerks up, and I smile when I see Beast. Despite the name, he's more like a giant teddy bear—*or at least he is to me.* He comes over to Pops sometimes with Skull or Torch. I first met him not long after Pops discovered I existed. Viper, the sperm donor, and some of his women kept me hidden.

Viper once told me while he was drunk that his father would disown him and have me killed because I was a mistake from a crack addict, club whore. He made it clear he didn't want me, but he didn't feel like I should die for merely existing. The day Pops found me, I thought my life would end. It turned out, it just began.

Maybe it's because of my past, I'm not sure, but Beast took up with me and has been nice to me ever since. It's always made me feel special, because he rarely talks to anyone; he was injured in an explosion. The man's always had a sadness about him, and I thought that his injuries were the reason, until Aunt Katie told me that he lost his daughter in the accident. My heart kind of breaks for him. He has scars, I know, but he's let his hair and beard grow so long you don't see them. You do see the ones on his hands, however, and they are pretty gnarly. Maybe they would turn off some people, but to me, I see them as badges of courage. Proof that he loved his daughter so much that he would walk through fire to try and save her. How beautiful would it be to have a man care for you that much? I mourn for all that he has lost, but even more for his daughter. I wish she could experience that love. What an amazing life that would be. It's just not fair.

"What's wrong, ladybug?" he asks, using his nickname for me that no one knows.

"Feeling a little out of place. Besides you, my aunts and uncles, I don't really know anyone here," I lie, but then again, I'm not sure I know Shaft, or that I could count him.

"Have you met Latch's sister, Lucy? She's about your age, and she has some friends over. I bet you'd enjoy getting to know them."

I want to tell him, I'm positive I wouldn't, but I don't. He's trying to look out for me and while I really appreciate it, I caught a glimpse of Lucy and her *friends* earlier. They look like the snobby, spoiled girls I do my best to stay away from. Still, if they're here and Beast can vouch for them, then the least I can do is meet them. It doesn't seem fair to judge them with no reason.

"I haven't yet," I tell him.

"Haven't what?" Jax asks, surprising me when he comes up behind us.

"She hasn't met Lucy and the girls. Was gonna take her over there."

"What for. Those kids are annoying as hell," Jax says cementing my first impression.

"They're close to the same age," Beast says and by this time his voice is getting gravelly. It hurts for him to talk, especially for extended periods. He doesn't mean anything, but I inwardly blanch at his use of words. Just what Jax needed. *Another reminder of my age.*

"Really? They don't seem it?" Jax says, staring at me strangely, and I have no idea what he's thinking.

"It'd be good for her to meet people her own age."

"You just wanna go flex in front of Lucy," a guy I remember Torch calling Briar says, joining us.

"Fuck you," Beast growls, and with his voice hoarse, he sounds what I imagine a bear would sound like when he growls. "I told you to drop it."

"Drop what?" Jax asks.

"Lucy has the hots for our man, Beast."

"Christ, you are like an old woman."

"Isn't she a little young for you brother?" Jax asks, and I wish I could kick him.

"She's not too young. *Hell*, she's out of high school and more than legal. I think she might be good for our boy," Briar says. "Might put a smile on his ugly mug again."

"Not if Sabre and Latch get a hold of him," Jax says.

"I'd think they'd be glad that Lucy has someone so amazing in her life," I tell them and Beast's hand flexes on my forearm as he puts his arm around me.

"Let's go, ladybug," he says gruffly.

"Ladybug?" Jax parrots annoyed.

I don't answer him, I couldn't anyways, because Beast leads me toward the picnic table where Lucy and her friends are gathered around. I spare a quick glance at Jax, his eyes are appraising me, but he makes no move to stop me from leaving.

The talk immediately stops when he gets close. I have to fight to keep from squirming when I feel all their eyes on me. I don't like crowds. Especially crowds that I don't know…*and crowds I'm pretty sure I won't like.*

"Lucy, this here is Skull's niece, Aubree."

"Oh. Hi, Aubree," she greets me sounding friendly enough. Her dark hair frames her face in feathered layers. Her green eyes shine with warmth.

"Hey, Lucy. It's nice to meet you," I tell her.

"She's new here, I thought it'd be good for her to meet you and your friends," Beast explains our interruption.

"You go to school here?" One of Lucy's friends asks. Her dirty blonde hair hangs in waves over her shoulders.

"I go to London-East," I tell her, naming one of the three high schools in the area.

"O.M.G.! you're still in high school?" That comes from one of Lucy's friends. Lucy blushes, and I start to feel a little better about her, because she's obviously embarrassed. Maybe she's not the snob I gave her credit for. "Getting ready to graduate," I tell her.

"Beast come over here for a minute," I hear Skull demand, and I immediately want to go with him.

"I'll be back," he says, not giving me the chance to tell him not to leave me alone with them. You can really tell his voice is bothering him now, because there's squeak at the end of his words. You can tell it's painful. I watch him walk away, wishing I could help him somehow.

"Thank God he's gone," one of her friend's sneers.

"I know, right? Someone really should introduce him to hair conditioner," another one says.

"Or a good barber," the last one adds. I look over at Lucy. I expect her to take up for Beast. I don't know…I mean Briar said she likes him. She should say *something*. But, she doesn't, instead she's laughing.

"Yeah, he's pretty hideous. You can't hardly see anything but hair."

"Girl! I know. You have to wonder if he's that hairy everywhere."

"Yikes," one of the other bitches' cries, and I've about had my fill.

"We better hush. We'll hurt Lucy's feelings. Everyone knows she was crushing on Beast hard."

"Yeah, she was going to be his Belle," another one adds, sarcasm so thick in her voice it makes me sick.

"Drop it, Kathy," Lucy says softly.

"What? She's just telling the truth. You were all gaga over him before we went to France."

"Yeah, but Lynn have you seen him now? He's repulsive. A woman would have to be drunk to want to be with him, and then that might not be enough," Lucy adds on at the end of the conversation. That apparently is when I go past having enough because I reach out and slap her so hard it feels like my hand is on fire.

"Wow, really? That's how you repay someone who has only been anything but good to you? I happen to think his scars, *hell*, everything about him is amazing. It shows how deeply he loves," I snap at her, all of them really.

"Whatever," another girl says and they all look at each other like I'm insane. Lucy is holding her cheek and looking at me, it's not anger I see in her eyes, but something else. Still, she doesn't say anything else which just condemns her further in my eyes.

"You know what? I feel sorry for all of you, but especially you, Lucy."

"Excuse me?"

"You feel sorry for us?"

"That's rich, a river rat feeling sorry for us," her friend chimes in, calling me a name I've heard often. It refers to the fact that I live on the North side of Laurel River, where the houses are mostly government funded. I don't know how they know I'm from there, and I don't care. Suddenly, I just want to tell Lucy what a loser she is and leave.

"Yeah, I feel sorry for you, but mostly for Lucy, because she had the chance to have someone amazing and wonderful in her life. Someone who loves unconditionally and she's throwing it away. Which is fine really. You don't deserve someone like Beast," I tell her. "You're not good enough for him," I stress to her lastly, and then I turn to walk away. Beast is standing two feet away from me and there's no doubt he's heard it all. His dark eyes are more than expressive. The tension is vibrating around us. Two other men are standing with him, and Jax is standing there too. I feel color creep up my face.

"Lucy, let's go," one of the men barks, anger so thick I jump at the sound.

"Latch," she complains.

"Now," he says, even sterner.

Beast comes over to me and kisses my forehead. He doesn't say anything, he doesn't have to, but my heart breaks even more for him. I watch as he moves away and then walks back toward the compound. I feel the tears leave my eyes. I don't even try to stop them, but I hate Lucy and her friends so fucking much right now.

"Let's go, baby," Jax says next to me, and I jump. His fingers come down catching one of my tears.

"They hurt him," I whisper the words that break my heart because Beast has been hurt enough.

"They did," he agrees, not bothering to try and lie.

"He's been hurt enough."

"That he has, sweet Bree. That he has," he says leading me away from the crowd. I go willingly, just wanting out of there, but I know in my heart that I'd follow Jax anywhere.

Chapter 17

Jax

FUCK. THAT'S IT. I'm screwed. I've been doing my best to stay away from her. I know what I agreed to, but I've spent the day at the party trying to back away. I have a list of reasons. She's too young and immature to even think of going there. I barely know her. I even convinced myself I could have sex with someone else and work her out of my system. Then I saw the way she took up for my brother. I saw the way it hurt her to know he was in pain, and I was a goner. Her reaction was not that of an immature kid. She might be young, but even with the limited time we've known each other, one thought has cemented inside of me. Aubree Davis is *mine.*

"Yo, Shaft! Where ya' going?" I look over to see Keys leaning against the building talking to Denise. I see the look in her eyes as soon as she looks at me. I feel guilty, for some reason, as if I've cheated on Bree—*which is crazy.* I hadn't even laid eyes on Bree the last time Denise and I did anything.

"Bree wants to go home, I'll be back a bit later," I lie.

"Well, when you get done babysitting come on back and we'll party," he says and the way Denise is hanging on him and smiling at me leaves little room to wonder what they're talking about. I know Bree understands, because her body goes taut against me.

"Not tonight, brother," I tell him and leave before he can say more shit that might set Bree off. She doesn't say anything as I lead her back through the club. We go out the front door, and I'm on my bike before she speaks up.

"You don't have to take me home. I can get one of the others."

"Bree—"

"You should go back to the party Jax. I can get home without you." I can hear the slight tremble in her voice, the jealousy she's trying to hide.

"Get on the damn bike, Bree."

"Jax—"

"Now," I order. I see indecision on her face and watch as she wars with herself. In the end, she gets on the back of the bike. I wait but when I don't feel her arms go around me, I have to speak up. She wants me? She will learn what I want. "Arms, Bree."

"What?"

"Put your arms around me," I demand.

"I'm fine."

"I don't want to have to tell you again, Bree." She's gonna be the death of me. Her smart mouth drives me wild.

"You're not the boss of me," she huffs, but puts her arms around me.

"We'll see baby. We'll see," I tell her, and I can't help but smile as my bike roars to life.

Her arms around me with her body pressed to my back is fucking perfect. I gotta admit I like the way I feel having her on the back of my bike.

Chapter 18

Bree

THERE HAS TO be something seriously wrong with me. That's the only explanation I can come up with. What else could explain how I hate the way Jax bosses me around, yet love it too? Even upset and confused I find myself leaning into him as we glide through the streets of downtown London, Kentucky.

All too soon we're outside his apartment. He doesn't speak when he shuts off his bike. I get off, feeling the nerves pulsate through my body. He hops off right after me, still not talking and his face looks angry. I have a momentary thought of just running away, but before my cowardice can win, he grabs my hand—pulling me with him. His steps are hard, solid stomps against the cement, and I'm more convinced than ever he's mad. I pull against his hold, trying to resist.

"Will you stop! You're walking too fast for me," I complain and he looks back at me and suddenly I think it's not anger…his eyes are heated and the look in them instantly makes my legs weak. Instead of responding he adjusts his speed.

When we make it inside, it takes a minute for my eyes to focus in the dark apartment. Jax walks around me and turns on a lamp that's by the old sofa in the room. His apartment really is in bad shape, but then it's not that different from any other home I've seen where the man is the only one who lives there. Pop's place is a real junk fest. There's things that could be done to this place that would make it feel welcoming, almost homey even. Would Jax flip if I took it on myself to do them? *Probably.*

"You're out of school in four weeks," Jax announces and it takes a few minutes for my brain to catch up with him. Talk about a quick change of thought.

"Close to that. So?"

"I'm not touching you for four weeks, not until you're out of school Bree. I'm a bastard, but I'm not that big of a bastard." He deflates me like I'm a balloon.

"I don't remember you giving me these terms when we discussed this earlier," I tell him upset and depressed all at the same time. I could tell he was different at the party, and I knew he was doing his best to renege on our bargain, but to hear him state it so calmly makes me want to scream.

"I am now."

"I see. What if I don't like the terms?"

"You don't really have a choice in the matter. They are what they are," he states.

"I don't have a choice?" I ask, taken aback.

"That's what I said. Didn't stutter, baby girl."

"Maybe my choice is to just walk away," I tell him and the very thought hurts me. My friends all talk about being in love and the need they have for their boyfriends. I've never had that, until I took one look at Jax. Then I knew. Instantly it hit me. *He's the one—even if he ends up destroying my heart.*

He looks me over, not answering. Fear curls inside of me, gripping my heart. I shouldn't have said that. Now, I'll have to walk away, because I'm positive he's not backing down. What's four weeks? I can handle four weeks, right? I never even wanted sex before Jax.

"Fuck! Women are difficult at any age," he growls turning away from me. I watch as he rakes his hand over his head. It's a motion that even in a short time of knowing him I know it's one he does in frustration. He throws his keys across the room, and I know without even asking that he's not going to back down.

"I'll just go," I whisper, wishing I could rewind everything. What was I thinking? He'll probably go back and party with that man and woman at the club. Jealousy burns deep inside of me. I make my legs move to the door, even with my heart screaming no.

Chapter 19

Jax

A SMART MAN would let her go. Hearing her footsteps behind me, I know the best thing to do would be to do just that—let her go. When I hear the doorknob turning, that fucking pain in my chest starts again. I don't want to let her go. That's my reasoning for turning around. Inside, I think it's worse than that though. I don't think I *can* let her go.

"Bree. Wait," I tell her and she looks over her shoulder at me, her hand frozen on the doorknob. "Your chance to walk away from me baby came before you offered me that body of yours." I'm an asshole, but fuck if I care.

"Jax—"

"I'm not giving you my dick until you're out of school, that's final."

"I don't see—"

"But that doesn't mean we won't find pleasure with each other." I grin knowing I have her.

She cocks her head to the side. "I'm confused."

"It's simple. I may not give you my dick, but I will definitely give you all the pleasure that sweet little body of yours can handle."

"You will?"

"Definitely. There's only one thing left for you to do."

"What's that?"

I raise my brow at her. "Undress for me."

"Undress…*now?*"

"You want this? You want me? Then baby strip. Right now."

"What's with all the baby stuff? What happened with calling me sweet?"

"I've decided you have a little bit of sour in you. Are you stalling?" This is where Bree surprises me again. She lets out a big sigh and then looks me straight in the eye.

"Probably," she says with stark honesty. Then, she slowly begins unbuttoning her shirt, her eyes never wavering from mine. With each button the blush on her face deepens. I see a fine tremble in her fingers, but she doesn't stop. She has no idea how truly beautiful she is right now in this moment. There's nothing fake about her. Nothing but her, and she's not trying to be seductive, but I've never been more turned on in my life. *Hell*, the zipper on my pants has a stranglehold on my cock. The damn thing can't have any blood flow at this point.

I can see small flashes of skin now that her shirt is unbuttoned. It's like the biggest fucking tease in the world. Her fingers have a death grip on each end of her shirt and her breathing is so ragged it's visibly shuddering through her body.

"Take it off, Bree."

"You're very bossy," she whispers so soft I have to strain to hear it, or maybe it's just I can't hear her over the way the blood is pounding in my ears and my heart is trying to beat out of my chest as the shirt falls to the floor.

Her skin is pale, white, virginal as if the sun hasn't even been blessed to shine on it. She's wearing a blue silken, lace trimmed bra that hugs her tits perfectly…*Fuck*. How am I supposed to keep myself from driving into that body for four weeks?

"The rest of it, Bree. Show me what you're giving me," I order, my voice almost as harsh as the hand I use to roughly adjust my throbbing cock.

Chapter 20

Bree

JAX'S VOICE IS so dark and rough, I feel shivers run up my spine, not stopping until even my hair tingles. I'm inexperienced, but even I can see the need in his lust filled eyes that's practically burning me alive when he looks at me. That gives me the courage to quickly undo my pants and push them down. I close my eyes, take a breath and then open them, standing in front of Jax in my bra and panties for the first time…*in front of any man for the first time.*

"Turn around," he orders, and I do it without a thought to argue. His voice is authoritative, but I think it would be easier not to face him when he looks at me. At least I was smart enough to wear a sexy bra. Unfortunately, I'm wearing panties that don't match. I really need to go shopping for more lingerie. I've never needed the sexy kind before, but I want to look my best for Jax. I stand looking at the door wondering what he will ask for next. I jump, letting out a gasp when I feel his hands on my shoulder. His hand moves along my neck, pushing my hair out of the way, and putting enough pressure I lean my head down. His rough, calloused hand feels incredible against my skin, but when his lips touch there my heart skips a beat.

Kissing down my neck and over my shoulders, his hands blaze the path first. Chills run through me, but I'm heated at the same time. He places a kiss at the base of my neck, his warm breath skitters across my skin, and I know I'm already wet along the inside of my thighs, but I can feel the moisture gather even more with his kiss and the tender way he's holding my arms. He keeps his lips there, every so often his tongue flicks against the skin, while his hands move down my arms and slide to my hips.

"Jax," I breathe, not sure what I want to say, just needing his voice to center me, because right now I feel like I'm floating.

"You're so beautiful, Bree," he whispers, his fingers flexing into my hips with bruising force. He pulls me back into him, the hard ridge of his cock pushing against my ass has me wishing he'd change his mind about giving it to me sooner. Even through his clothes he feels huge.

"Please…" I beg unable to tell him what I want.

"Please what baby? What do you want?"

So many answers spring to mind. Please, touch me. Please make love to me. Please don't let me go. *Please keep doing exactly what you're doing.* All I can manage though is a whimper. That's when one of his hands tangles into my hair and the other moves up to palm my breast. Excitement thrums through my body. Is he going to touch me? Has he decided not to wait? *Please, don't wait.* I bite my lip to keep from begging him to give in—to give me what I want.

His large hand moves over my breast, squeezing then releasing and repeating the action over and over. Desire bursts through me, even hotter than before. I feel his teeth bite into the skin where my neck and shoulder meet. *Not gentle.* Yet, right now I don't want gentle. I want whatever Jax gives me. I exhale at the desire and pain that runs through me, my entire body giving one slow, long convulsing movement.

"Oh…" I gasp as everything inside of me clenches tightly and evidence of my arousal runs from my center, wetting my thighs with sticky heat. If I could think, I might be embarrassed.

But, I can't think. Everything, every thought process, every touch, every breath is consumed by him. *Jax.* This man is owning me completely.

"I told you Bree, there were things I could give you until you're out of school. Things that will give you pleasure—*give us both pleasure*," he assures.

"I want it all," I whimper. Feelings of anticipation, need, and disappointment collide.

"You'll like what I give you," he growls against my ear, spinning me around to face him. When I come face to face with the desire and need written all over him, I can do nothing but agree.

I'll take anything he gives me, for however long he wants to give it to me.

Chapter 21

Jax

I'M BARELY HANGING on to control. I feel like a fucking pervert for even thinking of what I want to do to her young, untried body. I don't know what the fuck difference it makes that she is out of high school before I give her my dick, but somehow in my twisted mind it does. Who knows what the hell I'm doing. Maybe I'm hoping she'll save herself from me before those weeks are up. Maybe I'm waiting for someone to find out and kill me—put me out of my misery. There's only two things I'm sure of at this point. One is that having her and then being forced to give her up will kill me—which will definitely happen considering how young she is and *who* she is. The other thing is that regardless of it all, *I will have her.*

Her eyes look like liquid pools and the green is definitely brighter today, outshining the specks of brown and gold that mingle together. In all my years, I've enjoyed many women, but none have captured me the way that Bree has. And absolutely none have had eyes that even come close to how beautiful hers are.

This is all wrong. She deserves flowers, a soft bed, silk sheets, not a run-down rat trap with a worn out sofa and a bed that hasn't been slept on in months. I tell myself it's okay, because I'm not taking her virginity tonight, but I still feel like a fucking asshole. I pick her up and she instantly curves into my hold, her arms sliding against my neck, her breasts pressed against my chest. It might be fucked up, but holding her like this makes me feel like I've conquered the world.

When I get her to the bedroom, I'm torn between turning the light on, and leaving it mostly dark. There's enough light filtering through the windows that I can see her. I don't want her to be looking at how horrible the room is. I know she deserves better. I don't want her backing out because she sees what she's giving herself too. I need her tied to me before that happens. I want her completely mine, until her family and my brothers tear her away from me.

I slide her down my body, instantly missing the feel of her in my arms. I pull her away from me, just so I can get one more look. I can visibly see how a ragged breath shakes through her body.

"Jax?" she asks, but I don't have time to answer. Instead, I unhook her bra and clumsily push it from her body. Sweet Jesus, I wasn't expecting that. You think if you've seen a million tits, you've seen them all. But just like with Bree's eyes, that's no longer true. She's special. Pale white globes with dusty rose nipples so tight it looks physically painful. I can't resist brushing my thumb against it and watching as the point seems to strain toward me.

My eyes travel over her body, on the verge of breaking my own rule. I'm going to claim her eventually. *Why wait?* Then, my eyes stop at her underwear that is hiding that sweet little virgin pussy from me. *Jesus.* As if I needed another fucking reminder of just how young she is, suddenly, here it is.

Bree has on white cotton panties and over the front is a little daisy on it and the word *Sunday* written diagonally in frilly font and looped around the stem and leaves of the flower. She's wearing fucking days-of-the-week panties.

She must notice where my attention is, because her hand comes down to try and shield herself from me. I roughly grab her hands, pulling them away.

"Never try to keep me away from what's mine," I bark, like a fucking animal, but that's what she makes me feel. Like an animal and she's my prey. I'll fight and kill to keep her—*even my own brothers.*

"I don't want to stop you, I just…"

"Just what?" I ask, letting my finger follow along the rim of her underwear, dipping under the fabric every once in a while, loving the way her body tightens and leans towards me each time. She's already on the edge. *God*, how I'm going to enjoy pushing her over.

"I wish you'd just get it over with," she mumbles, her face a bright red. I want to laugh. She has no idea what I'm going to give her, or get her used to taking from me. Hurry will not be in my vocabulary. Well, possibly the first time, but the second time, I'll make sure lasts a good long time. Maybe until she begs me, or better yet until she can't do anything but cry from the need of what I'm denying her.

"In due time. Right now, you have too many clothes on."

"But, all I have on is my panties," she argues.

"Exactly," I tell her with a grin, before ripping them down the sides so I can claim my prize. I have plans for these later.

"Why did you do that? What am I supposed to wear now?" she asks, flustered.

"Me," I tell her, completely serious.

"But…" her sentence stalls on her lips when she watches me bring her underwear up to my face and deeply inhale her scent. "What are you doing?" She asks, her fingers biting into the bicep of my arm I'm using to hold her with.

"You smell like fucking air."

"Air?" she asks, but I can't explain, it would give too much away. How do you tell someone you are beginning to think you can't breathe without them? I don't want to discuss it. *Hell*, maybe I'm not ready to face it. Her hands move down to cover her pussy and she's looking around to avoid looking me in the eye.

I guess it's time to begin her training.

Chapter 22

Jax

I GRAB BREE'S hands, pulling them together, holding them hostage in one of mine, and forcing them behind her back. She doesn't even try to stop me. A fact that surprises, but pleases me more.

"I told you not to hide what's mine, Bree," I whisper in her ear. Her head leans back against me.

"Jax..."

"Don't worry baby girl, I'll give you what you need," I assure her. Letting go of her hands, I slide one of mine down her stomach and then further to cup her pussy. The heat rolling off of her envelopes my hand as I feel the wet evidence of her desire gather on my fingers. Excitement pounds through me. Not for the first time, I regret not being able to delve deep inside of her.

I push that thought aside and instead concentrate on the automatic way that Bree shifts her legs, making way for me to do whatever I want with that sweet body. I squeeze her pussy tightly, while my other hand palms and kneads one of her tits. When her hips thrust back at me, I feel like I've won a fucking war.

It's a dangerous game I'm playing, but I can't resist unbuttoning my pants and pushing them down so that my cock is free, pressing against her bare ass. I'm so hard and ready that my balls physically hurt. Pre-cum is leaking from the head and instantly slides against her creamy white ass. I take my cock in my hand, holding him roughly and stroke one smooth, long stroke, groaning as a stream of it slides against her cheek. Bree's breath hitches and her body stops all movement for a second as she feels what I'm doing.

I take my finger gathering the liquid on it and pushing it toward the crevice of her ass. My fingers bite into the fleshy cheek and I pull on it to reveal the small rosette opening, groaning as I push my pre-cum and finger into it. The circle of muscles clamps down immediately.

"Relax baby. Don't tense up. Let yourself go. It will feel good I promise." She takes a deep shuddering breath, but slowly she starts to relax, allowing my finger to go deeper inside. *Jesus.* She's so fucking tight. Exhilaration and need drum through me at such a rate, my body literally quakes. I'm going to have her in every way possible. *Soon.*

Raking my hand against her pussy, I push my fingers through the wet heat of her desire. She tightens down on my fingers, wanting to ride them. The urge to thrust them inside of her is there, but not yet. I slide them back and forth, never going inside but petting and combing through her sweet juice, while teasing her clit on each upward thrust.

"Ah," she gasps. Her hips are moving now in time with my actions. I can feel her legs tremble, as I rake back through. My hand is drenched in her desire. I want to taste her, but right now I need to do this. I've been thinking about it for days. I pull my hand back slowly, taking the time to scissor my fingers out and catching her clit between them. I push them together, so the throbbing little button jumps with each beat of her pulse. I can feel it against my fingers and again that feeling of power and control comes over me. What is it about her that makes me feel like I could conquer the world?

Finally, I pull my hand back through, and push a slick covered finger into her little ass. She takes it easier this time, maybe because she's excited, and maybe because my finger is so fucking soaked. She's so wet and ready for me, my dick hates me right now, and my balls are heavy. I need to give her my cum. My finger sinks up to the knuckle easily, and I pull it back out. I repeat that several times, getting her used to the feel of it, getting her used to my rhythm. Then, when I can tell she knows what I need from her, and what she needs from me, I let my finger leave that tight little cavern. Her whimper of despair makes me smile.

"Don't worry baby. Daddy's got you," I tell her. *Where the hell did that come from? Daddy?* What the fuck is wrong with me? That's never been something I've wanted. With her it feels as natural as breathing. This time I push two fingers inside her tight ass, tunneling in until they breach through the ring of muscles. Bree cries out and I hold them still for a second afraid I've hurt her. I'd rather cut off my right hand than do that. I've wanted her since the moment I first laid eyes on her. Now, I just have to figure out how to keep her without winding up dead. Not that I care. *Some things are worth dying for.*

"More. I need more," she whispers brokenly.

I think I could make her come like this. With nothing more than fucking her ass with my fingers. But, that's not how I want her first orgasm to be tonight. If things were different I'd want her first orgasm to be with my cock buried deep inside of her, so I can feel every fucking second of her pleasure. I decide to do the next best thing.

Regretfully, I take my hands away. She cries out in distress, and I place a kiss at the base of her neck in reward. I feel the need to make her work for every reward she gets from me—*and every punishment.*

"Shh…Bend over the bed, Bree. I'll make sure you get what you need."

"You will?" she asks, turning and looking up at me. The desire in her eyes makes me groan. She's hungry for so much more, and I want to give it to her. I cup the side of her face with my hand, kissing her forehead.

"You need to understand that you're mine now, Bree. I will never leave you needing more from me."

"Unless…"

"Unless I need to punish you."

"Punish me?" she asks, her eyes going wide as saucers.

"For misbehaving. Now lean over the bed, pull your legs apart and brace yourself with your hands."

She looks at me for a minute, as if undecided. Her eyes watch mine closely. Then she moves around me to obey my command. Once she's bent over the bed, with her ass sticking out, tempting me even more, I kick off my pants the rest of the way off. Then I drop to my knees behind her. I let my hands caress her legs, stroking as if I'm praising them. I turn so that my back is braced by the footboard of the bed and when I look up under Bree, my view is nothing but her sweet pussy and the glistening wetness marring her thighs. All for me…*All mine.* I reach up latching my hands on each of her hips and pulling her down to my face. Her body goes stiff in shock and she tries to resist. I give a slight slap on the cheek of her ass.

"What…"

"Sit on my face, sweet Bree. Give Daddy what he wants," I growl, my fingers tightening into her skin so much I know it has to cause her pain. It may even bruise her. *Fuck.* I want it to. I want my marks all over her sweet little virgin body. I want anyone that sees her to know she's owned by a man. A man who would fucking kill them if they touch her.

She does as I ask, but I can tell by her movements that she's unsure. It's okay. Soon she'll be lost to everything but sensation and riding my face until she comes. I use my tongue to slide along the inside of the lips that shield her from me. I take one hand from her hip so I can pull her pussy lips apart and gain better access.

The second her taste hits me, all thought of going slow is over. There's no way to describe how she tastes. She bursts on my tongue and as I swallow her down, I know it's a taste I will need for the rest of my life.

I concentrate on her clit. It's already jerking against my tongue—*pulsating with need.* I suck the sensitive skin into my mouth, holding it tightly, teasing it, and pulling on it, as if I'm going to release it and then sucking it all the way back in, ultimately mimicking what my cock will be doing someday. *Someday soon.*

Her once stiff movements begin to soften as her body picks up a rhythm as old as time. She's a natural, and I can't wait to show her everything her body can do. She pushes down against me, using my face to force friction against her pussy. I move my finger to her clit, holding it, while rubbing it back and forth with tight pressure. Her whimpers above me grow louder. Her sweet juice is running thick, coating my face. I can't believe how wet she is. Bree was made to be fucked. *God*, even though she's a virgin, as wet as she is, I know my cock could slide right in. *She's killing me.*

I stiffen my tongue and thrust it inside, fucking her with it, grinding her pussy down on me with even more force than she's using. Above me she's crying, calling my name—*sounding desperate.*

"Play with your tits, Bree."

I can sense her hesitation. "Do as I tell you," I growl against her clit, and in reward she clamps hard on my face. I move my hand down, sliding it through her cream.

Once I get my fingers covered, I seek out my cock, slickening my shaft with her arousal. I pump my hand up and down my length, imagining it replacing my tongue in her pussy. I suck her clit hard in my mouth and twist it.

I pump and stroke my dick in sync with my tongue as it devours her juicy pussy.

She shatters.

And I nearly explode.

The orgasm barrels through her and it's my name that she's screaming. She's so loud I figure my neighbors might call the cops. Turns out, Bree is not a quiet girl when fucked and damn if I don't love her even more for it. In fact, I think I will make it my goal to make her strip her vocal cords screaming my name. She tries to twist away from me, the pleasure too much, but I hold her tight, not letting her deny me and not stopping until she comes again and again, exhausted and begging for mercy.

My reward is licking her clean and promising myself that she'll never get away.

Chapter 23

Bree

I'M COMPLETELY WEIGHTLESS when Jax finally lets me rest. I come close to falling, except he's holding me up. Slowly, he maneuvers me so that I'm sitting across his lap. His hard cock is hot against my ass—so hard that it causes my insides to quiver. I'm completely wore out, but the feeling of his hard cock rubbing against my ass almost makes me interested in more. Instead, I moan. Jax pulls me so that my head rests on his chest. His fingers comb through my hair. I've never been treated gently in my life. *Never.* But, right now, Jax makes me feel like someone *special.* Someone *cherished.* Maybe that's normal after sex. I've never experienced it before, so I couldn't say. Right now however, I'm going to pretend that what we're sharing is special. When he kisses the top of my head, I don't stop the sigh that moves through my lips.

"Are you okay, baby?"

"Better than okay," I mumble against his neck, kissing it, sucking his salty skin between my teeth.

When he moves to get up, I groan in protest. I try to slide off his lap so he can get up without my added extra weight. He doesn't let me. Jax grabs me close to him, not letting me move and stands up like it's nothing. That simple fact makes me feel happy inside. To me it's proof that I picked the right man to give myself to. Carrying me back to the couch, he lays me on the cushions. I panic, thinking he's planning on leaving me alone. He grabs an afghan and covers me with it, gently. Placing a kiss on my forehead.

He starts to turn away from me and I grab his hand. "Where are you going?"

"I'm going to change the sheets on the bed before you lay on them."

"I could—"

"It's my job to take care of you. That's what I'm doing. You relax. I'll get this done and take a shower and come back and get you. Your job is to find some way to explain why you won't be home tonight, because you are not leaving here," he growls, sending chills running over my body, and the parts of me I swore he completely exhausted start to come to life with just the rumble in his voice.

"Shower? But…"

"A very cold shower," he says dryly. I can't help but look down noticing his hard cock jutting out towards me. Tingly awareness inside me brings everything female within me roaring to life. I want that… I want everything he has to give me. A voice inside my brain screams, *'It's mine!'*

"Let me take care…" I start to offer when he cuts me off.

"No," he commands, leaving no room for argument, but I try anyway.

"Jax, I want to…"

"To?" he asks and there's this smile on his face. *Satisfied…Arrogant.* I'd complain, but it's a really good look for him.

"To…" I deadpan.

"Say it, baby. Give me the words." Jax is all hot and demanding.

I look at him, my cheeks turning from pink to a red glow. "To make you come."

"You will, when it's time."

"It looks like it's time...*now,*" I argue.

He blows out a breath, his face contorted almost as if he's physically in pain. "I'm not taking your pussy right now. I told you that."

"Then I could...you know?" I tell him. His smile deepens and his eyes darken with laughter, but it doesn't feel like he's making fun of me. He's *happy.*

"I know...*what,* exactly?"

"I could use my mouth, like you did," I tell him, fighting down my blush and failing. He studies me, his smile slowly fading. He walks towards me, his dick bouncing with each step. I try not to get lost in staring at it, but again...*I fail.*

"Have you done that before, Bree?"

"Done what?" I ask, still hypnotized by his cock. I've seen a few before. I mean it's the age of the internet. I've never seen one in person though, and even if I had, I'm pretty sure they wouldn't measure up to Jax.

"Have you ever sucked a man off?" he growls, and I must have been really concentrating on his dick. So much that I didn't realize it was getting closer and closer. When he grabs the back of my hair and pulls my eyes up to his, I know, however. Gone is the easy look and smile on his face. Now, he looks vitally alive, electric even.

"What's wrong?" I ask confused, not sure why he seems...*angry.*

"Have those sweet cherry lips of yours been wrapped around another man's cock before?" his voice is so deep and the words practically rip from his throat.

"Are you serious?" I ask, starting to realize the thought angers him. That doesn't exactly make sense. I mean, I might be young, but even I know he's been with other women. *In fact...*

He glares at me, nostrils flaring. "Answer the question, Bree."

"Why are you changing the sheets?" I ask him, totally going with a hunch. Something flashes across his face, not an emotion, but maybe shock.

"I haven't been here in forever, they're dirty. Now answer my question," he growls, the tone vibrating through me.

"This couch isn't exactly clean," I continue to argue. Excitement spreading inside my body.

"Are you questioning me, Bree?" he asks, bending even further down. His hand moves from my hair to my neck, and he pulls my face closer to him, while keeping a firm hold on me. Maybe I should be afraid. There's adrenaline running through my veins. It's churning and drumming inside of me, making my heart beat faster, making my face heat, and anticipation spreads through me. It's not fear though. *It's excitement.*

"Maybe." I smirk.

"Answer my question, first," he says, his voice and face stern. It might be my imagination but I think his eyes are softer though.

"No. I haven't done that before," I tell him, giving in.

"Done *that?*" he presses daring me to say the words.

"Used my mouth on anyone before. I haven't wanted to until now."

"Good girl. Now give Daddy a kiss before I go shower and clean up," he says with a smile, and I can't help but hang up on that word again. *Daddy.* He's said it a couple times now. I shouldn't like it. I really shouldn't. Yet, every time he says it I get this funny feeling in my stomach, and my heart stops and then it feels like it tumbles in my chest. As wrong as it is…with Jax…*I like it.*

"You didn't tell me why you're changing the sheets," I push, not even bothering to hide the happiness on my face. I wouldn't say it out loud, but Jax was jealous about the idea of another man near me. *Me!*

"Because, brat, there might have been another woman here before, and I don't want anything to do with her, touching you. Including the sheets."

I celebrated too quickly. I knew—*or at least I was pretty sure*, why Jax wanted to change the sheets, but hearing him say that, causes jealousy to fire all the way through me. I don't like it. I don't like the idea of Jax with anyone else.

My face falls as my victory is swept from under me. "Was she special?"

"Bree," he sighs, a look of frustration coming out on his face. He brings his hand to his forehead, rubbing the crease above his right eyebrow in aggravation. He doesn't want to tell me. That means something. *It has to.*

Regret, jealousy, and hurt curl in my stomach. I shouldn't react, because whoever she was has nothing to do with here and now, but the emotion is still there, and there's nothing I can do to change how I feel.

"It's okay. I shouldn't have asked. Go clean up," I tell him, trying to keep the wobble out of my voice, because for some reason, I feel the urge to cry.

"Jesus," he growls, but it doesn't sound like anger. Especially by the delicate way he pulls me into his lap, afghan and all. Which is kind of a shame because it shields his cock from me. I want to cry and his dick is the last thing I should be thinking of. I try to hide my face from him, afraid of what he might see, but as soon as he gets me settled, his hand goes back to my neck, and he holds my face so I can't get away from him. "When a woman gives her body to you, that makes them special. A man isn't a man if he doesn't respect that."

Ouch. Message clear. I'm not unique I'm just one in a line. That's a slap in the face for sure. I jerk away from him, wanting away…just needing distance from him to regroup. Maybe he's right. I'm too young for this—at least emotionally, because I can't imagine doing what we did with any other person but Jax. On that note, I pull myself up, intent on finding my clothes and leaving.

Leaving, Jax.

Chapter 24

Jax

I SEE THE jealousy flair in Bree's eyes. It makes me happy. Has she already claimed me too? She's being unreasonable however. I need to nip that before it starts. I want her to be possessive of me, because she's mine, even if claiming her seals my death warrant. But *fuck*, I've got over twenty years on her. She's got to get used to the fact that there were other women before her.

She jerks, trying to get away from me. I'm on the floor and pull her down on my lap. I clamp down on her hips, keeping her still. Something about Bree, makes me love to cuddle her on my lap, holding her close to me, having her head against my chest, and her ass in my lap. It's where I'd keep her all the time if I could get away with it.

"Where do you think you're going?"

"I need to get up from here. I need to go to the restroom," she huffs, doing her best to avoid my face.

"What you need to do is settle your ass down," I gripe wanting to spank her ass and kiss her at the same time.

She tenses. "Let me up."

"Bree, I'm warning you." I know she's upset but she's gotta learn.

"I want up!" her voice screeches.

"If you don't stop acting like a child…"

"You'll what? That's what I am according to you. *A child.* I *need* to go to the restroom! That's not being childish."

"Unless you're using it as an excuse," I call her out on the bullshit. I'm a man. I don't play childish games.

"*An excuse?* You're crazy," she says, doing her best to appear innocent and failing.

"I don't think I am. I think you're acting like a baby all because you don't like the idea of me with other women."

She shakes her head, her hair falling over her shoulder, and I fight the urge to brush it away. "I think you're full of yourself."

"Maybe. But tell me I'm wrong."

"You're wrong," she huffs, anger flaring in her eyes and her cheeks flushed.

"You're lying," I tell her with a grin, and why the fuck I'm grinning I have no explanation except…*Bree.*

"You're insufferable," she grumbles, finally giving up on trying to get away from me.

"Kiss me, Bree."

"I don't want to," she says trying to twist her face away from me, and that's one lie I can't let her get away with. I put my hand on her neck, holding her head still and bringing her lips closer to me. Her eyes are still shooting daggers at me, and just to prove what a bastard I am, I'm enjoying it.

"Give me your lips."

"Why should I?"

"Because you want my lips on you. You want my kiss, and more than that you want to make me happy."

"You're full of yourself."

"Soon, you'll be full of me too," I tell her, grinning at the way her eyes dilate, as she catches on to what I mean. I let my fingers stroke softly against the skin on her neck. I lean into her ear, let my tongue run against the shell of it and then toy with the lobe. Her body shivers in my arms, but the whimper she lets out could drive me to my knees. "That's right baby. Soon, I'm going to slide my cock inside of you."

"Jax, I…" her voice comes out weak, hungry even.

"I'm dying just imagining how wet and slick you'll be for my cock. I want to thrust into you over and over. Do you want that baby? Do you want my cock inside of you, stretching you to fit me?"

"I thought you had to take a shower," she says, her voice husky and full of desire.

"Answer the question, Bree."

"You really are obnoxiously bossy."

"You have no idea. But quit stalling. Give, Daddy what he wants, and I'll shower while you figure out how to explain to Tucker that you're not coming home tonight." She sighs but there's a slight smile on her lips when she finally gives me what I want.

"Yes. Okay? Yes. I want all of that and more. It seems pretty clear to me, but then I'm not the one denying us right now," she says, and there it is. That sweet, bashful look on her face, but her sentence is delivered with a saltiness that makes my fingers itch to spank her ass.

"Salty…"

"You know that's a weird thing to say to a woman, don't you?"

"Babe, let's be honest. I'm forty years old. I'm a biker, and I am who I am. I'm not about to change now. I'm too fucking set in my ways. You seem so fucking sweet at times you make my teeth ache, and then all at once you throw something in my face, surprising me," I confess.

"Still…I mean, it's not really what a woman imagines her man will say to her. It's not how she wants her man to think of her."

"You're looking at it wrong. Have you ever had caramel that's so fucking good it melts in your mouth and makes you moan just from the taste?"

"Yeah…"

"That's definitely you, and after eating out that sweet little pussy of yours, I know just how true that is," I tell her, and I want to laugh when she squirms in my lap blushing. I've never been around a woman like her in my life. She's soft, delicate, and untouched. In my world that's unheard of. It brings out urges in me I've never experienced before. An urge to claim, to protect, and shield her from the rest of the world.

"Jax…" I love it when she says my name.

"But it's still a one dimensional thing… but salted caramel…You get the sweet, soft and delicious taste. But, the salt brings another side out. And somehow a fantastic thing, gets even better. That's you, Bree. Sweet, salty, flavorful, but always surprising."

"Wow."

"What?"

"You can call me salty anytime you want," she says deadly serious, which for some reason makes me laugh out loud again and kiss her lips. Then I forget what we are talking about. I forget everything, but the taste of her lips and the softness of them against mine. I suck her bottom lip into my mouth teasing it with my teeth, while letting my tongue brush against her delicate skin. I've never been one to do a lot of kissing. There's more important things to do with a woman. But, with Bree, I'm pretty sure I could spend days doing nothing but kissing her.

"Stop distracting me," I joke, suddenly feeling that pain return in my chest again. *Fuck*, forty years and it takes this small slip of a girl to knock me flat on my ass. I situate her back on the couch, spread the afghan over her body, and place a kiss against the inside of her neck.

"Don't leave me," she whimpers, her fingers tangling in my hair. I disengage slowly. She doesn't realize how hard it is to break away from her. I need to though, for my own sanity. *At least for a moment.*

"Where's your cellphone?"

"What? Oh…um…in the back pocket of my jeans. Why?"

"Hold that thought," I tell her and then walk into the bedroom to retrieve her cellphone. Holding it in my hand that guilt hits me again when I see the case; it's all glitter and crowns. *Jesus she's too young for me…Right?* Irritated for a number of reasons and wishing Bree could be older—not to mention have different family, I hand her the phone without touching her and kissing her again. *Which would have been my first choice.* "Call your grandfather or whatever. Make up some excuse he'll buy as to why you won't be home tonight," I order her gruffly.

"Okay…is something wrong Jax?" *Everything.* I rub the back of my neck roughly, knowing there's no point in telling her what's on my mind. She's too young to understand, and though she might be a Chrome Saint's Princess, she doesn't know my world…not really. I know Tucker enough to put money down on that.

"I just really need a shower and to get some sleep," I tell her gruffly. I see the worry in her eyes, and I don't really want that either. I'm worrying enough for both of us. "Now call. Make Daddy happy," I order her again, turning away.

"Daddy?" she asks, so softly I might have missed it. My dick, which was starting to go back to normal practically rages to life again. If she was calling me that right now, I know there's no way I'd be able to resist taking her right where she's at. *But she's not. Not really.* She's questioning me as to why I'm using the name. *Fuck*. That's the twenty-four-thousand-dollar question.

"What's wrong?"

"Is that…well normal?"

"Normal?" I ask pissed off, though if I stopped to think about it, probably more at myself.

"Should we be…I mean…you're not my father. I hated my father. I don't want you to be my father…I just…it seems strange," she says, flustered, her face red and her eyes avoiding mine.

"Trust me when I fucking tell you Bree, that I sure don't think of you as my child."

"I didn't mean to…"

"What I want from you, what I'm feeling with you is the farthest thing from *fatherly* that you can get and that's the fucking truth."

"Okay. I'm sorry Jax. This is all new to me. I mean, I know I am younger. I was just…"

"I mean I want to be the man in charge of you, the man who takes care of you, protects you, and sees to your needs. I will be your man, Bree. For…however long this lasts, I will be the only man you come to for *anything*. You got me?"

"I got you," she says, swallowing. I watch the movement of her throat and then slowly tear my eyes away so I can look into her eyes again. "I just didn't want people to think that…"

"That's where you need to stop. There are no people in this situation, Bree. None, except me and you. It doesn't matter what they think, because no one will ever know," I caution her and even though it needed done, when I see the look that flashes over her face, *fuck* if I don't feel that pain in my chest again. *Disappointment. She's disappointed.* If the situation were different, I'd do everything I could to make sure that's one thing Bree never feels again. This time it can't be helped. *Hell.* I'm disappointed myself. Disappointed, fucking pissed off, feeling cheated…

"Okay, Jax," she agrees.

"That being said, nothing two people do between each other can ever be wrong as long as they both are happy and find pleasure. I've never wanted this particular thing with another woman. I want it with you. That's as far as I'm questioning it. Understand?"

"You haven't? Never? Not even before…?" she asks, worrying the corner of her bottom lip with her teeth.

"Only you," I tell her, giving her too much, but feeling as if I did something right when disappointment leaves her face and happiness replaces it.

"Go shower," she says with a smile. "I'll make the call."

I stand there, looking at her smile unable to move for a minute, and wishing things could be different.

If wishes were horses…

I'd still be riding my fucking bike. Wishes are useless. Especially now. Especially for me.

Chapter 25

Bree

WAKING UP IN the arms of Jax is a new experience. Sadly, I barely remember going to sleep with him last night. I was out before he got out of the shower, and I can only vaguely remember him getting me and putting me in his bed. The only thing that I remember clearly is the way he spooned me from behind, wrapped his arm around me, and palmed my breast. He placed a gentle kiss on my neck and whispered, "Sweet dreams, baby," in my ear. For a woman who has never had any type of affection in her life—save a grandfather whose guilt leads him to buy me anything he thinks I might want, but whose idea of a hug is an awkward pat on the shoulder…this is a new experience. For the first time in my life I feel *wanted.* I was pretty sure that feeling couldn't be matched.

This morning, waking up with our naked bodies tangled together, my head on Jax's chest, and his hand wrapped in my hair holding me to him, I'm not so sure. I feel warm, wanted, and maybe even a little sexy. I feel like a…*woman.* Surely, this has to be the greatest feeling. It can't get any better than this. *Right?*

Jax is still sleeping and even in his sleep he's holding me tight. I move away slightly, ignoring the pain that happens as my hair pulls against his hold. I look at his face. He looks peaceful and carefree like this. He's a beautiful man, but I somehow miss the smile on his lips I've been able to glimpse a few times. He looks powerful. His chest is covered with a fine mist of hair, dark in color with just a small sprinkling of silver here and there. I always thought I'd prefer a smooth chest. Jax has proven me wrong. I love the way it feels when my fingers run through the hair, and the way it's crushed against my face while I lay here. His arm has this huge tattoo. I don't know about these things, but it looks military. There's an eagle on it. There's another tattoo I saw on his back last night of a bike riding through flames, with the words, *'Forged In Fire.'*

I thought that maybe it was his club tattoo, but I must have been wrong because there's a skull in flames that says, *'Devil's Blaze Soldier, Brothers Forever,'* on his side. I can't resist tracing the ink with my finger. He stirs in his sleep and grunts, which makes me grin. His hand slips from my hair and gives me more movement, and I can't resist taking advantage of that. This time, I trace the lines of his tattoo with my tongue, stopping only when I place a kiss in the center. Jax shifts, but thankfully doesn't wake. I get more time to play, because I'm really not sure which Jax is going to wake up. Will he be the Jax who regrets having me here, or the commanding Jax who makes me weak with desire? I know which one I'm hoping for, maybe I can help push him in the direction I want.

Nerves flutter inside of me and mix with excitement. I move my hand down past his stomach. My fingers brush against the hair I find there. One last look up to make sure he's still sleeping, and I build up my courage to push the sheet down away from the lower half of Jax's body. His cock grabs my attention first. It's not as hard as last night, though still in a semi-standing position. I watch as I drag my fingers through the fine, curled hair and encircle the base of his dick in my hand. It's soft to the touch. I didn't know what to expect, but this wasn't it. I squeeze him in surprise, then get worried that I might hurt him and loosen my hold. I look up to see his face and take a breath of relief when he still doesn't seem to be awake. His breathing pattern has changed, but remains steady; his eyes are closed.

I decide to push my luck and move my hand up, over his cock, leaving my grip firm—though not as tight. One stroke leads to another and then one more. I go slow, not wanting to wake him too soon, but more because I'm enjoying my time exploring Jax's body. After the forth upward thrust of my hand, a small bead of liquid forms on the tip of his cock. Curiosity flares through me, and I can't resist moving down and bringing my tongue across the head of his cock, taking the drop of moisture inside. Several things hit me at once. Salty, musky, and elemental. Man. *Jax.*

I want more. I want all of Jax. Everything he has, I want to claim as mine. Any other thoughts leave my head, and now the only thing I can concentrate on is one word. *More.* I work my tongue through the small crease on his dick, making sure I take every bit of the flavor that remains. I don't worry about waking him, I can't think that far ahead. I'm totally lost in Jax now. My hand automatically moves to pump his cock again, my grip is tighter now, but then I don't really care. I need him to give me all he has. His cock is firmer now, definitely harder and yet, remaining tender in my hand. But he's so hot. The heat from his cock alone could almost burn my hand. This time more of his pre-cum leaks. So much more, it drizzles against my fingers. Again, I don't stop to think, *I just do.* And what I do is bend down to take the entire head of his cock in my mouth, sucking on it hard, and moving my tongue over the head trying to gather all of the clear liquid I can find before swallowing it down. I barely notice that Jax has a firm hold on my hair again, until he uses it to lift me off of him. I release his dick, because I don't have a choice. The popping noise echoes in the room, and I force myself to look up at the man who is literally holding me hostage by my head.

"If you're going to suck my cock, Bree. You're going to do it right," he growls, his eyes dark with hunger. *A hunger I caused.* "Open wide," he orders and desire flip flops in the pit of my stomach at the tone of his voice.

Chapter 26

Jax

"OPEN THAT PRETTY mouth of yours," I tell her, taking my cock in my hand, and rubbing the tip across her lips and coating them so they're nice and shiny. Her tongue flicks against the underside of my dick and I groan, deciding to let her get away with it. I stroke my cock so some of the pre-cum slides out onto her tongue. She whimpers as I push just the head of my cock in her mouth. Her lips close around it and she sucks on it…*hard.* "That's it. Daddy will give you what you want," I tell her, tightening my hold on her hair even more. I push into that sweet mouth, bringing her head down at the same time.

I'm not a small man and her mouth stretches to accommodate me. When I hit the back of her throat, I hesitate. She's innocent. She's not like the other women I've been with. I need to hold back this side of me, at least until I get her used to sex…to sex with me…again that urge inside of me to claim her as mine gnaws at me. I keep going back and forth with what I want. I know what I'm going to do, but I keep hesitating. Chances are I won't survive the fallout of this long enough to keep her. But, I will enjoy the fucking ride while I can. Turns out it's Bree who surprises me when she moans around my cock and pushes it deeper inside. When it hits the back of her throat she gags. I start to pull her hair, forcing her off of me, when she moans around my cock again, resisting my hold, pushing me even deeper in her throat. I feel her throat muscles working around the head of my cock, and I growl at the pleasure. The urge is there to keep it going, but she has tears coming from her eyes, and I can tell she's pushing herself just to please me. I pull her back, rewarded by her whimper of displeasure.

"Jax," she complains, her voice hoarse.

I caress her cheek and tell her, "I'll teach you how to take me slowly. I don't want you hurting yourself. I don't want to see you in pain, I only want you to experience pleasure at my hands, baby."

"Jax, I was. I want more," she whispers, and the stark honesty in her voice is there, and it wraps around me.

"Bree—" My words cut off when she takes me back into her mouth. Her eyes stay on mine. I drink in the sensations for a moment. Nothing has ever felt this good. I've had a lot of sex, but the difference here is Bree. I hold her back and she grumbles around my dick. I want to laugh, but I'm too caught up in the pleasure. "Go slow, don't force it. Breathe through your nose and relax your throat muscles," I instruct her. She immediately follows my orders, but I'm lost in the way she's moving her tongue around my cock. It's not slow and measured, not calculated at all. No. I can tell what she's doing is unpracticed, full of excitement, and to be honest…it's never felt better. I stroke her hair gently in appreciation and praise. "That's it baby, suck that cock down," I encourage. "Oh fuck, yeah," I moan when she brings her hand down to my balls. She doesn't massage them, or tease them like any other woman would. Instead, she just pets them. It's innocent and yet sexy at the same time. I put my hand over hers and slowly show her how to handle my balls. She learns quick, while still managing to work my cock with her mouth, she takes me in until she starts to gag and then backs off, letting her tongue lick on the underside of my cock the entire time. "Suck harder, Bree. You won't hurt me, it feels good," I encourage her.

She groans, but does it immediately. *Fuck*, it really has never felt so good. My damned eyes could roll back in my head right now. I can feel the end getting closer. There's no way I can resist. I've lost myself in her, in more ways than I need to think about right now. I'm on the verge of pulling out, wanting to see my cum spread all over her tits and face when she takes me again. This time she swallows my fucking cock down so far that it works through every muscle in her throat and her face lands against my groin. I lose it. I can't feel sorry about it either. *It's too fucking good.* My hand twists hard in her hair, and I lift her off my cock until the tip is almost out and then push her down. Over and over I help her work my cock, faster and faster, and I fuck her sweet mouth knowing I'm on the brink. I'm *right* there.

"Shaft open up! Hurry man! I need to talk to you. The club is going to war, dude!" Keys yells, while pounding on my front door. I instantly freeze and Bree's mouth slides off my cock. I want to mourn the loss, but the word *war* stops all thoughts. I'm frozen. *What the fuck could have happened?*

"Bree, baby…" I start, when I see the disappointment in her eyes. I regret it, but I need to go to the door. My decision is out of my hands. The club has to come first. It always has. Until…

"Please. Give me your cum, Jax. Please. I need it," she whispers.

"Bree…"

"Shaft man!" Keys yells again and if there has ever been a man torn in two, it would be me right now.

"Jax, please," she whispers, but I can't, I have to go. I start to get up when she grabs my hand with surprising strength. "Give me your cum…please, Daddy," she whispers, and that fucking word ends it all for me. I stand, and I see the pain in her eyes, but she doesn't need to worry. Nothing could stop me from this right now. *Not a fucking thing.*

"Hold still, Bree. This will be quick, but I'll make up for it later," I growl, sounding like that damned animal that this woman seems to turn me into. I stroke my cock, hard and fast, wishing it didn't have to go this way. I want more time, more of her mouth, but this is needed. I jerk harder and harder, growling out my release as my cum shoots out and splashes on her chin. I watch as the creamy pearl liquid drips down her chin and runs down her neck. Another splash hits higher on her face and her tongue comes out to capture it. I'm mesmerized watching her tongue disappear in her mouth as she takes me inside there, savoring my taste. *Motherfucker.*

I jerk harder, this time aiming on her tits, and I jet out stream after stream of cum until my balls ache and my body is shaking. Once it's done, I don't even pay attention to Keys yelling in the background. Instead, I take my time rubbing my cum into Bree's chest and stomach. I massage and massage until it slowly disappears, and I know that my cum has absorbed into her skin and I'm a part of her. She has my scent. *She's mine—and God help anyone who tries to take her away from me.* The time for giving her up has passed. I can't let her go now. *I won't.*

Chapter 27

Jax

"DAMN IT, SHAFT! Open up!" Keys yells again. It's the last thing I want to do, but it has to be urgent for him to hunt me down here. I lean down and kiss Bree, regretfully.

"Stay here, I'll be back," I tell her before grabbing a pair of sweats off the bedroom floor and making my way to the front door while cinching them up. "This better be damned important," I growl, opening the door.

"Thank fuck. I was about to give up," Keys mutters. He's a tall lanky kid. We patched in together, but he's closer to Bree's age than mine at twenty-five. He has blonde hair, cut short and honestly if he didn't wear a Devil's Blaze cut, and have the tattoo's he'd look like he belonged in a business suit.

"Well, make it quick. I got shit to do." *Like Bree. Fuck, waiting—that ship has sailed.*

"We got problems, man. Skull asked me to get you because you weren't answering your cell," he says, and I rub the back of my neck. Shit, I don't remember what I've done with my phone. I think it's in my Blaze cut still and that's probably on the floor buried under clothes in the bedroom. Skull would have my ass for treating my cut like that.

"The battery died," I lie, though chances are it has now since I didn't charge it last night.

"You can explain that to the Pres. We need to get back. He

wants us with Beast and the others. We're rolling out to the Saints. It's bad brother. It's bad."

"What the fuck are you talking about?"

"The boys who went on the run last night with Tuck's club? Man, they rode straight into hell. They were ambushed outside of old county road 329."

"You're fucking kidding me? It was a simple damned run!"

"It was supposed to be. They were just picking up that load of—"

"I know what they were picking up," I growl, stopping him from saying it. I don't want Bree to hear it. That's club business and she don't need to hear that.

"Yeah well… There was a fucking shoot out."

"Shoot out? Who shot at them?"

"We don't have any answers, that's why Skull wants to ride out there. *Hell,* they may already be gone instead of waiting on us."

"I don't understand. Briar and Sabre haven't said anything?"

"Briar was taken to St. Lutheran, man. He's shot up pretty bad. It doesn't look good."

"Motherfucker!" I yell out. Sabre and Briar are probably my closest brothers besides Keys. The thought of them being hurt and injured and me not there to help them when they needed it, kills me. They're tough fuckers. I never thought of either one of them taking a bullet. "And Sabre?" I ask, frozen and unable to move to get dressed until I hear.

"He's missing. That's all we know. Tucker called Skull and they're meeting. I don't know man, we got to get going."

"I'll be right out. Just going to get dressed. Call Skull and tell him we'll meet him on road 899."

"Jax?" I stop when I see Bree standing at the beginning of the hallway. "What's wrong?"

"I thought I told you to stay in the bedroom."

"I heard you yelling and my grandfather's name," she says concern on her face.

"Her grandfather? Jesus, Shaft. Dude have you lost your mind?" Keys says coming up behind us. I turn to him, mostly to tell him to mind his own business when I see him staring at Bree. She's wearing my shirt and it swallows her. It's a T-shirt, and the short sleeves actually fall closer to her elbows. But, Bree is taller than the average girl, and the hemline falls just below her ass cheeks—giving too good of a view of her legs and thighs. I cross in front of her, blocking her from his sight.

"Keep your eyes to yourself. Fucking bastard," I growl, pushing his shoulder, and knocking him back a good foot, maybe more.

"I'm a bastard? You're sticking it to Skull's niece! Have you got a fucking death wish? Old man Tucker finds out, *hell*, Skull finds out, they'll take turns cutting the skin off your body—and you'll be breathing while they do it."

"You can't tell them!" Bree cries, moving around me. "Please. You can't get Jax into trouble."

"Jax? Fuck. Don't worry girl, I won't rat out my brother. Speaking of which, we better go, or Skull may venture out here to find you himself."

"I'll be right back," I mumble, pulling Bree back into the bedroom. I close the door when we're inside and go straight to find my jeans.

"Jax…"

"When I tell you to stay somewhere, Bree. You fucking stay."

"I'm not a dog," she whispers. I look over my shoulder and she's standing there, her face heated, wringing her hands nervously.

"Remember the deal? No one knows about us. It's not even been one fucking day and you already broke the damned rules."

"I think I'll just go," she whispers turning away.

"The fuck you will," I growl, buttoning my pants and turning around to grab her shoulders and holding her still. "You will stay in this fucking apartment and not leave. You do not open the door, you do not go anywhere."

"I can't stay here. My grandfather will be expecting me!"

"There's no way you're going back there until we find out what the fuck is going on. Did you not hear what Keys said? I have a brother missing and another in the hospital. Who knows what the fuck is happening, baby. You are not walking into a fucking snake pit until I know you'll be safe."

"Why do you care?" she asks and that makes me want to do nothing more than show her exactly how much I care, but I don't have time for that. My hand wraps against the side of her neck, pulling her face in close to mine.

"Don't push me on this, Bree. I need to know you're safe. You might not understand, but after what we've shared together, you're mine, and I take care of what's mine. So, do not push me, baby girl. You won't like how I retaliate." I watch as what I said registers with her. Her eyes widen, and maybe I gave too much away, but it doesn't matter. I'm keeping Bree, until the world comes crashing in on us—*and I have no doubt it will eventually.*

"I'll stay," she agrees, moistening her lips.

"Good. Now give your man a kiss."

"You'll be careful?" she asks, leaning into me when I loosen my hold.

"You'd care?" I ask her, turning her words back on her.

"I'd care…*a lot,*" she says, and *fuck* if that pain in my chest doesn't hit me again.

"Then I'll make sure to get back to you in one piece. Now,

those lips," I demand.

"Yes, Daddy," she purrs as our lips connect. My hand moves to her hair, and I can feel the way it trembles. She's wrapping me around her finger and she doesn't even know it. *Fuck*, I'm not even going to try to get away. *I don't want to.*

Chapter 28

Bree

I STAND LOOKING at the door where Jax left. He's been gone for ten minutes and adrenaline is pumping through my blood. He promised he'd be back. I don't know what's going on, but surely Pops wouldn't hurt them. He's been doing everything he can to build a bridge between the Devil's Blaze and the Saints. I may not get into that side of his life much, but he hasn't made a secret of that. He wants to be closer to his grandchildren. He wants me to have a relationship with Beth and Katie. Still, just to make myself feel better, I hunt my phone and call him.

"Breezy you okay?" Pops asks when he answers the phone. His nickname for me makes me smile. We may have not had a lot of time together, but he really has tried to make things up to me, and I love him; I'm starting to think he loves me too.

"Yeah Pops, I just had a favor to ask."

"What do you need?"

"I was hoping you'd let me stay with Roxanne a little longer. She's just getting over a cold, and I'd like to stay and help her."

"Breezy you're always trying to help save the world."

"Pops, you know I love Roxanne. She was good to me when I didn't have anyone else."

I should feel guilty here. I'm using Roxanne, who has been nothing but good to me, and I made her promise to lie to Pops if he called her. Roxanne was a club girl when my father was in charge. He treated her horrible. He beat her, he made her *service* men from other clubs who were quite literally monsters. I remember mornings she'd come in to check on me and she would be black and blue, her lips bruised and bloody, one of her eyes swollen and discolored, and burns on her body. The smart thing would have been to run. And she probably would have…if I hadn't been around. She stayed around to protect me and she somehow managed to.

When Pops made it clear he wasn't condoning anything my father did and hadn't known, she risked her life yet again to tell him about me. I can still remember Pop's face when he finally found me. I say found me because my father was a bastard and he went to great lengths to keep me hidden. I'm not proud that I wasn't strong enough to run away, but I wasn't. I was scared…a scared kid. It's something I never want to be again.

"How long you going to be gone?" Pops asks, and I shake off thoughts of my past.

"A week?"

"Okay. Just check in with me every day and let an old man rest knowing his girl is okay. But, when you get back we're going to have a talk about you traveling to Tennessee without letting anyone know. I have men whose life is dependent on making sure you're safe."

"Pops, I told you, Roxy called, and I just bailed without thinking. She's the closest I've ever had to a mom," I tell him, hating that I'm lying, but I want more time with Jax and desperate times calls for desperate measures.

"We'll talk about it later Breezy. You know I've only ever wanted to make you happy."

"I know, Pops. I am happy, I promise you. In fact, right now I can tell you I'm the happiest I've ever been in my life."

"You sure, Princess?" I can hear an edge of concern in his

voice.

"Positive."

"Okay. It's best you not come home right now anyways. There's some club business going on."

"Are you okay, Pops?"

"Yeah. My men were blindsided. We're fine though."

"What happened?" I ask, pressing and hoping he'll tell me something.

"It's club business, Breezy," he tells me, and I sigh knowing he won't say anything more.

"I have a right to know if you're in danger, Pops."

"Honey I'm a biker, not a fucking accountant. I'm always in danger. It will work out. I got to go now Breezy. Skull is here."

"What's he doing there?" I ask, trying again.

"He's bringing my grandbabies to see me of course, got to go. Call me tomorrow," he replies and now he's lying. It seems wrong that the two of us are lying to each other. I stare at my phone with a sigh. I know nothing more than I did before…

I look around the small apartment and curl my nose. It stinks. It's never been cleaned. I think back to my last conversation with Jax. *You're mine Bree, and I take care of what's mine.* It makes my heart pound in my chest, and I honestly can't imagine feeling happier than I am right now. That part wasn't a lie to Pops.

I get an idea in my head. I want to show Jax that he's *mine*, and I take care of what's *mine* too. Will he think it's stupid? Maybe, but I'm going to try. He told me to stay here, but I need to go to the store. I shouldn't be gone more than an hour. He'll never know it. With a grin, I head out the front door. Jax won't know what hit him. He'll never want to let me go!

Chapter 29

Jax

"ANY WORD FROM Briar or Sabre?" I ask the men when we meet up. The look on their faces says nothing and everything.

"No sign of Sabre. Briar's hanging on, but it's not looking good," Torch says. The words hit me like punches to my gut, robbing me of air and the ability to speak. I just nod my head to let him know I heard him. A couple of minutes pass before the roar of bikes can be heard.

Torch and about five of our best men, including Beast, Latch—who is in on leave, and K-Rex are here. We're waiting on Skull and a close friend of his who is visiting, Diesel. Diesel is the president of an ally-club that runs out of Tennessee. He's younger than me. I'd say mid-thirties, and if I didn't know he was a badass, I'd almost call him a pretty girl. He has long hair he keeps pulled up, or away from his face. He looks like a fucking fashion model playing a biker. The truth is however, he can out shoot, out think, and out drive most bikers that I've met.

The cracking sounds of the pipes on their bikes announce they're getting closer. When they pull up he's also got one other rider with him. Dancer, the VP from the Savage Brothers club a few counties over. *Fuck*, I look around at all of us and realize Skull is riding in like he's going to war. *Going to war with Bree's grandfather*. Shit could go bad fast.

Skull doesn't speak, he doesn't even stop. He punches his fist in the air and drives on by. We all immediately fire up our bikes, falling in line behind him.

IT TAKES AN hour to get to the Saints compound. The old man set it up once he found out Katie and Beth were alive. He wanted to be closer to them. Skull agreed to it and the two have been trying to start over and become two clubs that are allies rather than enemies. It's not been easy as old hates and attitudes die hard, especially among our kind. Yet, it seemed to be working. Which was why Briar and Sabre were on this run with Tucker's men. Now, it seems, everything is blown to hell. The high chain-linked gate to the fence that encloses the Saint's compound is closed. It's at least ten feet high with a string of electric enforced barbwire around the top. Tucker is standing on the other side with ten of his men. He's never been pretty, but today he looks like complete shit. His white hair looks as if it hasn't been brushed or *hell*, even washed. His shirt hangs tight over his beer-belly and is stained red…*blood.* He looks pale and worried and *fuck*, he should be.

He makes a movement with his hand and the gate slides back slowly, allowing us to enter. Once Skull, Torch, and Beast have entered and shut off their bikes, Dancer and Diesel follow suit while the rest of us fall in line behind them. Silence reigns for a few minutes as everyone sizes each other up. I watch as Skull gets off his bike.

"Do we talk here?" Skull asks, his voice hoarse. He's hurting. Skull is a hard son of a bitch, but he cares about his men and he, Sabre, and Briar have fought many a war together.

"Are we going to talk or did you come here to shoot first and ask questions later?" Tucker asks.

"Talk, but if your answers are shit, one of us isn't getting out of this alive," Skull says as if he doesn't give a fuck which way it goes.

"You and two others, only," Tucker orders.

"And who will be with you?"

"Only Granger," Tucker says, naming his VP.

The move is strange, and you can tell the rest of the Saints aren't happy with the decision. I'm sensing some undercurrents and my gut tells me there's something bigger going on here. I trust my gut. It's kept me alive this long.

Skull tells Dancer and Beast something and then he, Diesel, and Torch walk inside. It doesn't surprise me he takes Diesel in with him, nor that he leaves Dancer outside without a word to his other men. The main officers in our club are Skull, then Torch is the Vice President, Beast is our enforcer, and the other members of standing are Sabre and Briar…which leaves us fucking short of some good men. This whole thing is messed up as hell. I look behind me and see Keys staring at me. He's got a look on his face I don't like. I wish like fuck he hadn't seen Bree this morning. I have no idea how I'm going to contain him.

At the thought of Bree, I instantly remember this morning. Not that it has really left my mind since it happened. It's a foregone conclusion now that I'm claiming her. I'm just wondering how long I have with her before either her grandfather or Skull demand my blood. The reasons to leave her alone are staggering, but there's only one I'm listening to. *She's mine.* I never believed in fate, but the minute I saw her walk through the door at the club, I knew. It doesn't matter that it's only been days, it doesn't matter that I'm way too old for her. *She's mine.* Maybe it is fate. Maybe Bree is my destiny. I've always known fate has a twisted sense of humor. Bree is all wrong for me, but nothing else has ever felt so right, and I can't think past that right now. I'm not even going to try.

Chapter 30

Bree

OKAY, I KNOW I'm pushing it. I stayed out for about an hour going to the grocery store and buying some things to clean up Jax's apartment. I kept looking over my shoulder. More concerned my grandfather would find me than anything. I know Jax told me to stay here, but really, I just went to the store; there's not much harm in that. I stayed in the public eye the whole time. Men just tend to over react to things. Though, if I wanted to be honest, I like that Jax worries about me.

I'm getting a little worried. He's been gone for the better part of the day. I made him supper, though as I started cooking, I realized that I know nothing about what Jax likes to eat. For all I know he could be a vegetarian. Though, something about the man screams meat and potatoes to me. Well, really it screams let me jump on top of you and ride you like a pony, but that's beside the point.

Dinner is ready, and I've got the food sitting in the oven under the light to keep it warm. The oven is still heated from the cake that I baked. I was going to watch television. That's when I realized he doesn't have cable. There's a TV and a DVD player—but unless I want to watch porn, then it's out. I've watched porn before, but I don't really get into it, and it's not so much that I'm against it, but the titles don't inspire me to watch at all. There's a choice of three. It appears my man only likes compilation videos. We have the *Best Money Shots of 1999*, *Best Boobs on the Beach, and The complete works of Muffy Diamond.* Seriously. Muffy Diamond. *I can't even.*

I noticed a Redbox near the apartment and that brings me to why I'm pushing my luck. I'm walking to the local pharmacy. It's only about a five-minute walk, and the kiosk for Red Box is there. I wonder what kind of movies Jax likes? I can't see him watching romantic comedies. I hope he's not a horror movie buff. His porn was 1999, I think with a laugh. Maybe I can get the Die Hard movies. Everyone likes those, right? And it's close to Christmas so it fits.

"Aubree! Didn't expect to see you here!"

I look up to see Jeff standing on the sidewalk across the street. I smile, despite wishing I hadn't seen him. I don't want anyone to know I'm here. There will be less chance of Pops finding out I'm still in Kentucky if no one sees me and it's crazy, but I know this will make Jax unhappy. I have this need to make him happy—*to be the reason he smiles.*

"Hi, Jeff. What are you doing here?" I ask, while walking across the street to him.

"Out doing some Christmas shopping. I thought you were going out of town for a few days?" he asks and I frown. How would he have heard that?

"I am, leaving today actually. I just needed to pick up a few things. How did you know?"

"It's a small town Aubree. Everyone knows everything." His blonde hair is shaved shorter. He must've gotten it cut recently.

"But…I didn't tell anyone," I answer, still confused.

His blue eyes darken, but they don't match his tone as he talks. "Well, you had to silly! Or else I wouldn't have known. How about you grab a hot chocolate with me, before you leave me alone?"

"I don't know…I'm running late. I really should be getting back," I tell him. I get this strange feeling I shouldn't be here, only this time I think it's more than just the fact that Jax wouldn't like it.

"Come on Aubree. I got you something for Christmas. I thought I'd have to wait until after the holiday to give it to you. This way I can give it to you early. I even had the store wrap it." He winks and my stomach churns.

"But, it's early. Christmas is another three weeks away. I haven't got anything for you. Honestly, I've barely done any shopping." I fake a smile in return, trying to hide the off feeling I'm experiencing.

"It doesn't matter. You sharing hot chocolate with me will be my gift." He smiles at me and it feels…I don't know, fake.

"You do realize it's like sixty degrees today, right?" I fight the instinct to run.

"I know. This weather is awful. It's been warmer this month than it was back in September."

"I kind of like the weather, but yeah, it puts a damper on the holiday season, for sure. Okay, one drink, though it will be a cherry Coke."

"It's a deal. You like the weather? I want snow," he says putting his hand in mine. I try to jerk it away, but he doesn't let go. That feeling inside increases. I don't fight him though. The restaurant is just on the corner. We'll be outside, and I can break away quickly, get back to the apartment, all before Jax finds out…*hopefully*.

"I love it. I got to wear shorts a week ago. It reminds me of Florida."

"Well, I have to admit I do like you in shorts." His eyes rake over me, making me more uncomfortable.

"Jeff—"

"I know, I know, I'm a guy though," he adds with another wink. Jeff has been trying to get me to go out with him forever. I've never agreed, telling him over and over I've always thought of him as a friend. I thought everything was okay between us, until this moment. Today something is setting off my creep-o-meter.

When we make it to Weavers, an old restaurant downtown, Jeff pulls out a seat on one of the small outdoor tables. I sit down, looking around, expecting to see Jax. *Why does it feel like I'm doing something wrong here?* The waitress comes by, and I order a cherry Coke—*to go*, while Jeff orders a cheeseburger box. I realize immediately I'm going to have to be rude and leave while he's eating. It's annoying that he would order food when I told him I couldn't stay long. It's silly. I mean he might not even be expecting me to stay, but I'm just aggravated with him in general, and I don't want to be here.

"Listen Jeff, I better get going," I tell him, when the waitress brings back our drinks. "I need to finish umm…packing."

"You're going to your Aunt Roxanne's?" There's no way he should know that.

"Yeah, I leave tomorrow," I tell him, adding to my mountain of lies.

"She lives down by Cherokee Lake doesn't she?"

"Close, but no. Roxy lives on Douglas Lake. It's a beautiful place. I once thought about moving down there, but Pops begged me not to." I offer him a tense smile.

"Well, I'm glad he did."

"Yeah, I guess. I do like Kentucky. Listen, Jeff, I hate to be a broken record, but I really have to head out if I'm going to leave in time." I start to get up but he won't shut his mouth.

"Oh, come on, Aubree. You can give me ten minutes. You stood me up the other day when we were supposed to celebrate taking our SAT's."

"I just have a lot going on right now. Maybe we can have dinner when I get back in town." *Yeah, right. Not happening.*

"Five minutes, that's all I ask, *Breezy.*"

I shrink back. "What did you call me?"

"Breezy. That's your nickname, right?"

"Only Pops calls me that and a few other close family members. How did you know about it?"

"You've mentioned it before," he says coolly.

"But, I haven't," I tell him convinced of that. I rarely share anything about my life with anyone. I sure wouldn't be so forthcoming with anyone at school. I definitely wouldn't share my nickname.

"You must have, or I wouldn't know it, now would I?"

"I don't remember telling you," I say again, feeling really weirded-out.

"Geez, Aubree you're getting all paranoid. Can't we just sit down and enjoy each other's company."

"Another time, maybe." *Like when Hell freezes over.* "I really have to go now."

I stand up to make my getaway. I'm not sure what's going on, but I know I need to leave and get back before Jax comes home. I also know that in the future I'm going to avoid Jeff at all costs. I know I haven't mentioned my nickname to him, and I know that something feels really strange with him. What I can't figure out, is why I never picked up on it before.

Jeff reaches out and grabs my hand. His fingers encircle my wrist, hard with bruising pressure. His skin feels cold and clammy. I jerk my hand away and look up at him. Jeff is a good looking guy in that neat, sports jock, letterman sweater kind of way. He's nothing like Jax, and nothing that has ever appealed to me. He's also blonde. I've never really been attracted to men with blonde hair. Very few men can pull off that color for me. He's too clean cut, too…*nice* looking. *He's nothing like Jax.*

Right now, however, he has a coldness about him that turns me off more than anything. His blue eyes are overly bright, but there's no emotion in them. He's trying to smile and appear at ease, but it's coming across fake. There's an anger that I can see easily.

"Sit down Aubree. We need to talk."

I try again. "I told you, Jeff. I have to go. I'm heading to my aunt's, and I need to finish packing."

"You have time for me," he says, increasing the pressure on my hand and jerking it so I nearly fall into the table. It hurts, but I resist, yanking my hand back.

"I don't. I need to go," I grit attempting not to make a scene and draw attention to us.

"You need to—"

"*You* need to let go of Bree's hand while you still have your own, asshole," Jax growls from behind me. A shiver runs down my spine. His voice is deadly calm, but the anger I feel radiating off of him makes me almost afraid to turn around. Because, I'm not sure if his anger is directed at me, or at Jeff.

I'm afraid to find out.

Chapter 31

Jax

"I DON'T THINK what happens between me and Bree is any concern of yours," he smarts off.

"That's where you'd be wrong," I tell him, trying my best to beat down the urge to shoot off the bastard's hand.

"How do you figure?" the asshole asks.

"Anything to do with Bree has to do with me," I answer, putting my hand on Bree's shoulder. *A show of ownership*. I'm about one step away from fucking this punk's face up so bad even his mother won't know who in the hell he is.

"What the hell? Jesus Bree, are you letting him between your legs?"

"Jeff..." Bree gasps, and I don't have to see her face to know she's embarrassed. Honestly, I've had enough of this fucker. I walk around her and lock my hand on his wrist. He doesn't get the hint, so I apply more pressure, and when I hear him grunt in pain, satisfaction runs through me. He drops her hand, she immediately puts it on my arm, trying to stop me.

"Jax, it's okay," she whispers, because she sees the anger on my face. What she didn't realize is that in doing that, it would only make me angrier. There's marks on her wrists. Marks that I know will turn into bruises, where the fucker grabbed her.

I don't even think. I just snap. I clamp down on the mother-fucker's wrist, and when I feel something crack beneath my hand, I want to fucking celebrate. He's jerking around and whining like the little bitch he is.

"Jax, please! Let it go," Bree says again, and the stress in her voice gets through to me. Still, this asshole can't get away with this shit, so I twist his hand hard, satisfied that I broke something, or at the very least caused him enough pain he'll think twice before laying hands on my woman again.

"What the fuck dude? Where do you get off?" the bastard cries, holding his hand.

"Keep your hands to yourself," I growl, wanting to say a lot more, and barely containing myself. The only thing stopping me from going after him again, is the fact that Bree still has her hand on my arm. I bring my hand over hers, using my finger to rub against the darkened skin. "You ever put your hands on her again, I'll make you sorry you were born," I tell him, and it's not an idle threat.

"Who in the hell do you think you are?" he asks, still holding his hand.

"I'm her man!" I growl, not taking the time to think or to even try to stop my words.

"I can't believe you Bree. You're letting something like this between your legs? If I had known you were this hard-up I would have helped you out," the slimy bastard says. I lunge at him, but Bree, moves so she jumps in front of me.

"You need to leave, Jeff," she says, her voice tight with stress.

"He better get the fuck out of here, while he can still walk on his own," I threaten.

"I'm going. You can call your grandfather off. I thought more of you than this. You've disappointed me," the asshole says and that's it. *That's It.*

"I warned you asshole," I growl right as my fist connects

with his face. Immense satisfaction fills me as blood spurts from his nose, and he falls back on the stone covered patio. The chair he had been sitting in before I got here rakes loudly before toppling over itself. I kick him and would do more, but Bree is desperately grabbing at my waist, trying to pull me back.

"Jax, please! Please sweetheart, let it go. Please," she cries and I can hear her tears and that's the only thing that stops me. I look back at her and tears are running down her face. I don't know why she's so upset. Is she worried about this asshole? "He's not worth it," she whispers. "He's not worth word getting back to Pops," she whispers softer, so that only I can hear her.

I swallow down the objection boiling inside of me. I'm keeping her, but I don't want to have to deal with the fallout of what that means before we have to. As much as it burns me to admit it…*she's right.* I pull her into me, and we walk around the asshole that's still lying on the ground. My steel-toed boot connects with him one more time as I get Bree away from here. I don't want her breathing the same air as this asshole.

Chapter 32

Bree

I FEEL LIKE a nervous cat, walking back with Jax. We haven't spoken since the incident with Jeff. I can still feel the anger vibrating off of him. I don't know what to say to him. I have always heard people say don't poke a bear when he's angry. Right now, Jax definitely resembles a bear.

"What the hell were you doing there, Bree? I told you to stay at the apartment. Things are going to hell right now with the club, and I need to make sure you're safe!"

"Jax, I just needed to run out and get something. I wouldn't have been a minute if Jeff hadn't been there. I was just leaving when you found us and—"

"It didn't look like you were leaving. It looked like he was hurting you."

"Jax, you're exaggerating," I argue.

"Those marks on your wrist say I'm not."

Belatedly, I look down at my wrist and see the darkened skin. There will be bruises there. I don't know what happened. Jeff has never been like he was today. I'd try to explain that to Jax, but I don't think he'd listen—or that it would matter.

"Can we just let it go? It's done now," I say with a sigh, not sure how to end this argument, but just wanting it done. Tonight, was supposed to be so great. I envisioned Jax coming home and finding his clean apartment, and dinner and…

And what?

In my head, I had this vision of him hugging me while telling me that I was who he had been waiting on his whole life. It sounds crazy now. Like a stupid school-girl dream. Now, I suddenly feel embarrassed.

"What were you thinking, Bree? Jesus this is what happens when you deal with—"

"Don't say it," I warn him, I can't handle hearing him say I'm too young right now.

"Say what? That you're too damned immature to follow a fucking order?" he growls just as he opens the door to his apartment. His words feel like a slap in the face, and one I absolutely don't deserve. When he turns to close the door, I take a breath and back up away from him.

Suddenly, the dinner I fixed, the house I cleaned, and even the silly little miniature Christmas tree I put up seem stupid. So stupid I can't breathe. "Explain yourself Bree," he growls like he's talking to a four-year-old who has been caught writing on the wall with her crayons.

"*Explain myself?*"

"That's what I said."

"Go fuck yourself, Jax," I tell him, finally having had enough. I've taken enough crap in my life. I made a promise that I'd never do it again and I won't—not even from Jax.

"What did you say to me?"

"You heard me. I'm out of here," I huff, walking towards the door. I thought I'd be home free once I passed him, but he grabs me around the waist and hauls me back to him.

"You're not going anywhere," he growls, and I just want to slap the hell out of him. I try, and I almost connect before he grabs my hands, gathering them in one of his. He uses his hold on me to force me backwards. My legs hit the couch and he literally pushes me down on it, stretching out over top of me, and trapping me beneath him with my arms pinned above my head. I twist and turn, trying to get away, but it doesn't work. He moves his leg to push against mine, putting his in between both of mine. I try one last time to push away from him, but I can't move. "What did you say to me, baby?"

"I said go fuck yourself, asshole," I grumble, breathless from trying to get free.

"Little girls shouldn't use that language," he says angering me more.

I lose my cool. "I hate you."

"Good," he growls and then his lips crash hard against mine in a fiery passion.

Chapter 33

Jax

THIS WOMAN IS driving me crazy. When I saw her with that kid, I wanted to wring her neck. Then I realized he dared to put his hands on her, snapping his neck was a near thing. *Hell*, I still might for putting marks on her skin. The only thing that kept me from it right now was Bree. I needed her back under my roof, locked up, protected, away from everyone else. My dick was hard as a fucking rock, my control snapped when she told me to go fuck myself. The woman is killing me and tying me up in so many fucking knots, I'm never going to undo them. My tongue is plunging into her mouth, demanding she surrender, but she doesn't. She's trying to pull away from me. *Fighting me.* My hand clamps on the back of her neck, refusing to let her move her head. In retaliation, she attempts to kick me. I push her up against the back of the couch and wedge my leg between hers, bearing my weight down on her so she is basically my prisoner.

"You're such an asshole," she mumbles against my lips. Her hands are pushing against my chest, but I'm not about to move. I love that she's putting up a fight, but I won't admit that to her.

"I gave you an order," I remind her. "You disobeyed and it's time you pay the piper, baby."

"I'm not property or a dog, Jax. You can't order me around."

"That's where you're wrong sweet Bree. You let me touch you. I liked it baby. I liked it so much that I'm keeping you," I promise her.

"Jax," she gasps, and I can feel her pulse beating to death under my hand, rapidly and so hard it jumps under my touch.

"You're my property Bree and you're going to give me everything I want." My words are firm, directly to the point.

"What do you want?"

"You."

"But…" she hedges, dancing around the words.

"And you're going to give your body to me aren't you, Bree?" I narrow my eyes on her, demanding she bends to submission.

"I thought you said you didn't want to…until I graduated."

"Didn't want to what? Say it Bree. Give me the words."

"Didn't want to…"

"Say it. Let me hear the words from those lips that took my cock. *Say it.*"

"I thought you said you wouldn't fuck me?" she whispers, her face filling with color.

"I said entirely too much, and I think you need to know who you belong to. Fuck it, you're legal, and I'm sinking inside of you so deep you will be able to taste me in the back of that pretty little throat of yours."

Chapter 34

Bree

I BITE MY lip hard. So hard, I can taste the coppery tang of blood seep into my mouth. It's either bite or beg him to fuck me now. It's hard to breathe. Each breath is painful because it takes so much effort. I'm completely enthralled in Jax. He's holding me so tight I can't move. That should infuriate me further. Yet, looking into his brown eyes, which seem even darker than normal, everything fades except desire…want…*need.*

The way he talks only adds fuel to a fire that's already burning out of control inside of me. I'm so wet and every wicked thought and vision he puts in my mind, just makes me wetter.

"What if I say no?"

"You might say no, but your body says yes. It always tells Daddy yes, doesn't it?" He groans, taking my mouth again.

There goes that word. *Daddy*. Sensations fire through me, that have nothing to do with the kiss and everything to do with that word. *Why does he use it?* Why, when he uses it, does this knot curl in my stomach and heat flush my body. I shouldn't like it…*should I?* But…God…*I do*. It feels dark, forbidden, and hot. It feels like he wants things from me I never envisioned giving another man.

I watch helplessly as his free hand goes to the shirt I'm wearing. His warm, abrasive hand rests under it, lying flat on my stomach. My skin instantly heats, a ripple of awareness or need trembles through me. I know he felt it by the way those full lips of his curl into a smile. I wish I could wipe the look of victory off his face, but that would be stupid, because I want him to win.

"Want something, baby?" he asks. I rub my lips together to moisten them. His thumb comes up and brushes along the corner, finding the faint trace of blood I know must be there. "This won't do. I can't have you hurting yourself," he whispers. "Tell me the words, Bree. Tell Daddy what you want," he urges me. His eyes, the expression on his face, and the way he's caressing my lips, are all drugging me.

"I want your cock," I tell him—giving him what I know he wants. In response, he surprises me by stepping back. I know the confusion is written all over my face, it has to be. At least it is until he pulls his club cut off followed by his shirt. I'm frozen watching him.

Jax's body is a work of art. It's chiseled and lean with a rock hard six pack that would make the models on any of those romance book covers beg for mercy. But, he's not like them. He's not a model. He's not a *pretty-boy*. He's all man. I've admired it before, but again I'm drawn to the covering of hair on his body. Thicker on his chest, thinning somewhat as it goes down his stomach, and disappearing under the waist of his jeans. It's got touches of gray peppered through it and somehow, that makes him appear even sexier. Everything about him, calls to *everything* in me.

"Take your clothes off Bree," he demands.

I think about arguing, but I don't want him to change his mind. I've wanted to belong to this man since the first time we met. No. Since the first time I spotted him across the room. My hands are shaky as I undress. My shirt goes first. Cool air hits my body, but I'm way too heated, and the result is a delicious chill running along my upper body. I can feel my nipples harden—

almost painfully, through my bra. I leave my bra on, I'm not that brave, just yet. Instead, I concentrate on kicking off my shoes and pulling my socks off.

My eyes are glued to Jax who has already undressed, except for his jeans and the zipper on those has been undone. The hair that I was admiring on his chest is visible somewhat through the zipper of his jeans, and I lick my lips in anticipation remembering what he's hiding. We don't talk, the only sounds are our mingled breaths echoing in the room. The slightly erratic sound of his, that tells me he's as excited as I am, is the sole reason why I'm able to push my fear aside and undo my jeans. I'm standing in front of him wearing nothing save my bra and panties. They're not made to seduce—though slightly better than the first ones he's seen me in. They're cotton, a red and green plaid trimmed in black. I *really* need to go shopping. But, when I hear Jax's sharp intake of breath, my eyes jerk up to his, and what I see there steals my breath. Desire. Hot. Rabid…*molten*…and it's all for *me*.

"I ever tell you about this fantasy I have Bree?" he asks.

"N…no."

"You just get out of class. You're wearing knee high socks and the shortest fucking skirt I've seen in my lifetime," he tells me, as if he's describing the weather, except his voice has dropped into that deep timbre he uses when he's horny. He begins pushing his pants down, his cock literally bouncing as it springs free of his clothing. "The skirt is the same material as that bra you're wearing. You're walking in front of me and the cheeks of your ass can be seen with every step you take, and you were a bad girl that day, because you didn't bother to wear anything under that skirt."

"What do you do?" I ask him, no longer looking at his face. No. My eyes are glued to his hand which is moving slowly on the shaft of his cock. I've been curious. I've wanted to know how Jax got the club name Shaft. He refuses to tell me, but it should be because he has the most beautiful cock ever made. I haven't seen many. But surely, there can't be a better one than his. It's thick and long, and should scare me to death, but it doesn't. He's got these large veins that press out that look so hard, I wonder if it's painful. The head shines a darker hue, and as he strokes I can literally see the pre-cum bubble from the small crease. My tongue snakes out against my lips, wishing I could taste it too.

"Daddy's girl has to be punished for going to school like that."

"I do?"

"Definitely. You can't be out with nothing hiding that sweet little pussy from other men. It's all mine now."

"It is," I tell him, dropping to my knees without even realizing it. He's right there in front of me, and I just need one small taste. "How do you punish me?" I ask, leaning into his cock, hoping he will feed it to me.

"You try to run from me, but I don't let you. I'll never let you get away from me. Do you know why, Bree?" he asks, still stroking himself, and standing close enough that I can literally smell his pre-cum even if he won't let me taste it yet. I watch as the thick liquid beads on his head and then slides down to be devoured by his hand as he strokes himself.

"Because I'm Daddy's little girl?" I whisper, lost in this fantasy he wraps around us. Lost in the way he's stroking himself. I watch as a bead of pre-cum runs off the head and follows a large, throbbing vein down the shaft. I can't stand it anymore. I slide over on the floor the small space that separates us and catch the drop on my tongue, before it disappears. It's just a small taste, but I moan as it hits me, flattening my tongue and licking up his shaft—needing more.

"Fuck yeah baby," Jax growls, "You're all mine," he growls as my tongue laps along the head of his cock. He holds it still for me, and I let my tongue push into that crevice, seeking out more of him—needing it as I need air to breathe. "*Jesus*, always so fucking eager for me," he growls, his hand fisting in my hair. He tugs on the roots, a sharp burst of pain trembles through my body as I feel even more wetness gather along the inside of my thighs. There's nothing that Jax does to me that doesn't leave me hungry for more. "You're such a bad little girl. I should make you suck my cock and drain him dry."

"*God, yes,*" I moan, but the words come out garbled and end on a hum of pleasure, because he shoves his cock in my mouth right where I want it.

"But that would be rewarding you for being bad wouldn't it, baby. Cause you love sucking Daddy's cock." I don't answer, but the way I'm sliding up and down on him, definitely does. He tastes so good, and I love the way I can feel his dick throb on my tongue as I suck on him. When he uses the hold he has on my hair to pull me away, I cry out in protest, needing more and pissed off he's trying to keep me from it.

"Jax!" I plead, his name a prayer on my lips.

"You wanted to know how I punished you, remember Bree?" he asks, and I do, but I wanted to take his cock to the back of my throat and give him pleasure.

When we did that before, I never felt more powerful, more desired, and I want that feeling again. I want to see that desire erupt in him and know that I'm the woman giving it to him.

"Stand up," he barks, and I want to protest, but when I look up at him, I see the hunger on his face. His hunger…*for me*. He's as much a prisoner to our attraction as I am.

I stand on shaky legs, clenching my pussy as I feel a spasm

of need move through my body. I'm so wet, I'm pretty sure he can tell it just from looking. My nipples are so hard, they feel like they're trying to cut through my bra and the feel of the fabric against them is almost torture.

"It's time Daddy shows you exactly what happens when you're bad," he growls, picking me up and carrying me into the bedroom as if I don't weigh anything. I hold onto him, leaning up to bury my face in the curve of his neck. Kissing the pulse point I find there and stretching further so I can nibble on the lobe of his ear.

"Yes, Daddy, show me," I tell him feeling a tremor shoot through his body. He's not going to stop. Finally, I'm going to *belong* to Jax in *every* way possible.

Chapter 35

Jax

IT'S OFFICIAL. I'VE fucking lost it, but I don't give a damn. When Bree whispers in my ear and calls me Daddy, I can literally feel my balls tighten. Jesus Christ, I've never been this hot before. I don't know what it is, but with Bree, everything is different. It's better, it's more intense, and it means everything. I should be shot for binding her to me like this, and *hell*, I might be when her grandfather and the rest of the world find out. It's not going to stop me though. I'm taking her.

All thought stops when the little wildcat burrows down against my chest and takes my nipple into her mouth, sucking on it. I feel her tongue curl around the tip, the sucking increasing and then she captures it between her teeth. I moan as she clamps down, and I can't stop cum from leaking out of my cock. If I don't make her stop, I'm going to lose it before I ever get inside of her, and that's never going to work. I want in that tight little pussy more than I want my next breath.

I make it to the edge of the bed and set her on the ground. She still has my nipple, her head and body bent, refusing to let go. I wrap my hand in her hair again pulling her back up to face me. I refuse to come early like some wet-behind-the ears boy, getting his first taste of pussy—no matter how much she tempts me.

"Bend over the bed, Bree," I order her. She looks at me

pouting, her eyes heavy lidded, and her body heated a light pink. *Gorgeous. Mine.* She swallows, and again, I'm stuck watching the motion of her throat. Nervously, she licks her lips, but then nods her head in acceptance. She turns around, and I let go of her hair to let her. For a second, I do nothing more than look at her. Her back is delicate, sexy on its own. There's little dark marks dashed around here and there. I've heard some of the girls call them beauty marks and on Bree they definitely are. I'm going to spend hours memorizing where they are and using my fingers to connect them.

I quickly unlatch her bra, rudely yanking it away from her body, not liking that it's keeping one of those marks from me. I smile as I reveal it, having only been able to see it disappear behind a strap before. I reach down and kiss it, letting my tongue caress it, thinking this one is my favorite—at least, for now.

"Jax?" she asks, her voice shaking. In answer, I place my hand flat on the small of her back and gently push. Bree immediately leans over, bracing herself on the bed. I pet her in reward. Letting my hands slide along her naked back, moving along her sides, using my fingers to tease against her stomach, and trace the way her hips flare out. Just enjoying her body, because even that is telling.

My dark hand, worn from hours and hours in the sun, against that smooth pale white complexion. My hand scarred up and tatted, her skin virginal…*just like the rest of her.* She'll wear my name on her skin too. Low and on her back so that when I bend her over and fuck her, I'll see it. When we're out and her shirt rides up every other motherfucker will see it and know she's mine. I let my fingers drift over the area and vow that it will be done. Only then do I allow my eyes to go to her ass.

Bree has an amazing ass. It curves out into this perfect bubble. It's thick in all the right places, but fits her body completely.

Each hand finds a cheek, and I squeeze. My eyes close as I imagine fucking her from behind, this luscious ass cushioning me each time I slam inside of her body. *Christ almighty.*

"Do you still want to know how Daddy punished you for wearing so little to school?"

"Yes," she whispers, her body stretching, her voice sounding like she's purring.

I yank her underwear down quickly. I expected shyness from Bree. Maybe it's because she's not facing me, or maybe she's as worked up as I am, but she steps out of them, kicking them away eagerly.

My hands go back to massaging her ass, pulling the cheeks apart, and looking at the virgin entrance there. I'm taking that someday too. There won't be a part of Bree that I don't *own.* I lean over her, and my dick immediately pushes against her soaked pussy. I shudder as her juice coats my cock. Holy hell she's so wet. It takes all I have not to push inside of her and take her cherry now. I can't do that. I want to see her face the first time my cock is inside of her. I want this time to be different from any other I've ever had with a woman. My fingers slide into her hair again, unable to stop myself. I twist them in those long locks, forcing her head back. I find her ear, biting into it. Immediately her body spasms in response. *Why does everything about her and the way she reacts make me feel like a fucking king?*

"I pushed you up against a school bus and spanked that sweet ass until it was red with my hand print," I growl, slapping her ass now, like I have in that fucking dream so many damned times before.

"Jax..."

"That's not the words you were crying out, Bree," I tell her, connecting with her ass again. My eyes are drawn to the handprint I'm leaving behind each time. *Delicious.*

"Jax!" She cries out again, her ass bucking back into me, when I pause before the next one. She needs this almost as much as I do.

"What were you crying out, Bree? Tell me," I urge her, knowing she will understand. She doesn't fail me.

"Daddy," she huffs out, her breathing hard and erratic. "Oh God, I was begging you. Spank me harder, Daddy," she whimpers, her entire body moving, as she tries to grind without anything for that sweet pussy to cling to. She's going to go up in flames when I finally get inside her. "Jax…I need to come," she whimpers. "Daddy, please let me come," she adds as her body trembles beneath me.

I pull her back up, turning her to face me. Her eyes are dilated, her body on the brink of climax. I've never seen a woman more primed. Pride burns through me. *Like a fucking king.*

"I'll take care of you, sweet Bree. Daddy will always take care of you," I promise with a growl, letting my hand dip between her legs so my fingers can push through her cream. She's so wet, the inside of her thighs are painted with it. The minute she feels my fingers there, that greedy pussy tries to latch onto them. Her muscles clamp down on them, and I can feel how they immediately begin to spasm. One movement from me, one well-placed pinch on that swollen clit, that is practically vibrating and she'd go off like fireworks. I'm right there with her and as tempting as it is to let her come and get this part over quick before I claim her virginity, I can't.

I back up against the bed, changing positions and slowly lower to it, bringing her with me. She feels amazing stretched out on top of me. Her body heated and soft; better than any fantasy I've ever had. I shift us so that we're sitting up, looking at each other. I don't know if I'm doing this right. I've never been a woman's first lover before. I never wanted that. *Until*

Bree. Now, it's all I want. I comb her hair gently, and then her shoulders. I let my fingers drift over her face, a face that haunts me...*that owns me.*

"I don't know any way for this not to hurt, Bree. But, I promise you, if you just hold onto me. It will get better," I try to assure her, hoping like hell that I'm telling her the truth.

"I know, Jax. I'm ready. I want to belong to you," she tells me, almost shyly. Her hands move over my shoulders and face, much like mine did on her moments before and nothing has ever felt so sweet. I lay back against the pillow, moving her so that she's sitting astride me. Her pussy almost scalds my dick with its wet heat. She looks around, confused, not expecting this position and reacting unsure.

"Shh..." I tell her trying to quieten her fears. "We're going to do this slow, and you're in control."

"I'm in control?" Her face is a mirror of shock and elation.

"Exactly that. Now rise up on your knees," I instruct and she does as I ask. "Wrap your hand around my cock, Bree," I tell her, and *Christ,* the minute she does, I want to come. It takes more control than I ever knew I had not to, especially when she shyly strokes me. "None of that, baby. I'm close to the edge, and when I come it's going to be in that sweet pussy of yours."

"Jax... I'm not...I mean...I'm not on birth control," she whispers. "We need to wear...you need protection," she whispers and she's absolutely right. I do. I've never gone without a glove before. I wrap my dick up tight every damn time. Yet, for the first time in my life, I don't want to. I want Bree with nothing between us. When I take her for the first time I want skin against skin. I don't want a damn thing between us.

"I'm clean, Bree. I've never fucked a woman without a condom *ever.*"

"But...a baby..."

"I don't want nothing between us Bree. I need it to be my dick you feel for the first time, not some fucking latex."

"I want that too," she admits.

"Whatever the consequences, we'll face them together okay? I'll take you to the clinic, and we'll get you on birth control if you want. Whatever you want, but I need this from you now," I tell her like an asshole. I have no intention of letting her go on birth control. I want her pregnant with my child. I want her stomach stretched with my baby. The thought alone makes my dick jerk in her soft hold.

"Okay," she whispers, and though I can still hear how unsure she is, I want to scream in victory.

"Now, lower down on my cock baby. Take me inside of you."

She does and the minute the head of my dick slides into her, I know I'm not prepared. She's unlike anything or anyone. *Fuck*, it almost feels like my first time. She's so damned tight and her muscles are already milking me. Bree takes me in a little further. I watch her face. She's so ready that I'm sliding in easy, but I know I'm stretching her tight little passage.

"Jax…am I doing it right?"

"You're doing amazing, baby. Tell me how you feel?"

"I'm so…*full*."

"I know sweetheart, but does it feel good?"

"Yes…you're…you're inside of me Jax," she says, almost reverently. Her innocence makes me smile. I'm barely inside of her, but I know if I don't take over this will end way too soon. I hold my hands on her hips and pull her down slowly. I don't stop until the head of my cock is pushing against the proof of her innocence. I feel it, keeping what I want most in this world away from me. I stop and close my eyes trying to gain my sanity here.

"Jax?" she questions, and I can feel her trying to squirm in my hold. Am I already hurting her?

"I need you to play with your tits, Bree. Rub them like I do, and pull on your nipples," I instruct her and the crimson color on her cheeks deepen somehow. I watch as she shyly reaches up to do as I ask. I'm dying to have my mouth on them, but right now I can only concentrate on getting inside of her without hurting her too badly. Causing her pain, might kill me. "That's it. Does that feel good?"

"Yes," she whimpers, brokenly.

"Good. Now I'm going to show you how I need you to ride me. Follow my lead okay, sweetheart," I tell her, wondering if I shouldn't get sainthood for this shit. Any other woman but Bree and I'd just plow straight through, and worry about it later. *But this is Bree.* I use my hold on her hips to show her what I need. Soon she's following. She's so fucking hot…*slick*. It's like heaven and hell combined for me. Hell because I'm having to hold back.

Her hands come down to my shoulders and she braces herself, riding my cock hard now. I can feel her orgasm begin. She's about to skyrocket. It's now or never. "Bree. I need you to open your eyes and look at me," I tell her. "Look at your man," I growl when she fails to do as I ask. Her eyes open quickly then, and the pleasure I see there robs me of my breath.

"My man," she whispers, and I swear to fucking God that I feel those words all the way in my soul.

"I'm going to take you now, sweetheart. It's going to hurt, but I need you to keep your eyes on me at all times, and don't try to fight me."

"O…Okay," she whispers, but I feel her body tense.

"No, baby. Don't tense up. I swear with everything I am, I'm going to make this good for you. That's it, baby doll. Just relax that beautiful body of yours and let Daddy inside." I hadn't meant to say it like that. I can tell by her eyes that she's not entirely sure about that nickname yet. But, being inside of her, I can feel the way her muscles contract when I say it. She might be unsure, but her body fucking loves it. *She was made for me.* I do a couple slow glides, then speed her up. My eyes watch her face, but get distracted by the way her tits bounce up and down the nipples hard, puckered and reaching out to me. My mouth waters.

"God this feels so good, Jax. I'm going to come. I'm going to…" she breaks off with a slow whine, and I can feel her climax roll through her. It's now or never because she's taking me with her either way.

I know my hold on her hips is bruising, but I can't give a fuck. I'm too far gone. I slam her down on me, and the veil of her virginity gives way with a cry from her lips. I hold her down on me and wait, as much as it kills me.

"Shh…it's okay now baby. It's okay. I'm deep inside of you. Do you feel me?" I ask her.

"Yes, I feel you. It…it kind of hurts, Jax," she confesses and these big tears are at the corner of her eyes. I feel those damn things deep. I reach up to kiss them away, unintentionally pushing deeper. She gasps, and I want to kick myself. I freeze curled up into her, but afraid to move.

"I'm sorry, baby. I'll wait until—"

"That felt good…" she says, her voice full of soft wonder. If I were a religious man, right now is when I'd be praising my maker.

"That's it," I tell her when she starts moving, and the orgasm she started begins to take over again, pushing through her at the speed of light. She's riding my cock hard, squeezing so tight I'm surprised she hasn't broken him. I can feel my cum begin to push. I'm going to explode and when I do, I want to make sure she is with me. I reach down petting her clit with my thumb, and that's all it takes. She screams out my name and comes all over my dick. Her head is thrown back and her nails bite into my shoulders. I've never seen anything more beautiful in my fucking life. Her greedy little pussy has latched onto my cock taking everything I have to give it, and just like that, I'm a goner. My cum jets out so hard I know my balls will be sore for a fucking month.

"I feel you, Jax. I *feel* you," Bree moans like it's something awe-inspiring and maybe it is. Being with her like this is unlike anything I've ever experienced in my life. *Mine.*

"Mine," I growl out loud as I empty inside of her. "You're mine, Bree," I grit, my voice sounding more animal than man. Even after it's done, I don't let go of her, I pull her down to me and kiss her, trying to tell her without words what I'm feeling. When we break apart, she wraps her warm body around me, lying on top of me, her hand tangling into the hair on my chest as she lays her head on my shoulder. I still stay inside her. If I can figure out how, I'm never leaving her body again. It's that good, that vital.

"And you're mine," she whispers, against my skin, placing a feather-light kiss over my heart. The pain there blossoms and explodes until it's just heat where her lips were. As I feel her breaths even out, there's only one thing I know for sure.

Bree owns me—body and soul.

Chapter 36

Bree

"IS IT RUINED?" I whisper from behind him. Whisper, because after what we just shared, I'm unsure of myself and well, I did scream, so my voice is hoarse. *I screamed.* It's a wonder the neighbors didn't call the cops. *Does Jax think I'm weird now?*

"Where did you find food to fix?" he asks, looking at the pot roast.

"I went to the store."

"So, you've been gone all day, even knowing I asked you to stay put. I should spank your ass Bree."

"I'm not a child you can order, Jax. I went to the store, and then later, I was going to go rent a movie, because surprisingly enough I'm not interested in the misadventures of Muffy Diamond."

"What are you talking about?"

"Your porn collection. It's not my thing. So, I wanted a movie."

His eyes lock on me, heated…dangerous. "You went to the store."

"You didn't have any food here, and your place was dirty. I don't mind staying here, but I wanted food. So, I went shopping. And I wanted to make your place seem more like a home, and not a dorm room. It's not a big thing, and I wish you would quit bitching about it, because you're worse than an old mother hen."

"Old mother hen?"

I roll my eyes. "That's what I said."

"Do you know how many women I've let speak to me the way you do?"

"I shudder to think," I gripe, not wanting to think of all of the women that have been in Jax's life, and annoyed he would bring it up.

"Not one."

"Whatever," I sigh, turning around, I'm wearing his t-shirt and suddenly, I feel like I don't have enough clothes on. I've made it across the living room almost home free when I feel that familiar arm snake around my waist. My head goes down in defeat. I don't want to fight. *Not now.* Not after what we just shared. "Let me go, Jax," I tell him, and I'm talking about more than just letting me go so I can go change.

"I've never let another woman talk to me the way you do, Bree," he stresses.

"Great," I mumble in his ear.

"Did you hear me, Bree? Not *one.*"

"I heard you. What do you want? A cookie?" I sass.

"Will you listen to me woman? I'm trying to tell you that I care about you!" he yells, and I jerk my head up to look at him.

"You what?"

"I care about you, Bree. I'm yelling, because the thought of something happening to you when I'm not around to take care of you scares the hell out of me."

"I only went to the store, Jax," I tell him. His words squeeze my heart and they add fuel to the hope I feel inside, but at the same time, I don't understand why he is upset with me.

"Without me, Bree. Anything could have happened to you."

"Women and men go to the store every day Jax. I've done it hundreds of times. I love cooking, and I know it might not sound cool, but…I like taking care of people. I *want* to take care of you."

"Baby, I have a brother in a hospital room fighting for his life right now and another brother we can't find. Tensions are high between my president and Pops. I don't want to take the chance that you might get caught in the crossfire," Jax says, pulling me into him. His hand cups the side of my neck, and he pulls me into him so that our foreheads rest against each other. "I can't risk something happening to you, Bree."

"Hardly anyone knows who I am, Jax. It's not like I'm going to be caught up in some war."

"The men in my world, Bree, are not nice. It might not make sense, but that's the way it is. If you're with me, you need to be aware of that and help me take care of you. Please?" his voice has softened.

"Did you just say please?"

He nuzzles my cheek. "I'm being serious here, woman."

"If I say yes, will you feed me?"

"If you say yes, I'll feed you." He kisses my throat.

"Then yes," I tell him with a smile.

"When you say yes like that," he whispers against my neck. His hands gather his t-shirt up and whisks it off of me quickly.

"I thought we were going to eat."

"We are. *After…*"

"After?"

"Definitely after," he confirms, taking control of me, and laying me down on the floor.

"Thank God," I giggle as his beard tickles against my breast.

"What?" he asks, his fingers finding my pussy, and gently brushing them against my tender skin.

"Thank God I ran the vacuum on this carpet earlier," I gasp as his fingers push inside of me.

"Are you too sore? Does it hurt?"

"It feels amazing," I whimper, squirming trying to get his fingers to go deeper, instead of the teasing brushing he's giving me. "Jax. Quit toying with me. I need more."

"Thank God, Bree."

"What?" I ask, a little lost, my hips thrusting up trying to get him exactly where I want him.

"Thank God, you're mine," he grunts, unbuttoning his pants and pushing them down quickly.

"I am. I'm yours Jax. All yours," I vow to him, just as his cock slides into me. I'm more than a little sore. I might have lied to him, but not completely because he does feel amazing. He feels like I'm finally with the one person I was always meant to be with. *My soulmate.*

Chapter 37

Jax

"I CAN FEED myself you know." Bree laughs as I tear off another piece of pot roast, holding it to her mouth.

"I told you I'd feed you, and I will," I tell her with a grin. What I don't tell her is that feeding her is something that makes me happy.

"But you haven't eaten yet," she says once she swallows down the food.

"I'm eating now," I argue with her, and to prove my point, I take a bite followed by licking my fingers.

"I don't think I've ever seen someone eat pot roast with their fingers."

"I'm a talented man," I tell her with a wink.

"That I can't argue with," she says blushing, but also wearing a big smile. She's so happy, and knowing I made her that way makes me feel like I conquered the world; it helps ease some of the stress on my shoulders. "What's that look?" she asks.

"Look? I was just thinking how beautiful you are."

Her brows knit as she gives me a bullshit look. "Liar. What are you worried about? Are we going to have to talk about age again?"

"That talk would be a little late wouldn't it baby?" I whisper, leaning down with more food, hypnotized as I watch her tongue wrap around the meaty morsel—which I'm sure she's doing to tease me. *It's working.*

"Then what caused that look?" she asks.

"I'm just worried about my brothers and what's going to happen," I confide in her.

"Listen, I know you said Skull was upset with Pops, but I don't see Pops doing anything to Skull's men—especially if it put him seeing his grandkids in jeopardy."

"I know, they talked about that at the meeting I was at. You know the one, right? The one I went to while you were supposed to stay here and not leave?" In response she scrunches her nose up at me and sticks her tongue out. "Don't flash that tongue unless you're going to use it."

"I could be persuaded," she says wearing a sexy and devious smirk.

"Alright then." I grin.

"After you explain what's going on."

My smile fades. "Bree. Club business…"

"Yeah, yeah. But, I need to know what's going on."

"Bree—"

Those beautiful eyes hold me hostage as she glares at me. "Don't Bree me, Jax. You want me to stay here for the next week or two and not leave so I'm *safe*, then you better tell me why I need to be locked up behind your doors."

I take a drink of milk, washing down my last bite. "How about because you're supposed to be in Tennessee?"

She drops her fork—*the one I've yet to let her use*. "How about you quit stalling."

"God help me. If you're this stubborn now, what am I going to do when you get older?"

"You planning on keeping me around?" she asks, and she doesn't bother keeping the hopefulness out of her voice.

"If I'm able," I tell her honestly.

"I'll make sure your walker is in good shape," she jokes, mistakenly thinking I'm worried about our age still. I am a little, but only that she'll grow bored with me. I'll make sure that doesn't happen, even if it kills me. What she doesn't realize is her grandfather will probably kill me when he finds out what I've done. Maybe it would have been different if I came to him first, but I kind of doubt it. She's special and she was innocent. Someone that a dirty, used-up son of a bitch like me should have never touched. *But, I did.*

"I need to start spanking you more than just in the bedroom," I grumble feeding her again. She squirms and knowing that just talking about it gets her going, makes my dick hard…*well, harder.* You would think after the workout he just got he'd be dead to the world. *Not with Bree around.*

"Get that look off your face now," she sasses, wagging her finger at me.

"But—" I attempt to bite her dainty finger and she pulls it away.

"At least until you tell me what's going on."

"Like a dog with a bone…," I sigh.

"Jax," she warns.

I sigh. She's got me so fuckin pussy whipped. "Okay. It goes no further though, Bree."

"I'll try not to tell my friend the four walls your secrets," she grumbles.

I wipe my hands on the napkin lying beside the plate, trying to sort out my thoughts. I take another drink, getting my thoughts in order.

"Jax?" she prompts me.

"Tucker is in some trouble with his club, Bree."

"Trouble?"

"The men that were there when your father was President,

don't like having Tucker trying to rule them. They think he's past his prime and him leading the club can only lead to problems." I lay it out as openly as I can.

"What does this have to do with your brothers getting hurt?"

"Tucker seems to think some of his own men sabotaged him."

"His own men? Why?"

"To make him look weak to the other men and to other clubs."

Her mouth hangs open, and if we weren't in the middle of such a serious conversation, I'd be telling her how I'd put my dick in it. "Wow, and they thought this would work?"

"Bree, Skull has two men in trouble. Briar is fighting for his life. We have men out night and day trying to find Sabre. These are good men. Men with families who love them. Sabre has a little girl and his wife is a mess. It's all Latch can do to console her."

"Latch? Console?" she asks confused and really that's not a story I want to get into. What if she likes the idea of having two men in her life? Sabre and Latch might be alright with sharing Annie, but no one is touching Bree but me. I'll *kill* any asshole who tries.

"That's a long story. But, the point is, had Skull retaliated first, war would have broken out, and trust me when I tell you that it doesn't matter if Tucker is Beth's dad. Skull would end him without a backwards glance if he's the reason behind all of this shit."

"So, what are they doing now?"

"Tucker wants Skull to take over the Saints."

"Wow." Her mouth forms into a perfect O.

I wipe my hand through my hair. "Yeah."

"Is he going to?"

"Skull doesn't want it. He has his own crew, and he has Beth and the babies."

"So, what are they going to do?" She's looking at me as if I have all the answers.

I wish I did.

"Torch is considering it, but he's not really wanting the position either, and Skull needs him."

Bree sulks. "What's going to happen?" I know she's concerned for Pops, but don't know what more I could tell her really.

"I honestly don't know, sweetheart. I think until we know what is going to happen with Briar and find Sabre, we're at a standstill."

"Is my grandfather in danger, Jax?" she asks. I see the fear on her face, and I hate it. I wish I could reassure her that he's not. The urge is there to lie to her, but if I did that and something happened to him…I'd never forgive myself; I'm not sure she would either. I don't want lies between us—*of any kind.*

"Skull has Beast in charge of making him safe. He'll protect him."

"He will. He won't let anything happen to Pops," she assures.

It shouldn't, but her confidence in Beast pisses me off. *Hell,* it even makes me jealous. What would she say if it was me in charge of protecting her grandfather? Would she have the same confidence and faith in me?

"So, now that you know what's going on, I don't need to worry when I leave you alone tomorrow. Right?"

Her face falls and it kills me. "You're leaving?"

"I'm going with Keys to hunt for Sabre, unless they find him tonight." I don't enjoy the thought of leaving Bree, but I hate the thought of my brother laying out there hurt or worse…dead.

"Where will you be looking?"

"Old Route 80, along Turkey Ridge."

"Hmm…"

Cocking my brow, I mimic her, "Hmm?"

"You said your other friend…Briar?" she prompts, and I shake my head yes. "He was shot? So, you think that Sabre might have been wounded too?"

"Yeah, babe."

"The Laurel River connects through there…"

"We know. We have the sheriff's office working on that. It's hard to drag a river."

"You think he's dead?" she whispers as though the words hurt her to speak them.

"I don't think nothing but death would keep Sabre away from his Annie like this. So, yeah." I hate to say it aloud, but it's true.

"They're that much in love?"

I nod. "They're something."

"What does that mean? You don't think they're in *love*?"

"She's Sabre's world." I shrug, not sure how to answer that.

Her hair falls over her shoulder and she has this goofy grin on her face. "So, they're in *love*." I shrug again, uncomfortable with the L word.

"Can we just agree that you won't be out while I'm gone and make me worry?"

"It depends." Her goofy grin disappears, replaced with a smirk.

"Depends on what?"

"On if I'm too tired to move tomorrow," she answers quietly, her face betraying her embarrassment at being forward. I may have taken her virginity, but *my* Bree is still *innocent*.

"Is that so?" I grin, leaning down to take her in my arms. "I always did like a challenge."

"I was hoping," she says, her lips against mine, so that I swallow down anything else I'd want to say.

Chapter 38

Jax

"JAX! WHAT ARE you doing? I'm trying to make breakfast here!" Bree squeals when I come up behind her, clenching my fingers into her sides, pulling her ass back against my hard cock. I've got my jeans pulled up on my hips, zipped but the button undone. I know I have to be making Bree so sore she can barely walk, but I can't make myself slow down. I want her over and over. I'm not sure I'll ever get enough of her.

"It's your fault, woman. Pushing that ass out there, teasing me."

"Teasing you?" she laughs, and I swear to God every time she laughs that feeling in my chest comes back with a vengeance. I want her always laughing and happy.

"That's what I said woman. Now brace your hands on the counter top. This won't take long," I tell her shamelessly. Maybe someday I'll get enough of her that I can make it last longer and spend hours bringing her to peak after peak. That time is not now. Now, I lose my head over her too easy. I get lost in her body.

"Are you serious?" she gasps as I push my shirt she's wearing up, my hand stroking against her bare ass cheek.

"Fucking you is not something I will ever joke about, Bree," I groan, my fingers wandering until they find her pussy and are instantly met with her desire. She's always so fucking ready for me. Is there any wonder I can't hold myself back?

"But, we just had sex. Aren't men supposed to need recovery time or something?" she asks, her legs sliding out and making room for me, as she braces herself on the counter.

"Do you want me, Bree?" I ask unnecessarily. Her body is literally crying for me, and I can feel the way her body is trembling.

"Always…it's just…"

"What is it baby?"

"I'm a little sore," she whispers as if she's telling me a horrible secret. Regret hits me. I should stop. She's new to this. I can fix her a bath later though and let her soak. What I can't do is stop, and even saying it, I know that makes me a bigger bastard than I already knew I was.

"We'll take it slow and easy this time baby, I promise," I tell her, and I vow I will, even if it will kill me.

I pull my dick out, holding the base of my shaft tight in my hand. I push the head of it against her ass, and watch as I paint a clear stream of pre-cum against her ass cheek. Just seeing it on her soft white skin makes my balls tighten with the need to sink so fucking deep inside of her she can taste me. My cock slides against the lips of her pussy, pushing in. It coats the side of my dick in her slick juices. Her body quakes and even hurting she cries out my name, begging for more. I slide back through and prepare to enter her…

Just as Keys yells out my name and knocks on the fucking door. I'm going to kill him.

"Your friend has very bad timing," Bree whispers, her head going down to rest on the counter.

"*Fuck*," I growl, wanting to punch his face, "I know. Go put on some pants and underwear and cover yourself up," I sigh, wincing as I push my cock back in my pants.

She tilts her body to the side so she can still lie half curled into the counter, her head on it as she looks at me.

"You told me never to wear panties again."

"Your pussy is ready to be fucked. *Hell*, I still have your cream on my cock. That's something no other motherfucker gets to feel or smell but me. So, put them on."

"You're so bossy," she quips giving me a little lip.

"You love it."

"I'm finding I do like it…from you, *Daddy*." The naughty gleam in her eyes tells me she did that just to tempt me.

"Goddamn it woman. Quit teasing me and go clean up before I tell Keys to leave and fuck you here." If I had the time I'd spank her sweet, pearly ass for it, marking her with my handprints. She used Daddy just to get to me. I know she's not a hundred percent on giving me that. She does during sex—though sparingly. I'm okay with it. *Hell*, if I never got that from her, I'd still be okay. Bree gives me more than I've ever had. I've been jealous of what my brothers have found. I knew I was missing out, but I don't think I understood just how much, until Bree.

"I'll do it," she sighs, pulling herself up off the counter. Before she can walk away, I grab her and stop her.

"Kiss me before you go," I grumble. She smiles and then gives me a quick kiss. Of course, the minute my tongue pushes into her mouth I take more, deepening the kiss and losing myself in her.

"You kiss really good," she whispers when we break apart.

"Back at you, baby. Now go cover up my property," I tell her slapping her ass.

"Should I hide in the bedroom?"

"No, Keys already knows about us. It's okay he'll keep it quiet," I reassure her.

"Okay," she says quietly—too quiet.

"Bree," I start, knowing what's on her mind. I've never really talked to her about wanting what we have to go beyond our original deal and what I expect to happen in the future. I've resisted because she has to know her grandfather will go off. *Hell*, Skull and Torch might too. They like me, I'm one of their brothers, but they're protective over the women in their life. Skull and Beth have years separating them too, but will he be understanding about it all? *Fuck*, I still feel like a dirty old fuck at times when I look down at Bree when she's sleeping and her innocence and youth shine from her.

"It's okay, Jax," she says, giving me a soft smile.

"I'm not letting you go, baby. It's just not the right time to let people know we're in a relationship."

"When will it be?" she asks, and *fuck* if that's not a question I'd like an answer to.

"Let's get you out of school first, okay?" Her lips go tight, but she nods, walking toward the bedroom.

"Motherfucker, hurry up I'm freezing my balls off out here," Keys growls, and I shake off my thoughts, and laugh. He probably is. This fucking weather is crazy. December and last week it was actually seventy-two degrees. Today the high is thirty-two.

I watch as Bree disappears down the hall, and I listen for the closing sound of the bedroom door. Only then do I go let the fucker in.

Chapter 39

Jax

"SHE COOKS TOO?" Keys says watching Bree move around the kitchen.

I smile. "She's a good cook. Made me the best dinner I ever had yesterday," I tell him, bragging on her loud enough so she can hear. Asshole that I was, it hits me that I didn't exactly give her praise for going out of her way for cooking me dinner and shit...cleaning this place so that it doesn't look quite so sad. *Hell*, since Bree has been here with me, it feels...*good.* I rub that place in my chest that always hurts when I realize how much Bree is coming to mean to me.

"I can already tell she can clean up a dump and make it look good," Keys said, echoing a few of my thoughts.

I smile as Bree turns around with two plates and serves Keys and me omelets and hash browns. It might make me sound sad-assed, but other than a restaurant, I can't recall a woman—*hell*, anyone cooking for me. Well, besides Annie, or one of the other old ladies when we'd go to their house for dinner or something.

"Thanks, baby girl. You're eating too, right?" I say taking my fork in hand and watching her.

"I'm not real hungry. I was just going to go clean up in the bedroom and—"

I stop her from finishing out her sentence, by pulling her down into my lap. "If I'm going to eat, then you sure as hell are," I grumble, secretly happy that she's in my arms again. That's something I'm beginning to crave around the clock. I want her with me, all the time.

"Jax!"

"Shut it, you're going to eat," I order.

"Well, let me up then, so I can fix my own plate, and you eat yours."

"You fixed way too much. You can eat mine too," I tell her, already taking my fork, getting some food on it, and bringing it to her mouth.

"I can feed myself, Jax," she complains, but takes the bite.

"I know," I tell her, then I lean in closer to whisper in her ear, where only she can hear me. "Daddy likes feeding you. It doesn't matter if it's my dick or food." Bree giggles, and squirms on my lap. My poor dick is so hard, I feel sorry for him.

"You're such a freak," she laughs. I take a bite of the omelet myself this time and whether it's the food, the fact that her laughter is surrounding me, or that she's on my lap…it could be all three, but it's the best damn omelet I've ever had in my life.

"Where you going?" I ask Keys when he gets up.

"Getting a beer, you want one?" I look at the orange juice that Bree set down for us with a grin. Keys is not really an orange juice kind of man. *Hell,* I'm not either…but, because Bree did it, I'd rather have this orange juice than anything.

"Nah, I'm good, brother." *I'm more than good.*

I feed Bree some more and listen to Keys as he tells me about the latest happenings at the club.

"Boys are wondering where you are," Keys says, and he's looking at me and Bree strangely.

"You tell them I moved into my own place?" I tell him, without looking at him. I'm more interested in the way Bree's throat moves when she drinks the juice.

"Yeah, but Denise is really missing her time with *the* Shaft." His words chap my ass.

Motherfucker. He barely finishes his sentence before I feel Bree go still in my arms.

"You know yourself I haven't been fucking around with Denise months before I met Bree. You going to come into my home and disrespect my old lady like this after she fixed your ass breakfast?" I'm fuming.

"Jax—" Bree whispers, but I ignore her.

"I also know how you are with women. You'll be back when you get bored. It's not like you didn't get the name Shaft for a reason, brother." The bastard laughs and if that wasn't enough to make me want to punch his face in he adds to it. "Shaft here tell you about the twins that gave him the name Shaft? Or was that their mother?"

"Their mother?" Bree whispers, and I see the disgust on her face. I'm not ashamed of my past. *Fuck*, I am who I am. Still, I didn't want my past touching Bree. What I was before is not the fucking man I'm going to be for Bree.

"Yeah baby, you weren't the first young girl old Shaft here played around with. Only these girls liked to make it a family affair. Even the mother wanted in on the Shaft-action." Keys keeps on. I'm gonna kill him.

"You son of a bitch," I growl.

Bree jerks in my lap as if someone hit her. She gets up, and I let her, because I am going to fucking tear Keys apart.

"What? I'm just telling her the truth. Oh! I see! Nah, sweet cheeks, he never did the mom with the twins. At least not that I know. Though that one weekend we were both so wasted, who the hell knows," he says attempting to backpedal, but it's too late for that shit.

"Bree go to the bedroom."

"I think I will," she says and fuck, I can't tell what she's thinking. Mostly because she won't look me in the eye.

"Wow, you have her trained good. Maybe I need to find me a young piece of snatch. You always did like telling your pussy what to—"

He doesn't get to finish, or maybe he does because my growl might have drowned him out. I lunge at him, wrapping my hand around his neck as I slam him hard against the wall.

Chapter 40

Jax

KEYS IS NOT a little man. I'm a little taller, but he's wider, and a good ten to twelve years younger. He grabs my hand trying to push it away. My anger is stronger though, and I don't let the fucker go.

"You son of a bitch! You come into my home, disrespect *my* woman, and talk to her like that? What the hell is wrong with you?" I snarl at him, my hands tightening on his neck. I could end him right now, and the need is there. If he fucked things up with me and Bree…I will kill him. *Nothing will save him.*

"Jax you're killing him!" Bree cries from the hall. I look at her and see the pain on her face, but there's also fear. *Shit.* I don't want to make it worse. I give his neck one last squeeze before stepping back, watching the color leak back into his face. Keys starts coughing, his hand coming up to massage his neck.

"Bree your supposed to be in the bedroom," I grumble. Needing to beat the hell out of Keys, but not wanting her to see it and scare her more.

"Guess you haven't had enough time to train her," Keys says while coughing, his voice hoarse.

Fuck it. I've had enough. "You asshole!" I yell and strike out. My fist connects with his jaw, and his face goes sideways, his lip spraying blood. The hit feels good, so I go in for another before he has time to recover. Keys proves why he's good to have at my back in a fire-fight, he blocks my punch and charges with his body. We go backwards crashing me into a coffee table and the vase of flowers that Bree put on it. I hear the glass break as we crash to the floor. Vaguely, I hear Bree scream, but I'm too busy flipping Key's over, and slamming my fist into his stomach.

The bastard moves to kick me. I manage to avoid the majority of that, but he lands a hard hit, returning the favor by busting my lip too. Blood fills my mouth, and I spit it at him. We trade blows a few times, and I finally manage to get the upper hand. He's breathing heavy and still sitting on the ground. When we catch our breath, I'm up and manage to kick him. "Get up, motherfucker."

"I'm done Shaft, man," he says, but if he thinks it's going to end that easily, he's got another think coming.

"Who the hell do you think you are insulting Bree?"

He throws his hands up. "Will you listen to yourself? *Insulting Bree?* Who the hell is she? A piece of pussy! That's it."

I haul him up by the collar on his cut. "She's mine. *Mine.* And you will not disrespect my old lady," I growl my fist crashing into his jaw, and it's a hard hit. So hard, I find myself hoping it knocked his fucking teeth loose.

"Jesus, Shaft. Are you even listening to yourself? You've known this bitch for what? A few days?" his voice sounding incredulous.

I tower over him, my voice booming throughout the small apartment. "What happens between me and my old lady, or even how *soon* it happens, is none of your fucking concern."

"It is when you're setting yourself up, asshole. *Your old lady?* Shit, she's not even out of school," he spits at the floor and wipes his chin on his forearm.

"She's mine. I've claimed her motherfucker, I'm keeping her, and you need to show her respect."

"The only thing you've claimed is a *kid* who's going to get you *killed*," he stresses.

"Killed?" Bree asks, and I watch as she comes to stand in front of Keys. "What do you mean I'm going to get him killed?"

"You're a Chrome Saint's Princess. Do you really think your grandfather is going to sit still and watch a man twice your age lay claim to his innocent little girl?" he scoffs.

"Yes, if I'm happy. I'm not a Princess, either. You don't even know me."

He chokes out a winded laugh. "You're the *key* to taking over the reins of Chrome Saints. You're a Princess."

"The key?" Bree's eyes are an ocean of questions.

"Someone lays claim to you, that's like putting themselves in the running to be the next President," he elaborates.

"I don't see how. I thought those kind of things were voted on? Besides it's just a stupid club, what does that have to do with life?"

"*Christ.* She doesn't have a clue, Shaft man. And this is who you're claiming as your old lady?" he laughs, and then he turns to Bree with his hate. "You can't be that stupid, bitch. Do you even know how your Grand-daddy makes his money? Or *hell*, Shaft for that matter?"

I don't think I just hit, busting his nose and letting the sight of the red blood calm me, at least a little.

"Call her a bitch again, and you'll be breathing through a tube. *Brother or no brother*," I promise.

"You'd choose a piece of tail over family?" He attempts to get up from the floor.

I don't move to offer him a hand up, the fucker doesn't deserve one. "Bree is *my family*. You haven't got this, but you need to start."

"She's going to get you killed," he says sounding like a broken record, telling me shit I already know.

"Some things are worth dying for," I vow staring at my woman, knowing I'd do just that for her. She's worth it. I'd burn the world down and spell her name in the ashes when I'm through.

"No! Jax? He's wrong. Pops wouldn't kill you," Bree pleads mostly at war with herself. She doesn't want to think her Pops can be a bad man.

"Bree—"

"Sure he wouldn't sweet cheeks. Your *Pops* killed his own son without a second thought. *Hell*, he's killed enough men to fill up two cemeteries. He's not going to think about it when he puts a bullet between Shaft's eyes. He'll probably throw a party to celebrate," Keys says and Jesus, I need to kill that son of a bitch.

"You're lying," Bree snaps at him, but her eyes tell me she knows different, but isn't ready to accept the truth.

"Whatever. You ready Shaft? We're supposed to be out looking for our brother, remember? Or you too wrapped up in pussy to work for your club now?"

"Get the fuck out of my house. I'll be out in a few minutes."

"Yeah. I think I'm done in here anyway," he says and then leaves. I stare at the door for a second and only turn to face Bree when her question echoes in the air.

"Is he right? Will being with me get you killed, Jax?"

"Bree…" I have a hard time meeting her eyes. I don't want to hurt her.

"Will it?" she asks, but from the tears in her eyes, I think she might know the answer.

Chapter 41

Bree

"ANSWER ME!" I yell at him. His eyes are full of so many emotions. My stomach drops to my knees.

"Bree, sweetheart—" he attempts to placate me, but I won't stand for it.

"Jax, answer me," I order him, ready to beat the words out of him.

"He's not exactly going to be thrilled about it. *Hell*, how could he be?"

I don't accept that. "Because I found someone who cares about me? Someone I *love*?"

"Bree, you need to drop *that* shit."

"Drop…*what?*" I huff tapping my foot with a hand resting on my hip.

"This is not some damn fairy tale you grew up reading," he says to me, his tone exasperated. I don't know if it's due to the fight or this conversation.

"What are you talking about?"

"There is no *love* in the real world." His words hurt my heart.

I take a step in his direction. "That's not true."

"It is. Was it *love* that got your grandmother killed?"

"What are you talking about?"

"It doesn't matter. Let's just let it go. Listen, I need to go try and find Sabre. Are you going to keep your word, or do I need to find a man to watch over you?"

"We're not done with this discussion," I growl, wanting to have this out.

"I know, but baby, Sabre is out there somewhere. He has a family that's worried sick about him," he says earnestly. Guilt pools in my stomach. I couldn't imagine the hell that his wife must be going through.

I take a deep, steadying breath. "We will have this out when you get home."

"That mean you're going to stay put?" he asks, some of the tension leaving him.

"If I don't will you have an aneurism?"

"Possibly," he says his lips going into a smile.

"Then I'll stay put. You guys are wrong though. Pops will just want me happy and you make me very happy," I tell him, stepping into him, my arms reaching up to pull his face down to me. He gives me a light kiss. The coppery taste of blood hits me, and I pull back, using my thumb to wipe his bottom lip.

"We'll know soon, baby, because I sure as hell *refuse* to give you up."

"Is that so?"

"Completely. You're *mine* now. Remember what I told you this morning. Soak in a tub today and relax."

"Jax, I'm fine."

"I'm going to want that sweet little snatch again tonight and the work out I'm planning will need you to soak today."

"No playing until we have our talk."

"If you can hold out, I can," he calls my bluff.

"I can. It's *important*."

"Give your man another kiss."

"Won't it hurt you?"

His lip twitches. "It's worth the pain and then some."

"I don't like your friend," I whisper against his lips before I give myself over to our kiss. Jax's tongue slides into my mouth, tangling with mine in a sweet and slow movement that I feel all the way to my toes. Sweet agony.

"He's not my favorite person right now either. Don't worry. He won't talk to you like that again," his words are more than a promise.

"It's okay, Jax. Honest—"

"No. *It's not.* You're my woman, Bree. *Mine* and there is no *motherfucker* who will ever disrespect you while I'm around—especially my own brothers. That's not happening and Keys needs to learn that."

"When you go all He-Man like that, I have the strangest urge to strip naked and lay myself at your feet."

"Is that a fact?"

"Mm...hmm... Jax, my conqueror," I flirt.

"Oh. I like that. We'll play that little scenario out when I get home." The heat of his gaze melts me.

"I'll be waiting...*Daddy.*"

"Damn it woman. You're trying to kill me," he groans adjusting his dick. I watch him, filled with fascination. *I do this to him. Me.*

"Hurry back to me."

"I will, Bree. You can count on that," he says going to the door.

"And be careful," I warn him, worried, but not wanting to cling. I have been cut off from the club life mostly, but I know the last thing a man needs is a weepy, clinging woman.

"Always," he says carelessly, opening the door.

"I mean it, Jax. I need you to come back to me. Preferably in one piece, cause well I'm rather attached to all of your pieces," I tell him, blushing, but desperately trying not to. For his part Jax smiles. It's a real smile, one where I can tell he's happy.

"Roger that. I'll make sure to bring myself and all my *pieces* back. Trust me. It's never been more important to me than now. You just stay inside, please?"

"Yes, sir." I fight back the urge to salute him.

"Believe I like Daddy better," he grins.

"Get out of here, before Keys comes back. I'm not sure I can handle him anymore today," I laugh.

He nods and then with a wink he's gone. Suddenly, this small apartment seems way too big.

Big and lonely.

Chapter 42

Jax

"*MIERDA!* HOW IS it possible for a man to just disappear?" Skull growls, his hand going through his hair.

"We searched the entire section, Boss. There wasn't a sign of him," Beast tells him.

"Christ's big toe," Torch grumbles, lighting a cigarette.

"Can't you ever talk normal cabrón, your language is getting as ridiculous as those damn shirts you insist on wearing," Skull tells his vice president and brother-in-law.

"There's not a damn thing stupid about my shirt," Torch says looking down at his black shirt with large white writing that says: *I don't always make my wife scream, but when I do it's usually against the wall with my dick buried in her.* "It's completely true," he says easily while Skull flips him off.

"Shaft?"

"Nothing Boss, me and Keys went over our area backwards and forwards. There's no sign of Sabre."

"Was there trouble?" Skull asks, watching me closely. I look down at the blood stain on my shirt. I know I've got bruises he can't see on my ribs, and my jaw is still bruised and swollen. After I left the apartment this morning, Keys and I had it out where Bree couldn't see. I'm not sure if I won, or he did. We're pretty evenly matched, but I will say the fucker will be damned sore in the morning, and he will think twice before he talks *shit* about *my* woman again.

"Nah. Just some personal shit. Keys and I worked it out," I shrug. I hear Keys grunt his agreement in the background.

"See to it that you do. I don't need any more shit piled on right now," he tells me, and I nod in agreement, without saying anything else. It doesn't need to be said. We all need to have our heads in the game here. "Briar's still in a coma, still fighting. There's not much new to tell," he says resigned, and the pain of this news hits us all. A darkness settles, a black cloud hanging over the club.

"How's his old lady holding up?" K-Rex asks from the corner. Stephanie is a good woman, and we all think the world of her. She's been a basket case since Briar was shot.

"Doc had to give her a sedative. She's resting now. I've got a couple men standing guard at the hospital. There's some shady shit going on, and until we get down to who's behind it, you guys need to be watching each other's backs. Am I clear?"

All the men give their agreement by nod, grunt, or yeahs, but none of the men are happy that this is where things are. If we could just find Sabre, it would be better. Even if he was dead, at least we could move forward and maybe have a clue as to what the fuck is going on.

"It's close to Christmas. I want Sabre home with his family before then. We broaden the search tomorrow," Skull growls, knocking the gavel against the table. On that we're all in agreement, but there's not a damn one of us who knows how to make it happen.

I follow the rest of the men out, feeling like I'm letting my brothers down, but knowing fuck-all about how to fix it.

"Are we good?" Keys asks, and I look at my brother. I trust him above all of the others for the most part. We've been through the fire together. He's young though, and he's got a hell of a lot to learn, especially when it comes to questioning me.

"If you lay off my woman, we're square," I tell him.

"You really don't see the fucking mess you're going to get yourself into? Even if by some miracle we avoid going into war with the Saints, do you really see that old bastard welcoming you to the family and letting you touch his granddaughter? Shit man, you're setting yourself up, and I don't want to see you fall." I know his concern comes from a good place.

"I got it under control. The only reason I haven't faced it head-on is because of all the shit going down."

"It's your funeral," Keys says in resignation. "You got a death wish over a piece of ass, it's none of my concern."

"I'm warning you, Keys."

"That's my final thoughts on the matter, you just better make sure you watch your back, because I can't be there to guard it all the time." He slaps my shoulder.

"Point made," I say, suddenly feeling bone tired. I follow him out to our bikes, jump on and take off towards my apartment without a second glance. I don't want to talk to anyone anymore.

No one, but Bree.

Chapter 43

Bree

"YOU STILL CAN'T get her?" Jax asks, as I hang up my phone and stare at it. It's not like Roxanne to go this long without talking to me, or at the very least checking in.

"No. I'm sure she's fine. It's just..."

"You're worried?"

"It's been over a week. I haven't talked to her since that morning in your apartment, Jax. I can't remember going a week without talking to her, let alone even longer."

"What do you want me to do?" Jax asks. He was lying on the sofa, and I had been holding his feet while we watched a movie. Now, he does a half sit up and moves his legs so he can pull me back into him with my head resting on his stomach. I turn to the side so I can see the television, not that I really care. I let the heat of Jax's body relax me. His fingers go into my hair, and I allow my eyes to close, drinking in the moment. I've never had much tenderness in my life and Jax spoils me with it. I'm coming to crave moments like this as much, if not more, than anything else we do together.

"I don't guess there's much you can do, honey. I'm sure she's fine. She'll probably check in tomorrow. She may have found her a new boy-toy."

"I'll send a couple prospects down tomorrow to check on her," Jax says, and I turn to look at him.

I look back at him. "You can't do that."

His eyes crinkle around the corners. "I can and I will."

"How would you explain it?"

"I know a couple of boys that would keep it quiet, baby. But, even if they didn't, that just means whatever we have to face, we face sooner. You and me are together. That's not ending. I'm not letting you go. Everyone else will just have to get used to it."

"I felt more secure about that before your buddy Keys."

"It will be okay," he tells me, but I think for a minute I see doubt in his eyes. There's things we should discuss, but I find I don't want to go there again—at least not yet. I know it's stupid, but I want to remain dumb and pretend that Jax loves me as much as I love him. I know from his reaction to the word he doesn't even believe in the word. Maybe I can love him enough for both of us. I know I don't want to give him up. Although he may not love me, he wants me, and he's claiming me. Maybe in the badass-biker world that equates to the same thing? Or maybe I'm doomed to be like Roxy. Living on my own in another state with nothing but my memories. On that note….

"If you're sure," I tell him, turning my body so I'm on all fours and climbing over him. That gets his attention and he helps pull me up, his hand locking onto the back of my neck as he brings me in for a kiss. His face is intense, tight with desire. *For me.*

Jax kisses me, and I keep wondering how it's possible that every kiss is better than the time before. Surely that can't be normal, or else people would be kissing all the time and nothing would get done in the world. *Kissing Jax is that addicting.*

"*Damn*, baby." His tongue darts over his bottom lip. "You can kiss."

"I was thinking the same thing about you," I tell him, sliding my hand into the jogging pants he's wearing. I instantly find his cock and smile when I feel how hard he is. *For me.*

"And what do you think you're doing?" he groans as I stroke him.

"Showing my appreciation that you worry about me so much?" I whisper, not looking at him, because I'm busy pulling his cock out, and my eyes are glued on his length.

"Oh. Then I think I should tell you that I'm sore as hell and it hurts to move, but I got up earlier when you were napping and turned the heat up."

"Is that so?" I'm watching as the veins in his cock grow tighter with each stroke. I'm blocking out the sore confession, because his poor body is a bruised mess. He didn't tell me why, but I know he and Keys had it out more. I hope that *asshole* looks worse at least.

"Yeah, I didn't want you to freeze. Then, last night I was afraid you'd have a nightmare, so I pulled you on top of me and let you sleep with my dick inside of you—just so you wouldn't feel alone," he says and my body spasms at the memory. It's been three days since Jax took my virginity and, I've lost count of how many times we've made love since. What I do know is that none have been sweeter than when I woke up with his hard cock inside of me and Jax somehow sleeping. Waking him up while riding him is on my list of things I want to do again and again…*and again.*

"That was very thoughtful of you," I tell him, letting my tongue slide into the small opening on his head as I stroke him. Instantly, the taste of him hits my tongue. Male, salty, musky, and again…*all mine.* "I should probably reward you really good for that one," I praise him, flattening my tongue out, licking the side of his shaft.

"If you feel you must," he says, trying to sound like he doesn't care either way, but the way his body trembles beneath mine when I take him into my mouth fully, and the way his hand tangles tight in my hair as he pushes me further down on his dick tells me much more. Then I forget the game we're playing. I forget worrying about Roxy. I forget everything and lose myself in Jax. *My man. Mine.*

Chapter 44

Jax

I LOOK AT the clock above the table and frown. What the hell is happening to me. It's ten in the morning, and I've had two days off from the club. Normally, I'd be sleeping—most likely hung over, because *shit*, I was lying to Bree a couple nights ago. I'm sore as fuck. Keys got better hits in than I thought. The one bright spot I had was the fucker was in just as much misery. I know, because I texted him a few times. I need to report in today though. Skull has been good to me, and I definitely needed a couple days off to heal and regroup. We're short-handed enough though, and we need to figure out what the fuck happened to Sabre. My taking a couple days off in that respect was not cool, no matter how much it was needed. I sent a couple prospects down to Tennessee to check on Bree's girl this morning too. So I need to get my ass in gear. Yet, even knowing all this shit, I'm still not in a hurry to leave. I'm even starting to think of this crappy apartment as a…*home*. What the fuck is wrong with me?

I hear the shower turn on and smile. There it is. That's what the fuck has gotten into me. *Bree*. She brings a peace into my life I've *never* fucking had. Just being around her makes life easier, makes it…*good*. That might be proof I'm just a selfish fuck, taking her and keeping her when I should let her go. She'd be better off with someone her own age, someone outside of this life. *Hell*, even that wet-behind the ears kid who's panting after her would be a better choice than me. I can't give her up though, and the time for that has gone anyways. I need to tell Skull and Torch first. I owe them that. I have no idea how Skull will react. He and Torch both might decide to end me without giving me a chance to explain. I should have never kept her hidden—especially from my *own* family.

Pouring myself a cup of coffee, I think over my options. The best thing to do would be to come clean today. Put the wheels in motion for telling everyone about us. Yet, the club has so much shit going on right now. Waiting until we know what happened to Sabre might be best—not to mention Briar. I went by the hospital last night to check on him. There's been no change, but the doctors all agree the longer he stays like this, without showing any signs of improvement, means bad things. He'd been shot and lost a lot of blood, but what they are most concerned about is the swelling in the brain. When he fell, his head slammed into concrete. They think maybe he was standing on something, up higher than normal, so when the shot took him down, he fell.

I wish to fuck we knew what the hell had happened that day. We all assumed they had been on their bikes and been ambushed, but how could that be true if he fell from somewhere? *Motherfucker it's all just twisted to hell and back with no answers.* I know why Skull is so upset now. It's like banging your head against a brick wall repeatedly, only it would be worse for Skull because he feels responsible for sending my brothers out.

"Open up, hermano."

Fuck. Skull. *Here*. This is not good. I can still hear the shower. I'm gonna need to get rid of him…quick. I open the door, and do my best not to act like I want Skull anywhere but fucking here.

"Boss?"

"Sabre's been found, let's ride." *Motherfucker.* Sabre's found… even as that registers, there is one other thought that's stronger: *Couldn't he have called?*

"Is he…" shit, I can't even say it.

"He's alive. Fucked up, but *alive.*"

"Then why the hell hasn't he checked in? What the fuck is going on, Boss?" I ask, stepping into my boots and then running back to the couch grab my t-shirt and cut.

"He hasn't been conscious. He hasn't been able to check in. Unlike you, motherfucker—who apparently took it on himself to send two prospects to Tennessee without checking with me." I freeze, rubbing my hand along my beard.

"Boss—"

"Later el cabrón, first we talk to Sabre. The other men are waiting on us outside. I only came up to tell you alone that you and I are going to talk. You have access to the men, but *motherfucker*, you never act on your own without telling me what the hell is going on. You get me?" He pokes my chest.

Fuck, I gotta say something. *Now.*

"Yeah, man. Listen…"

"Later. More important shit going on. But, we will have this out. I'd just rather not call you out in front of the other men. If you leave me no choice," Skull shrugs. He likes me. I know he does and he's doing this as a courtesy. Most men he would have called them down and made an example of them. He's giving me trust here, and how will he feel when he knows I've betrayed him even more? *Shit.*

"Jax? Were you yelling? I couldn't hear you over the water, honey," Bree says coming through the hall. She reaches the kitchen, rubbing a towel through her hair and wearing nothing but another towel wrapped around her. *Motherfucking fucking fuck.*

I hear Skull's growl, but I don't look at him, instead I go and stand in front of Bree. No son of a bitch will see Bree like that, even my Prez.

"¿Qué mierda está pasando aquí?" Skull demands. *What the fuck is going on here?* I get a sick feeling that this will be the end of my time with Bree, if he has anything to do with it. *Fuck.* That can't happen. *She's mine.*

"Skull?" Bree, gasps from behind me.

"Go get dressed, Bree," I order her.

"What the fuck did you do?" Skull says, his voice deadly, looking ready to murder first and ask questions later.

"It's not what it looks like, Boss," I tell him, inside thinking, *fuck*, it's probably worse.

His dark eyes would kill me, if looks could murder. "It looks like you've been sticking your polla into my *menor de edad* neice."

"She's not underage, Boss," I growl, wondering if that sounds as lame to him as it does to me.

"She's in high school you sick fuck! Cristo, where the fuck did I go wrong here."

"Aunt Bethie was in school when you met her, Skull."

"Stay out of this, Bree," I warn her. "And for fuck's sake, go get *dressed.*"

"Seems I need to speak up. I love him Skull. He's my man," she confesses, taking up for me, but it doesn't matter.

"He's a dead man," he states, his tone resolute.

"I love him," Bree objects.

"Amor," Skull scoffs. "You're *too* young to know what *love* is."

"Was that true with Beth? She said she loved you from the moment you first met."

"And look what heartache that caused pequeño?" Skull returns, and I rake my hand through my hair, sure I'm losing my mind. I'm upset that my Prez, the man who understandably wants to kill me right now calls her little one. *No one* should have nicknames for *my* woman, but *me.*

"And if the family had respected her decision and you two wouldn't have had obstacles, none of that would have happened," Bree returns, stubbornly.

"Bree. Enough. Go get dressed," I order her.

"Si, Bree. Go put clothes on. I'll have my men take you back to the compound."

"I'm not leaving." Bree's stance says one thing, she's not going without a fight. That's my girl.

"She's not leaving, Boss," her and I say in unison.

"La mierda dices?" he growls advancing on me, but I stand my ground.

"She's mine, Boss. I've claimed her, and I'm not giving her up. You'll have to kill me to get her away."

"That could be arranged easily cabrón. I can almost assure it." The threat behind his words is loud and clear.

"Then so be it. But I'm not giving her up. *She's mine.*"

Bree—proving that she never does what she is told moves around me and holds close to my side, wrapping her arm around me. *Motherfucker.*

"I won't leave him and if you make me, I'll just find my way back to him." My woman is hard headed, and under any other circumstances, her defiant attitude would have me ripping her towel from her body.

"Son of a bitch, woman. Go get dressed. I don't want other men looking at what is mine!" I growl.

"Jax, he's my uncle, for God's sake," she attempts to argue.

"I do not give a damn! It's mine. Now go cover up!" I growl, my face tight, my hand in my hair wondering if I could pull it out and she'd listen to me.

"Quit yelling at me! I'm trying to save your life here!"

I look at her, those flecks of green and brown could hypnotize me. However, now isn't the time for it. "You're going to get me killed quicker!"

"Times like this I have to wonder why I love you," she mutters. She moves away from me though and looks at Skull. "I think you get I haven't had a lot of happiness in my life."

The look on Skull's face has changed. He's appraising the two of us differently and though anger is still there, I also see something else. He's studying us. I just wish I knew what the fuck that meant. He nods his head in agreement at Bree.

"For the first time in my life, Skull…I feel like I belong. I've never been happier. If I die tomorrow I'll be okay with it, because for a little while I had everything. Do you understand?"

"Motherfucker. Bree, shut the hell up," I growl, rubbing that area around my heart that always fucking finds a way to hurt around her. My voice is mean and harsh, and I can feel the tension go back in Skull and even hear him take a step toward us. I don't give a damn though. I'm too busy grabbing, Bree and pulling her back to me. "Shut the fuck up!"

"Jax—" Bree gasps, clearly confused.

I swallow the lump in my throat. "You will *not* die."

"I wasn't talking—"

"You will *not* talk about it, you will *not* do it, and you will never even contemplate leaving me. Do you understand?"

"Jax, sweetheart, I was just giving an example of why—"

"I don't want you talking about death in any way, shape, or form from this moment on. You understand?"

"Jax—"

"Do. You. Understand?" I growl. I'm holding her shoulders tight; I'm not even trying to be gentle. I'll probably leave marks on her skin, and I'm giving Skull more reason to shoot my dick off. I can't help it though. The thought of Bree *dying* is destroying me. *Destroying.* I'm staring into her face, my eyes captured by hers, and I won't let go until she gives me the words, until she somehow makes this raging fear inside of me better.

Bree's hand cups the side of my face. Her fingers brush through my beard and find my lips as if to stop my words. I wish she could stop this burning inside of me and these visions she started of her dying. My body is shaking with just the thought. I've seen too much death in my time. Too much fucking death, if that was to happen to *Bree*…to *my* woman…

"I'm not going anywhere, honey. I'm right here. I promise," she whispers kissing my lips gently. A kiss that is not one of passion, but one of a vow. One that calms a little of the fear she stirred inside. Still, my hand shakes as I bring her forehead in close and lay my lips upon it. I gather my breath in my body, realizing it's shaky, and I completely lost control here. *What the fuck is wrong with me?* Bree. Beginning to end…it's Bree.

"Now, go get dressed."

"Okay, honey," she says slowly walking away. "You won't hurt him," she says to Skull, and I just hold my head down, still not in control. I rub the back of my neck realizing that I'll never be able to control Bree. If I live through this, I'm not even sure I mind. I like her fire.

"We have club business. This will be tabled until that is dealt with," Skull growls, surprising me.

"You and Jax are leaving?" she asks.

"Yeah," Skull says.

"Boss—"

"But, he'll be coming back here. So, stay put," Skull growls interrupting me. Bree's face moves into the biggest smile. It blinds me for a minute.

"Be careful, honey," she says giving me a quick kiss on the

lips before all but literally skipping out of the room. I'm still rubbing the back of my neck trying to figure out what to say.

"Boss—"

"This isn't over *asshole*. But, right now Sabre, Briar, and the mess with the Saints takes center stage. You and me will have words later," he confirms turning around. "And for fuck's sake, hide your damn cock-stand for my niece," he says walking out the door.

I look down realizing during my haste to get ready and rush Skull out the door that I left my pants unzipped. And despite everything that happened, the fucker is sticking out of my pants, hard as a fucking steel rod. I do my best to situate the fucker, then carefully zip my pants up. I have a feeling this will be my life from now on. Being led around by my cock…but only by one woman…

Bree. Always Bree.

Chapter 45

Bree

"I'M NOT LEAVING with you. Absolutely not. Forget it Aunt Katie," I growl when I open the door to Katie yelling. When I open it, I see Beth peek over her shoulder. *Great.* "Not leaving for you either Aunt Bethie. So, if that's why you are here, you can just turn your cute little buns around to go home."

"You think my buns are cute?" Katie asks, looking over her shoulder at her ass.

"You know it is. Torch tells you all the time," Beth says with a snicker.

"Always helps to get a second opinion. Are you going to let us in or not?" Katie asks, and I sigh.

"Fine, but I'm not leaving." I step aside so they can come in.

"We know dear, you screamed it at us," Beth says quietly, closing the door behind her.

"Wow. This place is a dump," Katie says, curling her nose. Her comment annoys me. I thought I had the place looking pretty good. I cleaned and cleaned. I'm actually kind of proud with how it looks.

"It's better than some of the places we stayed at when we were in hiding," Beth says with a shrug.

"Nah, I just think it's cleaner. You didn't clean house very well," Katie says with a wink.

"I was sick and pregnant. Quit being a pain in my ass," Beth grumbles and sits down. "Pregnancy always makes you a bitch," she teases on a sigh.

"No. Lack of sex makes me a bitch, and Hunter won't touch me until the doctor says we're all clear."

"All clear?" I ask concerned.

"She had some spotting last week," Beth answers as Katie sits down on the couch beside her.

She shrugs waving her hand out. "It was nothing. I told Hunter he was going all to hell over nothing, but he wouldn't listen. He's so on edge over Briar and Sabre he's over reacting about everything."

"Yeah, Skull's the same way."

"Still, Aunt Katie, if you're spotting that's kind of serious."

"It wasn't much and just one day. I didn't cramp or anything. The ultrasound and things turned out just great. I go back next week and then maybe Hunter can calm his ass down."

"Where are the kids?" I ask, letting it go because if she's not real concerned I'm sure she's fine.

"Mattah has them. Now, how about you tell us how in the world you ended up shacking up with one of Skull's men," Beth asks, and I sigh flopping in a chair.

"We're not exactly shacking up."

"Oh, I'm sorry. You mean you haven't been living here while Pop's thinks you are at Roxanne's?" Katie asks, and I know I'm blushing. *Crap.*

"I love him," I tell them honestly, looking at them so that maybe they can see something on my face to convince them.

"Pfft. You're not even out of high school yet, Breezy. What do you know about love?"

"Don't be like that. You weren't exactly over the hill when you first met Torch."

"It wasn't about love when we first met it was about bumping uglies."

"Bumping uglies? I swear Katie you're beginning to be more like Torch every day—and before you ask that's *not* a good thing," Beth grumbles. "Bree we're worried about you. I know you *think* you *love* Shaft, but—"

"I don't think, Aunt Bethie, I know. I *absolutely* know. I knew the moment I first saw him."

"But—"

"You said that's how it was for you and Skull," I defend.

"It was, but honey look how that turned out? The *hell* Skull and I went through? I wouldn't wish that on anyone. We nearly destroyed each other." She looks down at her hands in her lap.

"But, look where you're at now. Would you have changed anything knowing you get what you have now?"

"Bree, honey. Pops will kill Shaft for touching you, and you've been around enough to know he will."

"Not if I love him. I don't understand. Have you guys forgotten what I've been through? Why can't you trust me to know that this happiness I have right now means everything? I'm owed this! I've never asked anyone for anything, but I need this guys. *I need Jax.*" *God, I need him and I want to keep him.*

"Breezy," Katie breaks in, but Beth puts her hand on Katie's arm and looks at me. *Really looks at me.*

"You're sure he's the one?"

"He makes me laugh. He makes me feel like I'm alive for the first time in my life. We laugh, and Jax doesn't smile a lot. He has this half-smile he uses with everyone when he wisecracks, but he hardly ever laughs and gives a full smile. I make him do it all the time. He holds my hand when we're watching television. And he does it in a way that I really don't think he's aware of it. He cooks for me…"

"Shaft cooks?" Katie appears skeptical.

"Well, he heats up soup and makes a mean hotdog."

"Wow," Beth says.

"Don't make fun," I grumble, because I love that Jax does those things for me.

"I wasn't making fun. Poor Skull doesn't even know how to turn the stove on."

"Same with Hunter, even the microwave is beyond his basic knowledge."

I stare the pair of them down. "The point you guys, is that he's good to me. Good to me in a way that I know I always want to be with him."

"You love him," Beth concludes.

"With everything inside of me." My eyes must have a dreamy look about them, but talking about *my love* for *my man* does that to me.

"I hate to be a broken record here, but you're so young Breezy. You might find the same thing with boys your own age. You've not even finished high school!" Katie grumbles, and the *high school thing* is really starting to grate on my nerves.

"I'm just as old as Beth was when she met Skull, and I'll be out of school in January. I'm graduating early because of my core work and scores. I even have eight hours of college credit under my belt. I'm not some kid you guys." I can't seem to stress that fact enough. "No matter how everyone insists on seeing me. I know what *I* want and that's *Jax*."

"Breezy, at least allow yourself to date and see what is out there—"

"Stop it! Just stop! Do you hear yourself? Do you know how many boys I've been attracted to in my life, Aunt Katie?"

She flinches. "No, but—"

"None. Not one. I've never been like the other kids at school. I've been through too much. I've seen too much darkness. I can't pretend to want to be around those people. I don't. They may be great people…but we have *nothing* in common."

"Who's to say that down the road you might find someone who will—"

"Do you honestly think that if you lost your husbands today that there would be another man who would even come close to who they are to you? Today? Ten years down the road? Twenty? Even fifty? I know in my heart that Jax *is* the man I'm *supposed* to be with for the rest of my life."

"Nothing we say will change your mind, will it?" Beth finally says after we sit in silence for a few minutes.

I confirm, "Nothing whatsoever."

"Good. Then we need a game plan on how to tackle the men and Pops, because we're going to need a united front here," Beth says, and I stop.

"Good? You mean you were okay with this all along?"

"Honey, I love Skull with all my heart. That kind of love is special. I have it, Katie has it—"

"I do, even if he's an idiot, he's my idiot," Katie jokes, and I have to laugh. It lightens the mood.

"All we wanted to do is make sure you had that too. Skull told me he thinks Shaft is completely gone for you. He's sure risking a hell of a lot by being with you. So, now we need to make sure we can contain Skull and Torch."

"I'm afraid they may be the easy part in all of this. The one we really have to look out for…" Katie adds.

"Pops," we all three say together and the worry can be heard echoed in each of our voices.

Chapter 46

Jax

MY BROTHER LOOKS like hell. If I didn't see the tattoos I wouldn't even know it was him to be honest. He's bloated, bruised and more than battered. Sabre has broken ribs, a broken arm, his jaw is broken, his eyes are swollen shut, while his chest and stomach are all varying shades of maroon, blue, and purple. I don't know what the fuck he has been through, but it's clear he's been tortured, and tortured by someone huge. I can say that because there's about a size fifteen boot impression against one of Sabre's ribs. It's a miracle he's still breathing—even if it is by a machine. Sabre's a hell of a fighter though. He's moved his good hand twice since the brothers have been here, so we know he's in there *somewhere*. That gives more hope than we have with Briar at the moment. Unfortunately, because he can't talk, we still have no idea what happened to them, or how the fuck he ended up in a small county hospital four counties away from where the first attack happened. Something is stinking here, and I sure as hell wish we could find out what the fuck is going on.

When I look over at Skull and see the tension on his face, seeing it mirrored in each of my brothers, I know I'm not alone.

"I don't understand how the hospital knew to call us? It's not like Sabre is telling them anything."

"One of the nurses on duty recognized the tatt on Sabre's

back as belonging to the Devil's Blaze," Torch answers, his eyes never leaving Sabre's.

"Where the fuck is his Devil's Blaze cut?" I ask.

"That's the hundred-dollar question," Skull growls.

"What do we do now?"

"We leave two men here watching Sabre's back. The staff is getting him ready for transport. He'll be back home by the end of the night and in the same hospital as Briar. That way we can lockdown that place and make sure they're safe," Skull says.

"I can stay," I pipe up, not wanting to, but feeling like I owe Sabre. I took two days off while he was here alone, without someone at his back.

"You and I have business. K-Rex, and Sway can stay here," Skull answers. I knew it would happen. Still, a part of me was hoping he'd let me and Bree slide. *Looks like it's not going to be that easy.*

WE SLOW DOWN and the crew pulls into the old meat packing plant that our crew and the Savage Brothers usually do business together in. Skull makes a motion with his hands, and everyone turns in. He turns off his engine and we follow suit.

"Torch and I have some business with Shaft. You guys head on back to the compound," he orders, and *fuck,* that bad feeling I had just exploded. *Son of a bitch.* They all are looking at me, including Beast and he doesn't look too fucking thrilled with me either. Will he be my next beat-down? They're all gone within a matter of minutes.

"Prez man, I'd like to stay here," Keys says and my eyes go to him. *Motherfucker*, is he planning on joining them when they kick my ass?

"We got it covered," Skull says, arms crossed at his chest,

leaning back on his bike.

"Just the same. Shaft is my brother, and I want to be here... *for him*."

Skull and Torch ignore him and push me towards the plant entrance. I follow, keeping an eye on Keys who follows behind me. It takes a minute for my eyes to adjust to the darkness, but then Skull flips on the old florescent shop lights, and the buzz of them fills the room.

I'm still in shock. Partly because of what's getting ready to take place here, and partly because of my brother. Here Keys was putting his neck out there for me. What the hell does someone say to that? I love my brothers. Being part of this club is all I've wanted in life. It's one reason I didn't mind prospecting at my age, even when the rest of the brothers were a fuck of a lot younger. I knew in my heart that this club was where I was meant to be. But now, to see Keys stick his neck out for me, when there was no reason to, I feel that bond in my blood. We've always had each other's back in battle, but this... *This is different.*

"No," I tell him my voice hoarse because I'm charged with emotion. It's not a comfortable feeling for me. *Shit,* since being with Bree, maybe I'm going soft—at least with everything but my dick. "I'm fine. You don't need to be here, brother."

"I'm not asking for your permission," Keys grumbles. His face is a mask of stone.

"Maybe not, but I'd rather not have any other witnesses when I get my ass kicked. You could go back and watch over Bree, until I get back."

"What makes you think you're going to go back motherfucker?" Torch growls, and I guess Skull found time to clue him in on this morning. *That's great.* Are they going to end me? God knows *that shit* has been done here before. I knew it was a possibility when I got involved with Bree, I just kind of figured it would be at her grandfather's or the Saint's hands and not by my own club. I don't want to go down like this. But, I'm not going to beg them. I wouldn't even change shit if I could. Bree is *my woman* and no matter the time we've had together, no matter how short lived, it has been worth it.

"Then so be it. Then let Keys watch her and make sure she's okay for me."

"You got shit backwards chico. We don't owe you a mother-fucking thing. You were the one who should have come to us before you laid a hand on Bree."

"Pres—" Keys starts, but I wave him off. This is me. *All on me.*

"You're right. I should have." I own it, I own it all.

"Then why didn't you, motherfucker?" Torch demands.

"Because you would have tried to stop me."

"Damn straight we would have! She's a fucking kid."

"She's not. Bree's more adult than people twice her age, but the truth is, nothing you would have said could have stopped me. *She's mine.* What happens here tonight won't change that. I claimed her, and she's an old lady of the Devil's Blaze. *Whatever* the fuck you do to me, *nothing* is going to change the fact that she's *my woman.*"

Torch grabs a baseball bat that was leaning in the corner, palming it in his hand. His face doesn't leave mine, and I will not give him the satisfaction of blinking.

"You know what I'm thinking, Skull?" he asks.

"What's that hombre?" Skull answers.

"I'm thinking Shaft don't get that if he's not breathing that Bree is up for grabs." His voice is gravely.

"The fuck she is," I growl.

"Si. Especially since every snake out there is crawling

through the grass with the hopes of being the next leader of the Saints," Skull adds in.

"Fuck them all! *She's mine,*" I roar like a damned lion. "That makes her the club's. She has your protection," I growl going after them, only to have Keys try and hold me back. It doesn't work, I act like a wounded animal. I almost make it to Skull when Torch sweeps my legs out from under me with the fucking baseball bat. I fall to the ground hard, knocking the breath from my lungs.

"Look at that Skull. The bastard has enough balls to come at you, but not enough to tell you he's going to be fucking a kid."

"She's not a motherfucking kid!" I scream.

"She's in high school, you sick prick!" Torch grits as Skull's foot connects with my chest.

"Oomph." What little air I didn't know I had left in me blows from my open mouth.

"Prez, maybe we can stop and talk about this," Keys says and he looks a little green. *Shit*, he should be on this end.

"You need to leave Keys. I'm already fucking pissed at you for not coming to me. Cristo, do my own men not know who they answer to?"

"He was coming to you, it's why we fought," I gasp, trying to cover for him. "Let him go be with Bree so she won't be alone."

"Bree is not alone, estúpido. Beth and Katie are with her."

"Boss. I know I don't deserve it, but I'm asking—"

"Asking what?"

"Let me keep her. I promise you I'll bust my back every fucking day to be the man she deserves."

"What do you think Torch?"

"I think he's a sorry sack of shit." He laughs. *The motherfucker laughs.*

"Si. But then so were we once, el cofrade, were we not?" Torch rakes his hand across his beard and the son of a bitch actually smiles.

"I suppose we were, but you were a sadder sack of shit than I was."

"Whatever, cabrón," Skull laughs. "Keys your idiot brother is safe. Go on back to the compound," he orders. Then they both squat down to look at me.

"Then it's over? You're letting me go home to Bree?"

"Oh, it's not over. Far from over. We're still going to beat the shit out of you. You should have never touched her without our blessing," Torch warns.

"You never would have given it." I breathe out regaining air in my lungs.

"Probably not," Skull shrugs. "But, she seems to *love* you and she could do *worse*."

"Maybe. I still say she could do better. She's short changing herself," Torch adds.

"Who understands women? Beth and Katie both settled when they picked our ugly faces."

"Speak for yourself motherfucker."

"Okay, time for the pain," Skull growls, standing up.

"But, I thought you said…" Keys trails off, lost as to what's going on and *hell,* he's not alone.

"I'm not going to kill him, but he kept secrets from his club. Secrets that involved his President's family. That's no good. That buys him a beating, and it just so happens I got a lot of pent up frustration."

"He gets to come home though, right?" Keys asks.

"Sure. If he can drag his ass on his bike when we get done with him," Torch says, hauling me up on legs that will barely hold me. "Let's see how bad you really want her, fuck-head,"

Torch sneers.

"I'll make it home to her," I vow. In response Torch and Skull both just grin.

Shit. This is gonna hurt.

Chapter 47

Bree

"YOU'RE LATE! I was getting worried!" I exclaim going to the door when I hear Jax's gruff order to open up. I'm not prepared for what I see when I do. Jax is being held up by Keys. He looks like he's been run over by a herd of elephants. "What happened?" I cry, immediately trying to help hold him. Keys moves him through the room with my pitiful help and lays him on the couch. Jax breathes out in pain and groans. He coughs and you can literally see the pain his body spasms in. He closes his eyes, and I can't stop the tears that fall from my eyes. "What happened?" I ask again, looking at Keys.

"Nothing, baby. I'm fine," Jax mutters, trying to pat my hand to reassure me.

"It doesn't look like nothing!" I cry. "Oh, your poor face." Tears are battling to fall down my face.

"Skull and Torch decided to welcome him into the family," Keys says.

"They *what?*" I screech. Anger and sadness rush through me.

"Reckon they welcomed him in really well," Keys says and it pisses me off. I bury my elbow in his stomach. "Hey! What was that for?"

"For being an *asshole*," I grumble.

"Baby, calm down. I'm fine," Jax chokes out. He's not fine.

"You don't look fine."

"Well, I am, and I'd be better if *my woman* would come over here and give me a kiss."

"In a minute. Though I'm not sure where I'm supposed to kiss you. Your lips are all swollen and bruised," I wonder, grabbing a bowl from the kitchen. I fill it with hot water in the bathroom, grabbing some alcohol and antibiotic cream. I add a whole box of bandages thinking there's no way it will be enough.

"Baby—"

"Don't you baby me. Where were you? Why didn't you help him?" I look to Keys for an explanation.

"He tried," he tells me, defending his brother.

"Funny, he doesn't look like he's been ran over by a pack of wild animals," I complain.

"Honey—" his voice is so hoarse.

"Don't you *honey* me."

"What are you mad at me for?" he asks, like an idiot.

"You're trying to get yourself killed. You promised me you would be okay!"

"I wasn't trying to get myself killed."

"I don't think I want a woman," Keys states grabbing a couple beers out of the fridge. He hands Jax one, but before he can get it, I grab it and set it on the table, settling on my knees in front of the couch so I can try and clean him up.

"You can have it after I get done bandaging you up," I tell him.

"Baby, no offense but the beer might help the pain more than what you're doing."

"Will the beer help you when these cuts get infected? Oh crap, Jax! Is anything broken? We should get you to the hospital and let them check you out. I can't believe you!" I shake my head as I assess him, debating where to start.

"I don't have anything broken, and honey getting home on

that bike was about all I had in me. I'm done here."

"You drove home?" I ask, and yes, I'm definitely still screeching.

"No. He rode, on the back of my bike, like a chump. He did better than I thought. Of course, I handcuffed him—"

"You handcuffed him? Oh my God! You let him handcuff you to the bike? Are you crazy? What if he had wrecked or something?"

"Why are you yelling at him for? Technically, it's your family who did it and this was nothing compared to what they could have done," Keys grumbles falling back into the chair so that it scoots a good six inches. I've decided I really, *really* don't like him.

"It was nothing?" I ask Jax, and I've gone from screeching to whispering in no time flat as it starts to dawn on me what Jax has endured.

"They took it easy on me baby," he whispers softly, his eyes fluttering. He's spent. Not even a nickel left of him.

Easy? He looks like they almost killed him! Suddenly, the gravity of the situation—of *everything* begins to settle in. *My* family did this. *My* family almost killed him. *This is all my fault.* With that thought tears begin to fall. I fall back on my ass and just let them well up and flow like a steady rain over my cheeks. I can't stop them. It's like a dam broke and more and more just keep flooding.

"Come on, sweetheart, don't cry," Jax says doing his best to sit up even if he is in all kinds of pain, and *that* makes me cry harder too. He wraps his arms around me as sobs rack my body. "Bree, baby, you're killing me here."

"*Christ.* I know I don't want a woman now," Keys says to no one, and if I wasn't in the middle of a meltdown I'd throw the bottle of rubbing alcohol at him.

"Bree—"

"They hurt you!" I sob.

"It looks worse than it is," he tells me, trying to smile, but his poor lips won't let him give me *my* smile. The one that spreads completely and makes my stomach tingle.

"Because of me! This is all *my* fault. Everyone's right. I should have stayed away from you," I cry in despair, my head dropping down. *I got Jax hurt.* In response, Jax's hand tightens up around my neck until it's almost painful. I pull my watery eyes up to him, and his beautiful face is blurry from my tears to the point I can only see the bruised colors that are starting to bloom further along his skin.

"Listen to me, woman. Nothing anyone could do to me would make me regret being *your man.* Fuck them all. I *have* you and that's all I *need*," he growls, his voice suddenly sounding stronger. I'm trying to get myself under control. I need to be stronger too. I need to be the kind of woman Jax can be proud of. I need…*to kill my uncles.*

"I'm sorry, Jax," I whimper through my tears. Feeling like I've let him down, feeling guilt he's hurting, and just a million other things and none of them good.

"I'm not. I'd take this and more for you. You hear me?"

"I *love* you," I whisper giving him the only thing I can.

"Then dry up those eyes. I don't want my woman crying."

"*Christ.* I'm never claiming a woman either," Keys mutters from behind me, and I take a shuddering breath, using the back of my hand to wipe my eyes.

I see the light in Jax's eyes now. Just me getting a hold of myself has made him happy. Then I grab the bottle of rubbing alcohol, hurling it hard as I can at Keys. I played softball in school, so it's pretty much a direct hit. I did close the lid so it didn't pour all over him. *He should be thankful.* It however hits his beer and he spills that on his pants.

"What the hell did you do that for?"

"You're an asshole," I yell at him, and I feel a little better when Jax gives a laugh, even if it does sound painful. Keys scowls at me, but doesn't say anything else. Now, I just need to kill my uncles…*and maybe Pops.*

Chapter 48

Jeff

AUBREE LIED. I hate that she lied to me. It's that man making her do it. He's a bad influence on her. He's trying to take her from me. Take her innocence, her purity. I can't let that happen. I look out of my car window and see Roxanne. I've only met her once or twice when she's come to the school for events Aubree has been in. I've never heard good things about her. I know she used to be a club whore. That kind of influence can't be had on my Breezy. I'll have to cut her out of Breezy's life. There's no other way really. I'm glad she's done her best to protect her, and it's good that she helped me get her away from the idiot who thinks it's cool to call himself Shaft.

Maybe I'll be nice to her. I'll make sure she doesn't have to suffer the things I go through. Aubree could have made this easier. Everything was going fine, until she met *him*. We could have gone about this slow. She's made me change my plans. She's the reason there has to be pain. I hope she understands the lengths I will go to just to protect her. To keep her safe.

Roxanne lives in one of those small, government housing apartments, where each one looks the same. Dark brown brick, no more than three windows and the same colored brown door. Luckily for me however, her apartment is on the end. I'd rather not have a lot of people see me here. I don't even like the fact that Bree is seen here. She's too good for a place like this.

I walk to the door, and I can feel the adrenaline pumping inside of me. It takes the woman a few minutes to get to the door. For a minute, I'm hoping it is Aubree who opens, but it's not.

"Can I help you?"

"Hi Roxanne, it's great to see you again."

She squints at my face. "I'm sorry, do I know you?"

"It's me, Jeff? Remember? We met when you came to Bree's award ceremony a few months ago."

"Oh," she answers, her face scrunched up in confusion. "Is Bree okay?" I study her for a moment. Her skin is starting to sag, especially around the neck. She's got tired green eyes that are too heavily covered in eye-shadow. Her once vibrant red hair is starting to give way to gray. She's tall and slim. Passable. She's not a beautiful woman, but maybe in her prime she might have been, before she spread her legs and became a biker whore.

"Actually, I'm here to surprise her. She said she was visiting you for Christmas."

"Oh. Well yeah, she was, but she got held up. She's not here yet." Roxanne holds the door close to her body.

"When will she be here?" I demand, a sick feeling of heat flushing through my body. *She lied to me. She's still with him. She's not here at all.*

"I'm not sure. Listen, I have to go. My boyfriend is on his way over. I'll tell Bree you're looking for her," she stutters, and she pushes the door to close it. I stick my foot in, not letting her shut me out.

"I need to talk to Bree today."

"I'm not sure what to tell you," she answers. "But, I really need you to go now. I'll call Bree, and if she wants to talk to you she'll call you."

"That's not good enough for me Roxanne."

I watch as her eyes go big. I see the moment that the fear hits her and it soothes me. I keep things so tightly compacted, I have to keep control. The fear in her eyes allows that control to snap. I grab her hand before she can completely back away from me and then push my way in the doorway as if I was out on the football field. This is going to be easier than I dreamed. I'll take care of her, get rid of her car and set about luring Aubree away from that man. She'll have to pay for letting him near. *She'll have to pay dearly.*

As I snap Roxanne's wrist, I smile because I can hear the crack of the bone even over her screaming I find myself hoping that Aubree doesn't make me do to her what I'm going to do to Roxanne here.

Don't make me, Aubree. There's so much more I'd rather do to you…

Chapter 49

Jax

"FEELING SORE ARE you?"

"Fuck off, asshole," I growl at Torch. The bastard just laughs harder. Skull sits down beside me, but his face is definitely more somber.

"We didn't beat you down enough, you're moving too soon."

"Beth and Katie came over to take Bree shopping. I couldn't stand to look at the empty walls. I really need a better place."

"You do if you're going to keep Bree," Skull agrees and manages to piss me off. There's no *if* to it, she's mine.

"I'm keeping her," I grumble at him.

"Si. Then you better find a new home. She deserves better than that dump," he says, and he's not wrong. She does. Hell, she deserves better than me, and I'm pretty sure that's what he's thinking too. I take a pull from my beer and lean back. "How is my sobrina?" he adds.

"Worried. She still can't get a hold of Roxanne. Have you heard from the prospects I sent to Tennessee?"

"They reported back about an hour ago. There was no sign of her. The house is empty, and the woman's car is gone. They checked inside, just to make sure. A few dresser drawers were open as if clothes were taken out in a hurry, and the closet door was open. Maybe she just needed to leave in a hurry?"

"Maybe, but from the way Bree talks they're super close. I can't imagine she'd leave and not call her."

"So, it's like the rest of the shit around here lately. Another mystery without answers," Beast growls, and it's hard for me to get used to his darker voice. He's changed a lot since his accident. He was trying to get out more and become part of the club again—besides just being the main muscle. Yet, since that day at the picnic when Lucy said crap about him, he's retreated more. *Fuck*, he's so hairy now I can barely see his face and he's added so many tattoos there's no skin visible anywhere. He's definitely more *beast* than *man* now. He puts his heavy body down in the seat, and I'm surprised the fucker doesn't cave under his weight.

"Amen," we all seem to say together.

"You look like a fucking train hit you," Beast says, and *shit*, I must be bad if this is coming from him.

"It looks worse than it is," I mutter resisting the urge to kick the shit out of Torch for laughing. *Fucking bastard.*

"Where did Beth and Katie take Bree?" I ask, trying to change the subject.

"Who the fuck knows, Katie's not talking to me," Torch bitches.

"They went into Somerset," Skull answers.

"That's a hell of a long drive for shopping," Torch complains. "I should paddle her ass for not telling me."

"I've got Bruno driving them," Skull answers. "Or Beth wouldn't have told me either. I told him to take them there so they wouldn't run into any of Tucker's bunch."

"Fuck," I mutter.

"Si. There is a can of worms you do not want to open just yet, motherfucker."

I scrub my hands over my face. "Fuck. I know," I answer.

"I ought to beat you again," Torch says giving me a dirty look.

"Then your wife really would be pissed," I joke, hoping that's enough to change his mind, because *hell,* I'm so damned sore I haven't even been able to love on my own woman. I'm hoping that will change tonight. It's been two days, and I still had trouble riding my damn bike over here.

"That's not why she's not talking motherfucker," Torch answers, and Skull snorts in disbelief. "Well it's not the *only* reason. She's mad cause I won't give her my dick."

"*Jesus,* I don't want to hear about your sex-life," Beast growls.

"Screw you. The woman is addicted to me, what can I say?" Torch brags.

"That you're an asshole?" Skull answers and we all laugh. Skull's phone rings though and takes his attention. He barely has the phone up to his ear before he's hanging up. "Briar's awake. Let's ride," he orders already going to the door, leaving us to follow behind.

Chapter 50

Jax

"FUCK BROTHER, YOU had us worried," Skull says grabbing Briar's hand in his inked one and giving it a squeeze before letting it go. We're in Briar's hospital room. His old lady, Stephanie is sitting at his side, holding his other hand, her head resting on his chest.

"Too fucking mean to die," he jokes, his voice is hoarse and really weak. They took the breathing tube out when he came to, hopefully that's all it is. He's so damned pale, he doesn't even resemble the man who was giving me hell over Bree.

"Do you feel like telling us what went on?"

"He needs his rest," Stephanie says tearfully.

"Need to tell them, babe," he argues and she stares into his face for a minute.

"I'm not leaving," she argues. Skull must not object, because he sits down and waits.

"Drove to the meeting place," Briar says and starts coughing. His old lady helps him drink water from a straw and just seeing that hurts. This bastard could best any man that came his way. *Son-of-a-fucking-bitch.* "It was empty. Chains said the crew had messaged they were going to be late. Someone suggested we check everything out, scavenge the area and make sure it was secure and no cops waiting for us."

"Who suggested that? Chains?" Torch asks, talking about

Tucker's sergeant-of-arms and the man that was supposed to be in charge of the run.

"Nah. One of the others," Briar says wheezing. I watch as Stephanie rubs his chest while still holding his hand. Her grip on him has her hand white because she's holding on so hard. "We parked up. Sabre and me stuck together—*shit*, how's Sabre?"

"He's alive brother. Better shape than you, but whoever did this beat the ever-loving-fuck out of him," I joke.

Briar's eyes go to me. They take a minute to focus, you can tell, but then he does his best to smile. "They get a hold of you too."

"Nah man. Skull and Torch had to teach me a lesson about women," I joke. Understanding dawns on him and he shakes his head.

"Told you she wasn't for you. *Jailbait*." He chokes out with a wheeze.

I tell him with pride, "She's my old lady."

"*Damn,* how long I been out?"

"Too long."

"Be careful. Tucker didn't do this, but after the shots were fired…" Briar stops taking a breath, his face cringing as if he was in pain and his eyes go cloudy again.

"Who fired shots?" Skull presses.

"Don't," another deep breath, "know who was first it came from the woods. But, my bullet came from one of Tucker's men," he says, and he tries to move his hand to his chest.

"Who shot…are you okay, el hermano?"

"Feels…."

He doesn't get the rest of the words out. Briars head goes straight back as if in pain and his eyes go wide. His entire body shakes to the point the bed rattles. Stephanie starts screaming. Skull is hitting the call button for the nurse. They barely get there before the heart monitor changes from a steady beep to one long continuous sound. The doctors and nurses work, as we fall back around our brother. Keys helps pull Stephanie back who's cries and screams may haunt me for years. Our eyes are glued as they take the crash cart out and prepare Briar.

"Clear!" a doctor yells and they hit him with the paddles. We all hold our breath, but the sound doesn't change. "Charge!" he says again and just a few seconds later. "Clear!" *Again no change.* A repeat of the same, brings the same conclusion. The doctor looks at the clock on the wall, putting his hand on Briar's face, closing his eyes. *Fuck. Fuck. FUCK!* "Time of death—"

I don't hear the time. I don't see anything but my brother lying on the bed in front of me, *gone.* Stephanie breaks free from Keys and collapses on top of Briar, screaming, "*No,*" as if it was torn form her very soul.

"No…." she cries, the sound dragging out as if the word lasted forever, and then a shuddering breath, "Oh, God, no. Not my man. Not my man," she sobs, her whole body shaking.

Fuck. Fuck. FUCK! I've lost my brother. I've lost my friend.

Chapter 51

Bree

"HONEY? ARE YOU okay?" I ask Jax, lamely. He's sitting in our room, staring out the window. We're all on lockdown since Briar's death. Jax has been so quiet, withdrawn really. I don't know how to reach him. He barely eats, he doesn't talk much. If he didn't come to our bed at night and hold me, I would worry that he is done with me. We've been moved to the club, into Jax's old room. I wasn't happy about it, but I wasn't about to argue either. He's going through enough. It took me a complete day to clean and scrub it. Jax promised he hadn't been with a woman in there since it had been cleaned last, and I know he hasn't touched anyone since we got together, but just the idea that something in there might have been left over made me uneasy. I even had one of the prospects get me new sheets. *Better safe than sorry*. Still, I can't wait until the day we get back to the apartment. There, it was just the two of us, and I loved it. Now, I barely speak to him all day. We've been on lockdown for four days, but it feels like a year.

"Fine, Bree," he says, as if I haven't heard that answer each time I've asked it. It's enough to make a woman cry.

"Honey—"

"*Damn it, I said I'm fine*!" he growls, and I'm standing behind him getting ready to put my hands on his shoulders. When he barks at me like that I jump back, holding my hands together instead of putting them on him. I know he's upset about Briar. *All the men are.* Katie and Beth said Skull and Torch are a mess. The only difference is they're holding onto their women. Jax isn't. He keeps pushing me away.

"Okay. Dinner is served in the main kitchen," I tell him, trying again. "You really should eat."

"I'll eat when I get hungry. It's not your job to make sure I eat. We're not married, Bree and you sure as hell aren't my mother."

"What's going on with you?"

"Nothing. Just forget it. Go eat and visit with your family," he mutters.

"I spend all my time with them. I want to be with you," I tell him, and I'm doing my best to keep the tears at bay.

"Well, I don't want to be with you. Understand?" he growls, looking over his shoulder at me. He looks so cold. I can almost feel my heart physically break. I was fooling myself. This is what happens when you love someone and they don't love you. I thought I could be enough, could love him enough, so that this relationship would be good for both of us. What a fool I was. *Maybe I am just a stupid kid.*

"Yeah, I think I got it, finally," I mumble, hating that I feel the sting of tears at the corner of my eyes.

"Bree—"

"I think you've said enough. I'll be out of your hair in a minute."

"What are you doing?"

"Packing."

"Packing? Where the fuck you going to go? We're on lock-down, and I doubt very seriously Skull and Torch want you in their room with their women."

"It's none of your business, is it? You've made it clear you don't want me, I'm sure someone out there will."

"Fuck no. You get your ass back here," he yells, but it's too late. I've given up packing, and I just march outside. I don't want to be around him. I make it to the main room, which is really just a giant bar complete with music, tables, a dance floor, and stripper poles. I've decided these places are designed by men who are really little boys who never grow up. Jax grabs me just as I get there, pulling me back against him. I fight, pulling away trying to get free, but he clamps his arm around me.

"Let me go, *asshole*," I hiss. I'm really tired of everything.

"Bree, damn it! Get back in the room. You can stay there. I'll sleep somewhere else tonight."

His words feel like a kick in the stomach, momentarily robbing me of breath. I thought I was hurt before, but now the hurt is so much more. *Sleep somewhere else?* I think on those words, mostly because right now, I can't do anything else. I can't breathe. Slowly, I turn around on him. I've gone completely still, so maybe that's why Jax lets go. I'm not sure, and I don't really care. I face him, and I hope he can see the pain he's caused, but more than that I hope he can see the anger.

"And just where would you sleep, Jax?" I growl, and I don't do it quietly. It echoes in the room, mostly because the room has gone quiet now.

"Bree mad," I hear Diego say in the background, and my little cousin doesn't even know the half of it.

"It doesn't matter. I'll find somewhere. Just get back in there."

"You'll find somewhere?"

"That's what I said damn it." *Where did that man I was falling for disappear to? The man I gave myself too, the man who claimed me.*

"You can bunk with me honey. I sure have missed having you warm up my bed."

My head turns when I hear that, and it's the woman that was with Keys that day at the picnic. The thought of him sleeping with that cunt-bag makes me sick. This is what he prefers to me?

"Well there you go Jax. You can go climb in bed with your whore and relive all the reasons why they named you Shaft."

"Hey! Who you calling a whore?"

"Three guesses and the first two don't count," I growl turning to face her.

"You can't talk to me like that!" she snaps.

"I'd rather not talk to you at all, you're the one who stuck your big nose in where it doesn't belong."

"Big nose? What are you? Twelve. No wonder Jax is bored with you." Her attempt to insult me is pathetic.

"Big. Nose. It's the only thing bigger than those fake boobs you're carting around."

"My boobs are real honey, and your man's dick has made itself at home over and over in them."

"*Jesus Christ, Denise*!" Jax roars, and what she said brings visions in my head that I do not need, and they're only made worse when he calls her by her name.

I march over to her. I think that shocks her, because for a minute she steps back and seems worried. *She should be*. She's at least two or three inches taller than me, and definitely has about twenty pounds on me, but I'm mad enough to spit nails, so I figure that evens us out.

I grab her by her blonde hair, which could use a good conditioning, and yank hard. She screeches so loud you'd think I was killing her. I'm not—*not yet*.

"Damn it, Bree! *Let her go*!" Jax demands from behind me. I sense him there, and before he can grab me, I turn around, dragging blonde bimbo with me. She's bent down trying to get her hair free, and she's clawing at me. Everyone thinks because

I'm innocent and quiet that I'm not a spitfire. They forget that I had to fight for my life from the earliest days I can remember. Even more than that, they forget that when Pops found me, he made sure I could take care of myself. I wrap my arm around her neck with my other hand, squeezing it tight enough that she can't move as much. Her fingers are scratching into my arm and the movement hurts like hell, but I can take it.

"Damn it, Bree. Let her go, before you get hurt!"

"I'm sorry, were you wanting to make sure I didn't damage her fake boobs so your dick could play?" I stare Jax down as his whore struggles to break free.

"*Fuck*. I'm not worried about her tits."

"You should be, because if I find a pin or a knife I'm going to pop the damn things!" There's laughter around me, but I'm too mad to pay attention to it. Jax's face changes and he looks at me differently, that barely registers over my anger though. I'm seeing nothing but red now.

"She can't breathe, Bree," he stresses, trying to coax me into letting her go.

"Ask me if I care, Jax!"

"Let her go, baby."

"Don't call me baby! You don't have that right anymore. If you want rid of me, at least be a *damn man* and *say it*!"

"I'm no good for you!" he growls.

"What are you talking about?" I cry, and Denise is starting to claw at me again, and it's pissing me off. I change my hold then push her away, hard. I might accidentally forget to let go of her hair so that when she goes sailing the other way, she leaves my hand full of stringy hair with a bad dye job. *Yuck*. I let that nasty shit drop to the floor fast.

"I watched a brother die! I just finished riding in his funeral and toasting him goodbye!"

"I know! I was there, maybe you couldn't tell since you've been ignoring me."

"It could have been me!" he shouts.

My voice softens, but I'm still hurt. "It could have been anyone, but it wasn't."

"You deserve better, Bree. Haven't you seen the hell that Briar's old lady is going through? You deserve better than that. Everyone's right. You deserve better."

"*God*, you're such an idiot."

"Amen a eso!" Skull yells.

"Damn it—"

"No one knows when they're going to die, Jax. I might not wake up in the morning, who the hell knows. We take what we're given. What you don't do is push people who love you away."

"Bree you deserve better," he says, but I can tell I'm getting through to him.

"You bitch! I'm going to kill you!" Denise screams, finally picking herself up off the floor.

"Touch her and you're out of here. I ought to kick you out for talking in front of my babies like you have," Skull growls, and I decide to let him deal with her. I apparently have bigger issues.

"You're right. I deserve a man who has balls enough to live," I tell him, suddenly freaking tired. My eyes want to close and my body wants to curl up in bed.

"Where are you going?"

"To my room, you can sleep with Denise, maybe she'll let you glue her hair back on her head," I tell him, just wanting out of here.

Chapter 52

Jax

"MAYBE WE NEED to fuck you up again," Torch threatens.

I'm standing frozen where Bree left me. My heart feels like it's beating out of my chest. I don't think I've seen her like this. I pictured her as young and naïve, someone I needed to take care of. Tonight, she was all woman and more capable than I have given her credit for. She also made sense. I know she did, but ever since Briar died from that blood clot...ever since we lost him, my brain has been fucked up. I can't get over watching him draw his last breath and the cries of his old lady will haunt me to my fucking grave. I've never been afraid to die. In this life, it happens. Let's face it, ain't a fucker around going to get out of this world still breathing. But, I've never had anything or anyone I'd regret leaving behind. I've never had someone I wanted to protect from hurt before...*until Bree.*

"You two have done enough," Beth tells Skull and Torch as they continue discussing how stupid I am, and I can't even deny that. I do feel stupid. She walks over to me and looks me in the eye. "Are you going to go after her or what?"

"I'm trying to protect her," I tell her, wishing I could make her—*hell, everyone,* understand.

"From what?" Beth asks, and maybe I could have handled her alone but Katie is suddenly there.

"Yeah from what? Because there's no protection from male

stupidity. I ought to know."

"Sweetness don't make me spank that ass," Torch yells out, trying to sound pissed, and failing.

"To do that *snookums*, you'd have to touch me and that doesn't seem to be something you are up to doing lately."

"I'm trying to protect you and the baby!"

"Christo, you could have said anything but that," Skull mutters.

"Seems like you and Shaft both have shit for brains," Katie grumbles.

"You need to go after her," Beth says, still staring at me and her eyes feel like they're peeling back layers that I try to keep hidden. I find myself trying to avoid them.

"Mi cielo, maybe you should leave them alone. Let them work their problems out, si?"

Beth turns on her husband. "If I had someone yell at me, perhaps we wouldn't have gone through so much hell, Skull."

"You were young, and I was estúpido," Skull admits.

"Doesn't that just sound like someone else," Beth says, and that's her style. Katie is more in your face, slap you across the head. I'm used to that shit. Beth? She's scarier. She's logical, she plans her words, and *fuck*, it's hard to argue or fight that. I watch her walk back over to Skull. He pulls her down into his lap, holding her close, and you can tell that in the moment the rest of the world has drifted away for them. It's only the two of them.

"Eres mi mundo," Skull whispers before taking her mouth in a kiss that finally makes me look away from them. *You're my world.* I always thought he was laying it on thick, seducing his woman, but now I know I was stupid. Bree is my world. *My whole world.*

"Don't be a dickhead, like my old man," Katie tells me slapping me on the chest and getting my attention back.

"Did you just call me a dickhead?" Torch growls, and I hear the chair scrape back as he stands up.

"Yeah full of cum and no room for brains," she growls, before looking back at me. "She loves you. Go fix this and make Bree happy, or I swear to God you'll wake up one morning a eunuch," she says and I know her threats aren't empty. I almost want to reach out and protect my dick from her, but instead I walk around her and go after Bree.

"I'm going to paddle your damned ass so hard you won't sit for a week," I hear Torch behind me, and Katie's reply is lost to me, because I open the door to my room and find Bree sobbing on the bed, and now her cries may be the ones that haunt me.

Chapter 53

Jax

"BREE…" I START, but then stop not knowing what else I can say. I rub the back of my neck in aggravation. This is why I haven't done relationships. Women are too damn complicated. Even as I think it, I know it's a lie. I've never done a relationship because there's never been a woman for me besides Bree. I thought life had passed me by. Turns out my woman just hadn't been born yet.

"Go away," she says, the sound muffled by the pillow that she's been crying into.

"Baby, I'm sorry, it's just…"

"I said leave! Go play with your balloon-boobed blow-up doll!"

"We really need to work on your name calling," I half laugh, walking to the bed.

"I got a name for you," she growls yanking her body up to face me as I sit beside her. "Asshole! Because that's what you are, an asshole! And I hate you!" she cries, and she slaps my chest hard, and then must decide it felt good, because she lays into me connecting again and again. I let her get a few good licks in, because *fuck*, I deserve them. Then I carefully grab her hands and hold them by her wrists so she doesn't hurt herself—or me. "I hate you!"

"You told me you loved me," I remind her, hating the tears

in her eyes.

"I lied! I could never love a—"

"An idiot" I fill in for her.

"You are! You're an idiot and I hate you and—"

"*And I love you*," I say softly, meaning it with everything I got left in me.

"You are made for that tramp and—*What* did you say?" She blinks, wiping at her puffy cheeks.

"I said, *I love you*."

She shakes her head. "You don't."

I nod. "I do, baby. I love you."

"You've got a funny way of showing it!" Bree pushes at my chest again.

I grab her in my arms, tempted to shake her, but I tell her again, "Like I said, I'm an idiot." I relax a little when she stops trying to pull out of my hold, her body definitely less tense.

"You hurt me."

"I was scared," I confess.

"Yeah, sure."

"Bree, you're so innocent and beautiful. You're made for a world other than the one I'm in. You deserve better than to be crying at my bedside some day when I draw my last breath."

"We all die, Jax. Eventually, we all do. It's why you should cherish the time we have with each other, so that when the time comes—"

"Bree…" I start but she interrupts me.

"When a time like that comes, you have no regrets, no wasted time, *nothing* but love."

"You make it sound romantic. I was there, Bree. There's nothing fucking romantic about watching my brother die and the woman who adored him crumble into pieces."

"Maybe not on the outside, but would she have hurt any less

if he died in a car wreck? Or a heart attack?"

"That's not the point."

"I think it is. And even if Stephanie hadn't been there, do you think she would have hurt less, or more at having been denied the chance to hold his hand one more time and to tell him she loved him one last time?"

"Fuck," I mutter letting her hands go and rubbing my beard in frustration.

"What?" she asks, studying me.

"Just my luck you're going to be logical like Beth."

"What does that mean?"

"Just that I'm in trouble," I sigh, bringing my hand up to brush along the side of her face. I hold it, staring into her eyes. "I love you, Bree. I know I fucked up and I'm sorry." Her eyes widen.

"I'm not sure I'll get used to that."

"To what?" I rub her back, moving my fingers in soothing circles.

"Hearing you say you love me."

"I'll try to say it more often. Can I kiss you?"

"Since when did you ever ask?"

"Since I hurt you."

"So, you're saying you want to kiss and make it better?" she asks and she's got this grin on her face now that instantly warms me. A sign that she's better. That she's good, and that I haven't been such an ass that I can't make her happy.

"I'm sure as hell am wanting to try," I whisper against her lips before pushing inside and claiming her mouth. I've gone days without her, but it seems like a lifetime. I can taste the salt from her tears against her lips and my heart hurts. I need to make up for each one that dropped. I don't deserve her. I never will, but fuck, if I won't try to earn her love from here on out.

"Jax," she breathes when our lips break apart.

"Yeah, baby?"

"I know just the spot that needs Daddy's kiss," she grins and *motherfucker,* just like that my dick wants to explode. I growl, pushing her back on the bed. She's got me by the balls and she knows it.

And I don't even fucking care.

I love it.

I love her.

Chapter 54

Jax

"YOU LOOK LIKE a man well-satisfied with life," Torch says when Keys and I walk into the garage area. I flip him off, but I don't argue. What can I say? That I have everything a man could want? Bastard already knows that.

"From all the screaming coming from his room last night, I'm surprised the bastard can still walk this morning," K-Rex adds.

"*Suficiente!* Christo this is my niece you are talking about, hijos de puta," Skull mumbles. He looks over at Beast who is staying behind. "Keep them safe, hombre. Then we will discuss your plans." Beast nods, but doesn't talk. There's a look on his face I'm seeing more and more lately, but that's not what's bothering me. It's the fact he's not wearing his cut. I've never seen Beast not wearing it. His club is always emblazed on his back. *Son of a bitch.* It doesn't take a rocket scientist to figure out what his plans are. Beast wants to leave the club. The truth and bitterness of that burns in my gut.

I put it out of my mind as we gun our bikes up and head out. The doctors have Sabre up and alert. He still can't talk, but he's been trying to write on a board. Annie has been able to communicate with him, and he demanded to talk with Skull. He briefed us this morning about what was said. It wasn't nothing we weren't expecting. The ambush was by Tucker's own men.

They're getting ready to overthrow the asshole. They wanted to cause a war just to make him appear weak and to have the war with the Blaze break out again. Basically, his fuck up of a club wanted Skull to take out Tucker and pave the way for them. *Weasels.* That's all the motherfuckers are. Too weak to take what they want and face the war.

They'd rather step back and let others do it for them. Well, they bought themselves a war, just not the one they were suspecting. By the time we leave Tucker's compound today, he's going to have to be out recruiting new members. I hope the bastard is prepared. I know the only reason Skull isn't taking vengeance out on Tucker for being too weak to control his club is Beth. A woman changes things. I couldn't end the motherfucker either, not knowing how much Bree cares about him. I'm sure the same thing holds true for Torch. So, we find ourselves here, riding toward a meeting which will most likely end in a blood bath. Hopefully, all their blood and not our own. We've lost enough to this damned bullshit.

The boys are subdued when we make it to the compound. I stand, stretching out the kinks. It's not a bad ride here, but as sad as it is to admit it, I'm still hurting from the beating Torch and Skull put on me. They might have pulled their punches, but they made sure their point got across. *The hard way.* Skull's watching me stretch and the bastard knows why. *Damn him.* I can almost see amusement on his face, except he, better than anyone knows what we are about to face.

We're parked about a mile from the compound. Skull got a message through to Tucker privately, and hopefully, that means none of his club was forewarned. We'll know pretty damn quick if they were, I guess. My hand goes to the gun on my side. I promised Bree I'd do my best to come back in one piece to her. I hope like hell I can keep that promise.

Skull gives the signal and we fall back in groups when we reach the open clearing that was agreed to. It takes about fifteen minutes for all of us to hit the positions we discussed in the meeting. Skull and K-Rex are in the lead. Torch takes five of the others and hides behind the tree line, that also hides our bikes. Me, Keys, and four others are all behind Skull. It doesn't take long before Tucker and twelve men show up on their bikes. Tucker stops immediately.

Skull and the rest of us have our guns drawn. I don't see the need for this damn show. To me this is another reason Tucker is too fucking old and weak to be running a crew. If it had been me, I'd have blown holes in the bastards who dared to double cross me. Then I would have taken the leader of it all and punished him in front of everyone for weeks. He would be my message. I relayed that information to Skull, but he told me this was the way it was going to go. It's not my place to question my President unless he starts to lead me wrong, and that's just one reason the Devil's Blaze is my home. Skull never has. *Not once.*

"What the fuck is going on here, Skull? What's the meaning of this shit?"

"You and your crew caused me to lose a man I trusted and respected."

"You can't come on our property and ambush us like this. You fuckers won't live to see the sunset," Tucker's Vice President growls. Skull shuts him up with one shot, clear through, right between the eyes.

"Podrías pudrirte en el infierno," Skull says, telling the bastard to rot in hell. Since, according to Sabre, he was the one behind the ambush, I completely agree.

Unfortunately, that's when the others try to get brave and go for their guns. I make note of the ones who don't. There's not very fucking many of them—four by my count and that includes

Tucker and two of those are members that had to be here when he started the damn thing. Whoever takes this club on is going to have shit on his hands for a long while. Torch and his men come out from behind and make sure the other members have been subdued before a firefight can break out. There's something to be said for catching a man without his back being guarded. Still, Tucker giving us the code to the private gate his crew uses got us here.

He finally turns around to face the men who were trying to get him killed, by sticking a knife in his back and not in his heart. I think I see the moment reality hits the traitors. You see it come over their face.

"You motherfucking shit-sacks? You didn't have the balls to get rid of me? You thought you could involve my family? My daughters? Have them be the ones who knifed me in the back?" He walks to the man that Skull shot earlier. That one probably hurts the most, because Tucker thought he could trust him out of all of them. Maybe that's why the old man decided to finally step down. That would be a fucking hard pill to swallow for sure.

"It was your man killed, son. What do you think I should do with them?" he asks Skull.

"It's your club."

"I'm too old for this shit, brother. I'm surrendering to the Devil's Blaze."

The older men, the ones who knew what was happening even seem a little shocked at what's happening. Maybe the old fucker didn't talk things through all the way. We all knew and most of us accepted it. We knew Skull was going to remain the head of our club, he assured us of that. I was surprised Torch agreed to go to the Saints. Maybe he felt he had no choice—"

"Then I appoint my second over your damn club. He'll decide who lives or dies." Skull says, looking way too relaxed. Torch comes around and slaps Skull on the back as he stands beside him.

"You just want rid of me, brother. But, it's not going to be that easy."

"What are you saying?" Tucker growls and this time the old man looks as surprised as the others.

"I don't want the club. My place is with my brother."

"A thorn in my fucking side."

"You'd be lost without me asshole," Torch laughs back at Skull.

"Si. Probably so."

"What the fuck does that mean for the Saints?" Tucker asks, clearly not prepared for what just happened. I have to say it surprised me too. I thought it was a done deal.

"It appears, it's up to my men what happens to the Saints," Skull says calmly. "Does any fucker care what happens to this piece of shit club?"

"Listen now, damn it. This wasn't what we—" Tucker starts to interject, but the men drown him out, all by saying the same thing—no. It's worded differently ranging from *not a damn thing,* to *hell, no.* Yet, the sentiment is the same. With Bree in mind, I don't answer. This club has taken so much of her life, but she loves Tucker, and there are times when she talks about some of the other members enough for me to know she cares about them. So, I remain silent.

"Looks like no one cares if the rest of you draw a fucking breath," Skull says, and Tucker's face gets so red I think the bastard may have a heart attack.

"You son of a bitch! We had a deal! I trusted you to—"

"Wait a minute brother," Torch interrupts Tucker and something is happening here. I may have not been in on the conversation, but I can see it in Torch's and Skull's faces. "I don't really care what happens to the Saints, but my old lady might be a tad upset if I turned my back on her father."

"Si, I could see where Beth might do the same."

"Yep, and I don't know about you, Boss-man, but I like for my woman to be all smiles when I crawl in bed at night."

"Can't argue with that," Skull says, walking around. "It seems we have a problem here," he adds and it might be my imagination, but I think the bastard is looking at me. *Fuck is he going to tell Tucker I'm sticking it to his granddaughter? Shit. Bree will not be happy if I kill him.*

"Seems we do," Torch says.

"No, we don't. I'll remain President of the fucking club and if you lying assholes ever step foot on my property again, I'll—"

"Might want to watch what you say, Tucker. Seeing as how you'll never see your grandkids again if you don't let me on your property," Torch says.

"And I'm feeling offended. I could not worry about what Beth demands and just end you and the rest of your crew now. It is not like I care," Skull answers.

"*Damn,* you're a hard man, brother. But, I have a solution for everyone I think." Torch smiles.

"What is that, hermano?" Skull asks Torch.

"I nominate Shaft to oversee the Chrome Saints."

Motherfucker.

"Si. I think this could work. Shaft is a good man. Can't take a punch worth a shit."

"Well, to be fair he had a baseball bat to the knees right before your punch," Torch defends.

"Eh…maybe so," Skull says, and he's almost grinning.

Me? My heart is hammering in my chest. What the fuck is going on here? What are they doing? Are they serious? They want me to take over my own club? *Motherfucker, a club that is sunk so deep in shit I'd be smelling it for years.*

"No fucking way!" Tucker growls. "I will not accept this! I don't even know this asshole!" he yells and well that pisses me off. I stalk forward, without even realizing it.

"The way I see it gringo. Shaft here is the only way you and your men live to see another day," Skull answers.

"We will fight. I will not accept someone who is not family and has not proven himself fit to lead my crew."

Oh shit. I see the exact moment Skull and Torch are silently congratulating themselves, and I know what the fuckers are up to. The shit-kicker of it all is that it settles on my shoulders, and I don't even mind. This is what Bree would want. *Hell*, if I'm honest, it's even what I might want. The thought of my own crew, of building something to be proud of for me and my brothers, for the sons I could have*…it feels good.*

"Funny you should say that old man," Skull answers, grabbing me by my shoulder. "Meet the man who your granddaughter claimed as hers in the middle of my club last night." I hold my head down. Fucking hell, *I've been played.*

"What the fuck are you talking about? Bree isn't even here! She's in another fucking state."

"But, she's not. Seems she's been shacking up with old Shaft here," he says patting me on the back like he's doing me some big motherfucking favor.

"I'll kill you!" Tucker yells at me, and I swear I can see a blood vessel burst in his eye turning it red. *Shit.*

"Well you might, Tucker. I'm not going to say you can't. But, he outlasted both me and Skull having a wail at him," Torch says.

"Si, and at the same time," Skull adds. "It was mostly impresionar," Skull says, with a grin.

"Mostly?" I ask, my voice hoarse with emotion and thoughts of what is about to happen. Am I really going to agree to take my own club? Fuck it. It's time to lay down the law if I'm going to be. There will be no room for second guessing me. *I won't allow it.*

"Si, you had a few missteps, gilipolla." He laughs.

"You touched my granddaughter! She's a baby!"

"She's not. She's a woman and damn fine one, old man. And listen to me here, she's mine, and I'll *kill* any son of a bitch who tries to take her or touch her. What's mine stays mine."

"She claimed you?" His eyes tighten as he looks me over.

I stand proud. "She says she loves me, fuck if I know how that happened."

"She's obviously loco," Torch says.

"If she is, she takes after her aunts," I grumble back. All the while we're talking Tucker still has his eyes trained on me, and I don't back down.

"I'm going to fight you. It is my right as grandfather and President of this club."

"Wouldn't have it any other way," I tell him, knowing this was coming.

"Why should I trust that you even know how to run this club?" Tucker asks.

"The way I look at it, Tucker, I can't do any worse than you, or that shit for brains Viper did."

I watch as the words hit home as sure any bullet would have.

"What would you do to the men who have betrayed me?" he asks, and *shit*, what is this? Am I applying for the fucking job now?

"I'd have made sure your VP was tied up and strung up out front of the club, and every fucker who helped him would be forced to watch me torture him for days, probably weeks. Then when I felt I had enough fun, I'd let him swallow a bullet and then turn my men loose on the others."

The old man seems more than satisfied with my answer. He takes a step to me.

"Then it seems we have a fight on our hands, Shaft. May the best man win," he says.

Motherfucker. I can't beat him like I normally would, Bree would never forgive me. I can't exactly let him have a cakewalk though. That's the one thought I have before a fist slams me in the face, and I swear I can hear Torch and Skull laughing. *Assholes.* I can't worry about them though, because Tucker's already hitting me again.

Shit this is gonna hurt.

Chapter 55

Bree

"HE'S GOING TO be okay? Right?" I ask Beth for the hundredth time.

"He's fine, Bree. If he wasn't, Skull would have told me.

"Then why are they demanding Beast drive us to Pops? Why couldn't we just see them when they got home?" I question again. I can't keep the panic out of my voice.

"That, I'm not real sure about," Beth admits, and I can see the way she's wringing her hands. *She's worried.*

"Maybe Pops found out you gave your cherry to a man old enough to be your father?" Katie adds helpfully blowing a bubble with her chewing gum. "And he's got Shaft waiting there for you in pieces?"

"Katie!" Beth cries.

"What? It's a distinct possibility." She shrugs.

"Pops wouldn't kill Jax," I tell them wistfully.

"Oh honey," Beth whispers.

"He wouldn't. At least not until he talked to me first. And besides Aunt Katie, Jax is not *that* old."

"He's old enough to have been your sperm donor." She snorts.

"Oh, stop it."

"Hey, I'm not judging, I'm just saying. But, it kind of works if you think about it."

"What are you talking about," Beth asks.

"Well, technically he is donating his sperm to her and *damn,* the whole club heard her calling him *Daddy.*"

Beth laughs, and I hold my head down feeling the color red bloom all over my face. *Shit.*

"They did not!" I argue, but I do it rather weakly because chances are they did. I may not have much experience, but any woman could tell Jax has a magical tongue, even if they were nuns.

"I've been so bad Daddy. Lower Daddy, lower," she moans, imitating my voice, or at least attempting it.

"Shut up," I growl.

Katie eyes me. "No! You shut up," she says. "That shit's gross."

"Oh please. Like you and Torch don't tip the scales over in the kink department."

"Shut up, Beth," Katie grumbles, and I think I can almost see a blush on her face.

"I'll pay good money if all three of you shut up," Beast grumbles.

"Sorry," all three of us answer from the backseats.

"There's some things a man doesn't need to know about the men he hangs out with," he says as he comes to a stop at the gate to Pop's place.

It just takes a minute before the gate is rolled back, and we pull through. My nerves are shot, and in my head I'm imagining the most horrible scenarios that I can come up with. The one thing they all have in common is Shaft being hurt…*or dead.*

"Beast?"

He looks at Beth through thc rearview mirror when she calls his name. The look on his face pulls my attention away from all my worries. He's broken. I've known it forever, and after that day at the picnic he seemed to get worse. Yet, right now he looks so different. It takes me a minute to realize why. *He's not wearing his club cut.*

"Beth," he answers.

"You know we love you, right?"

"You better get out, your old man will be wondering where you are."

She nods in agreement, but the car is filled with sadness. We get out, and I stop by his door.

"You're leaving, aren't you?" I ask him.

"I don't belong here anymore," his voice is rough as he speaks, but resolute.

"Where do you belong?"

"Nowhere and that's the problem. Be good ladybug. Make sure Shaft treats you good."

"Will I see you again?" I ask, not bothering to hide the tremble in my voice.

"I don't know," he says, and he rolls up his window.

End of conversation. I send up a prayer for him. If ever a man needs peace, it's Beast. I catch up with Beth and Katie at the door. They each grab one of my hands and we walk inside.

Please let Jax be okay…

Chapter 56

Jax

"WAS ALL THIS necessary? The damn place was fine before!" Pops growls.

"It is if I'm going to be President of the club," I growl back. "And keep your voice down old man, my head is killing me."

We're sitting in the bar room of the Saint's main room. The men (that we didn't dispose of) along with some of my brothers are cleaning out every room, especially the bedrooms. We're taking everything out and starting over. I'll keep what is salvageable, but *damn*, there hasn't been money put in this shithole in forever. That's only part of my reason though. I want to make sure there aren't any secret entrances, or fucking surprises that might bite me in the ass. The best way I know to do that is search the place from top to bottom. After we secure the main compound I'm going to have to completely redo the fences and security. The electronics equipment looks like something from the damn 1980's. *Hell*, the television monitor actually had rabbit ears and aluminum foil on the back for reception. I would be helping them, except I can barely fucking walk after letting the old geezer beside me wail on me.

"I can't believe my granddaughter would pick a man who can't take a punch."

"Fuck you. I just have a headache. It's nothing to do with the fight. You hit like a girl."

"It was hard enough to knock you on your ass," he says with a laugh taking a drink of his whiskey. I flip him off and he motions his drink at me as if to say cheers. *Jesus.* I think I'm starting to like the bastard.

"Your club is a shit-hole Shaft. Any idea where you're going to start first?" Torch asks, and Pops gives him a dirty look. *Yeah, I'm starting to like him.*

"Men. I'm going to have to rebuild the men for sure. There's four left, and I'm not sure which of those are real fucking trustworthy.

"I'll loan you some prospects till you get on your feet. We're fucking short-handed too, though, so that's the best I can do," Skull says with a sigh. Some things might be settled, but no one knows more than him what the cost has been. Which makes what I'm about to ask shitty, but it's there just the same.

"Been meaning to talk to you about that, Boss."

"Not sure you should be calling me that now amigo." Skull runs a tattooed hand through his dark hair with a smile.

"What would you rather him call you?" Torch asks like the ass he is. "Uncle?"

Skull appears horrified at the thought. "Fuck, no."

"You better be marrying my Breezy, or I'll give you a worse whipping than I already have," Pops growls.

"I already claimed her as my old lady." I smile.

He evil eyes me. "Breezy deserves a wedding."

"I'll be seeing she gets one," I tell him.

"See that you do."

"You want to take him back to the clubhouse?" I ask Skull, a hopeful look on my face, even though I know the bastard will shut me down.

"I'm staying right here and making sure you don't fuck shit up."

"You do get we're doing you a favor here old man?" I grumble, thinking this will be my life every fucking day now.

"You do get that my granddaughter is way too good for you? *Fuck*, she's better than any of us sorry fucks. Same goes with my daughters." The other men nod their heads in agreement along with me. Some things a man can't argue with.

"So, what did you want to ask hermano?"

"I want permission to ask Keys if he'll be my second."

"You trust him?" Pops asks, but I ignore him. I'm busy staring at Skull.

"I expected as much. Si, ask him. I don't imagine he'll say no. The two of you have a strong bond, you need that."

"Like you and me, right Skull?" Torch smirks. The two of them are like daylight and dark. Where Skull is dark and menacing, Torch is airy and funny. A real joker that one, but don't get it twisted, that fucker is mean as they come. Even if you'd never know it looking at those damn t-shirts he wears.

"Fuck off."

"He's crazy about me." Torch laughs.

"And you're just crazy," Pops mutters.

"Jax?" Bree asks from the door, and my attention goes to her. I haven't seen her in two days and except for a quick text to tell her I was okay, we've not spoken. She looks even more gorgeous than I remember. *Fuck*, Pops is right. She is too good for me—so far out of my league it's not even funny.

"Come here, baby," I tell her. *Shit*, I'd already be by her side, but as much as I hate to admit it, I'm so fucking sore I move around like an eighty-year-old man. She hurries to me, only to stop and stare at Pops.

"Breezy. How was Tennessee?"

"I'm guessing you know the answer to that," she says when she's almost in front of me. I reach out and grab her, pulling her to me.

"Jax!" she whispers as if she's embarrassed and maybe she is with her grandfather here. But, when she looks down at my face she gasps. "What happened to you? *Oh my God*! Your poor face!" she cries, moving her hand over the bruises and cuts there.

"I'm okay, baby. It looks worse than it is," I assure her.

"Not hardly. You got the shit kicked out of you, boy," Pops declares proudly.

"He did at that," Torch agrees, as Katie climbs in his lap. Skull doesn't bother to add anything, he's too busy kissing Beth.

"Damn it, Jax. Are you trying to get yourself killed?" Bree mutters, still looking at my latest battle scars.

"I'm fine honey. Your grandfather hits like a girl."

"The fuck you say!"

She turns on the old bastard. "You did this? Pops! How could you?"

"Pretty fucking easy considering Skull and Torch had to be the ones to tell me that some over the hill bastard had laid claim to my granddaughter. A granddaughter, I might add, who was supposed to be safe in the next state over!"

"Watch who you're calling over the hill, old man," I grumble.

"I'll watch when you roll down the other side," he barks back. "Breezy, I expect an explanation."

"You're not getting one," she says, surprising everyone, except maybe me. That's my woman, stubborn and takes no shit. I saw it the night she yanked Denise bald, and I love this side of her.

"I deserve one."

"No. You don't, grandfather. I love you, and I'm grateful to you, but the truth is what's between Jax and me is nobody's business but *ours*. I love him, and he loves me. I'm not giving him up for anyone." *God*, I love her.

"Kids these days show their elders no respect," he mutters. "You're finishing school young lady." His voice stern and fatherly.

"I will Pops," she grins and then looks down at me. "If you don't quit getting your face beat in you're gonna damage those good looks of yours I love."

"You'd love me anyways," I say wincing as I smile.

"I probably would," she agrees.

"Kiss your man," I demand.

"Thought you'd never ask," she grins and then gives me her lips.

Perfection.

Chapter 57

Bree

"FUCK, BABY, I love your ass," Jax groans a second before I feel his fingers bite into my cheeks, kneading it.

"I thought you were sleeping," I whisper, smiling.

"I was. Then I woke up and my woman was lying across my body, her pussy fucking close to my dick, and her ass turned up waiting for me."

"You're warm, and I wanted to be close to you."

"You could have laid down beside me, instead of lying on your stomach across me."

"Are you complaining?"

"Fuck no," he says, and I laugh out loud this time.

"Go back to sleep, Jax. You're supposed to be recovering." In response he pushes my body against him, rubbing me slightly against his hard dick.

"Does it feel like I need to recover?"

"No, but you look like you do," I observe casually.

"Your family keeps trying to beat the shit out of me. Not my fault," I half tease.

"Maybe I'm not worth—*Jax!*" I squeal as he slaps my ass so hard it immediately feels like it's on fire.

"Stopping you from saying something stupid." He rubs the spot he just set on fire.

"That hurts."

"You like it like that." His tongue brushes over his bottom lip, wetting the skin.

"Not without a little foreplay," I pout, not entirely telling the truth.

"Sorry, baby. I'll kiss and make it better," he laughs and bends down to kiss my ass, though it's more like he bites a cheek while undoubtedly leaving a mark, and then lets my skin go with a soft kiss.

"You're crazy."

"Over you. I want my name tattooed on you."

"You do?"

"Fuck yeah. I've been thinking more and more about it. I want it right there," he says, his voice dropping down to that tone he uses when we're loving on each other. I'm looking over my shoulder at him, wanting to see his face. He's gazing intently on the space above my ass. It's the area at the small of my back. His large, inked up hand moves across my skin slowly as if he's seeing something already there. "I want it right here, baby. So, that every time you bend and your shirt rides up, fuckers will see you're mine. *Property of Shaft.*"

"Shaft? Not Jax? Not Daddy's girl?"

"Smart ass. It is a thought," he grins looking at me rubbing his chin. "But no. Jax and Bree that's who we are together, just the two of us."

"And Daddy?" I smirk.

"Something you bring out in me that I've never wanted before, but I sure as fuck ain't going to apologize for it. When you call me Daddy it goes straight to my cock, and I need to fuck you until you're so full of my cum it's running down your legs," he growls, kneading my ass again. His words are so intense, his voice so dark that a shiver of need rolls through my body, and I can feel my thighs wet with need. "Nothing is wrong in bed as long as we're both legal adults and find pleasure in it together, Bree. *Nothing.*"

"So, you're not still hung up on my age?" I question.

"I'll admit I'm going to sleep better once you're out of fucking school."

"A few short weeks away," I singsong.

"Thank God," he groans falling back on the pillow.

"Are you really going to be happy taking over the Saints from Pops?"

"I hadn't planned on it, but the longer I'm here the better it feels. I can make this club into something to be proud of."

"I didn't doubt that for a minute."

"The bigger question here is you," he tells me, his hand moving between my legs before he lets out a groan when his hand comes in contact with my thighs. Guess my secrets out. Not that it was much of a secret. I'm *always* wet around *Jax*.

"Bigger question?" I gasp as I feel his fingers search out my clit. His cock is a hard indention against my stomach and the heat from it warms every part of me.

"Are you going to be happy here? This place doesn't exactly hold great memories for you, s*weetheart.*"

"I'm happy as long as I'm with you," I whimper, spreading my legs to allow his hand more room to move when suddenly, two of his fingers push inside of me. The insides of my thighs tighten against his fist trying to ride it, as his fingers continue to plow through my wetness and thrust into my pussy.

"You certainly feel happy. My baby is all wet, and your poor little clit is throbbing."

"I know," I moan, trying to push myself up so I can ride his hand better.

"Does Daddy's girl need to come?"

"I need fucked," I whimper, already lost to the feelings that only Jax can get from me. I hear his groan, knowing he loves it when I tell him to fuck me. His fingers leave me, and I cry out in despair. *"No! Jax, I need you!"* I beg, my whole body shaking with the loss. In response, he tightens his hands on my legs and pulls my ass toward him.

I'm grappling with my hands trying to help support myself, as he moves my body exactly where he wants me as if I'm light as a feather. That coupled with the manly growl he lets out makes my body quake. *And then his mouth is on me.* My legs are resting awkwardly on him, knees against his shoulders, his hands are digging into my hips as he holds the lower part of my body suspended in the air, and then his face is between my legs. I feel his hot breath first, then his tongue slides along the lips of my pussy, and he hums as he licks the cream I know he's found there.

Jax's face presses inside. Then I feel his tongue move against my clit, teasing it, licking it over and over, and then plunging inside of me. He's fucking me with his face. There's no other way to put it. Pushing against me so hard and eating with so much hunger, I'm already on the verge of coming. His hard cock is leaking pre-cum against my neck, and I push myself up on one arm while wrapping my hand around him. If he's going to play, then I'm going to, too.

I stroke his cock once, then again. I'm rewarded with his groan that vibrates deep inside my pussy as he continues fucking me with his tongue and devouring me. I clamp my thighs so tight against his face, I wonder if he can breathe. His pre-cum is raining down on my hand as I stroke him. He's as close to coming as I am, and I want every drop. I slide my mouth down on him, taking him to the back of my throat. The taste of him explodes inside my mouth. I'm cupping his balls, and I can feel them swell and jerk, making me suck harder, wanting to give him pleasure, but more than that, just wanting *him*.

I feel the first of his cum shoot into my mouth, at the same time his body jerks underneath me. He bites my swollen clit, and it's too much as my climax thunders through me harder than it ever has. It's intense, it's earthshattering, and so raw that I'm scared. I try to jerk away from him, but he doesn't let me. Frustrated, I move my head up and down on his cock, using my mouth to stroke him as he empties himself completely, and I drink him down. He licks me through my climax, using his tongue to slowly bring me down, and just when I think I might survive, he finds my clit again wasting no time bringing me back to my peak. The second orgasm feels like it might destroy me, but I've barely started, and he's moving me again…this time he flips me over lowering me down on his already firm cock.

That's when my lover destroys me. Just like that. My back to Jax's front. His arms wrapped around my waist and breasts, his cock deep inside of me, a second orgasm melting into a third, as his teeth are biting into my shoulder. I see stars and lose myself so that all I feel is him and nothing else exists, that's when I know, that's when I'm absolutely sure. There will never be anyone else in this world for me but Jax. There's no going back.

He owns me, body and soul.

Chapter 58

Jax

New Years Eve

"EXPLAIN AGAIN WHY this has to be done?" Pop's rides my ass.

"Old man, you're wearing on my last nerve. I told you your security sucked. That fence is so fucking weak, I wouldn't be surprised if you couldn't drive through it on a bike."

"You sure are emptying out the bank account. Hope you fucking got a plan to make more green."

"It's covered," I tell him, not adding that most of this shit is coming from my pocket and not the club's. Skull takes care of his men, and *fuck,* I've never had anyone to spend it on but myself, and I sure as hell don't need much. I watch as Bree comes into the room. Her hair is in a messy bun on the top of her head, she's wearing flannel pajamas in peach and green with a gray shirt that says, Sleep Machine. I've seen women dressed and undressed in a hundred different ways, but Bree like this would be my pick hands down. She takes my breath away and it's probably better, because she's not even trying. "Besides, protecting what is important shouldn't have a fucking price tag," I tell the old man.

"You may grow on me yet, boy. You just might," he says, and I can't do anything but shake my head. Bree and I have been here for two weeks now. We spent Christmas here, and I swear if I didn't know better I would have thought at one point the old man cried. Skull and some of the boys came over. Pops had his girls and Bree all here, and there was a big dinner. I gave Bree a diamond engagement ring, and I think it made her grandfather happier than she was. Though she did show me her appreciation when we were alone later that night. There's only one dark spot surrounding any of us right now.

"Any word from Roxy?" Bree asks as she makes it to the table. She leans down to kiss me and her breath is fresh with the taste of toothpaste and woman.

"Not a fucking thing. I'm telling you it's not like Roxanne. She'd always check in and she'd never just leave without letting us know where she's going," Pops reiterates.

"I sent some prospects down there, they didn't find a trace of her," I tell him again, needlessly.

"I'm worried," Bree sighs, sitting down in my lap. I reach down and get a fork full of my omelet to feed her. She rolls her eyes at me, but she eats it.

"You two are disgusting," the old man grumbles. Bree and I just grin.

"Get used to it. It's not about to change," I tell him, and it's not. *Fuck*, if I could keep her in my lap with my hand feeding her all the time, I would.

"What's your plans today, Baby?" I run my hand down her arm, trying to behave in front of the old man.

"I need to run a few errands, including picking up a prescription I had filled. They close early today, so I guess I need to start moving, but it's cold outside. I was putting it off."

"I'll take you."

"That'd be foolish, you have a bunch of stuff to get done here today, and you promised that you would ring in the New Year with me, I don't want anything to get in the way of that. I'll be fine by myself."

"No, honey. I don't know what's going on with Roxanne, but something feels off. Until we know what's going on, I don't want you going anywhere alone." I swallow down my orange juice.

"Jax—"

Pops starts in on her and I chuckle under my breath. "I agree with him girl. You don't need to be gallivanting everywhere alone. You got a man now."

"Really Pops? I would hardly call going to the pharmacy gallivanting, though I'm not sure exactly what that is."

"Quit being smart, Breezy," he chastises her.

"Fine, then get one of the men to take me into town. That way you still get your work done, and you know I'm not alone. Problem solved," Bree tells me. Her face is so frustrated at coming up with a compromise, I have an urge to kiss her. So, I do, brief but hard, and with feeling on her beautiful pale pink lips.

"You're my woman. It's my job to look after you. I don't want to give that privilege to another fucker. It's all *mine*," I practically growl at her, but try to tone it down. The day's young.

"Yeah, I think you're growing on me, boy. I do believe you are," the old man says, slapping me on the back. This time I roll my eyes, but Breezy just curls into my chest with a happy sigh.

"Boss! We got a problem!" Tubby says coming in. Tubs is a prospect that has been with the Saints for a while. At least that's what the old man says. He said he always meant to patch him in, just never got a chance to—which is code for didn't care enough to worry about it. He's working his ass off, and I got a good feeling about the kid. He's probably going to be one of the first men I patch in. He needs some work, especially in the weight room. He's not exactly fit, which is how he got the road name

Tubs, because his stomach didn't leave much room between him and the bars on his bike. But, the kid definitely has promise.

"What the fuck is going on now? I swear I can't see a minute of peace around here," Pops growls.

"He's talking to *me*, old man. I'm the boss here now, you keep forgetting that for some reason."

His eyes narrow like a beady crow on me. "Maybe I could remember it better if you didn't have a glass jaw."

"Fuck you," I grumble, wishing I hadn't let him think he was winning for as long as I did. I have a feeling he's going to ride my ass about that fist fight until one of us draws our last breaths. "What's up, Tubs?" I ask, ignoring Pops, especially when Bree is kissing my neck lightly and holding me close. There's much better things to think about.

"You told us to replace the fence on the private side, that we use as our secondary entrance."

"Yeah, I want the steel enforced that is up to code with the electric ran across the top. We need that shit done before Torch starts installing the cameras for me."

"We found a dead body there. Looked like it had been dumped fresh."

"*Motherfucker.*" I bang my fist on the table.

He wipes his hands on his pants. "What do you want us to do?"

I sigh inwardly. "Let me ride down with you to see if I know who it is, then we'll decide."

"I'll go with you," Pops pipes up, and I figure I'll let him. If this body has some significance, he would know.

"Bree—"

"Go honey. I'll be fine. Just be safe," she says standing up. I give her a quick, heated kiss and we head out.

I hope this isn't a sign of things to come as President of the Saints.

Chapter 59

Jax

"POPS! IT'S ROXY!" one of the older men shouts before we're even out of the SUV. His words bring a chill over my whole body. I'm out of the car and over to the body in no time, but the old man beats me. He hits the ground and pulls her head into his lap. That's the only answer I need to assure me that this is Roxanne. *Fucking hell, what does this mean? How the hell do I tell Bree, this will crush her.*

I lean down to inspect the body, but it doesn't take a doctor or coroner to discover what killed Roxanne. She's got a hole through the back of her head that screams close range shot. Since she's in the woods, close to the compound, I know she's been sent as a message. What I don't fucking know is what that message is.

"I want whoever did this found, and I want them fucking brought down!" Pops growls out, holding Roxanne, even knowing there's nothing that could be done for her now.

"Let's canvas the area, spread out boys. I don't care if you just see a cigarette butt. I want to see it. We need to know who the fuck did this, anything might help."

We spend the next forty minutes going over the place with a fine tooth comb. A few things were out of place, most notably a lighter. It was just one of those cheap disposable ones you buy when you're waiting in the aisle at the checkout lane when the line doesn't seem to be moving. It's there staring at you, so you just grab it. It's plain and bright Kelly-green. It could have been dropped by one of Pop's men before I even come along. *Hell*, it could have been dropped while the men have been working on the fences. Something about it though is bothering me. I can't even say it looks familiar, because it's just a fucking lighter. Still, something in the back of my brain tells me I'm missing something.

I'm palming the lighter in my hand while the boys load up their trucks with the tools they've been using to reinforce the fences with. I'm palming it while Pops insists on carrying Roxanne to the back of a truck and covering her up in a blanket. I'm turning that damn lighter over again and again in my hand, trying to will my brain to sift through my memory and find out exactly why this damn thing is bothering me.

I'm still puzzling on it, as I'm driving and listening to the old man swear vengeance on whoever did this. We drive down the road to a local garage ran by Colton Seiver. He isn't a member, but he does a lot of work for the Saints. He's a tall man, standing well over six foot. He's got dark hair that falls a little too long and a beard. He's covered in ink and he's got the look of a man who has seen hell and survived it. Pops introduced me to him a couple days after I took over. He seems like a good man to know. *Hell*, I'm even hoping I can talk him into joining our ranks.

"Pops, Shaft. What's up?" Colton greets us when we get out of the SUV. He has to figure it's something. Two visits in one week from the club isn't coincidence.

"Someone dumped a body out by our back gate. Figured if anyone saw a vehicle out this far it'd be you."

"Well the road is pretty fucking deserted, one of the tricks of living back on a dead end holler. About the only company I ever get is people needing machine work," he says with a shrug. "You call the cops? *Hell*, seems like every day someone is finding a body in the backwoods of Kentucky. This place surely ain't what it used to be, been thinking I need to move to Florida."

"Yeah, I'm sure there's nothing like that there," Pops growls.

"Well, I figure there may be more what with the gators and shit, but at least I'd have my ass in the sun instead of this fucking cold." He grins.

"So, you haven't seen anyone?" I ask him, bringing the conversation back around.

"There was one little red car, but I've seen it before, so didn't think to tell you guys. Little red Ford Focus. You know Pops, I asked you about it once. Had the dent in the left quarter panel? You told me it was club protected." I look at Pops for confirmation. His head goes down like someone sucker-punched him. His hand visibly shakes as he wipes the top of his head.

"Roxy," he growls. "That's Roxanne's car."

He cups the back of his neck. "It wasn't a woman driving, Pops. It was a man. *Hell*, a kid really."

"What did he look like?" I ask quickly, and the more Colton talks, the more that sinking feeling in my gut intensifies. *Son of a bitch.* I look at the lighter in my hand, and I remember the day I found Bree in town, and that bastard had his hands on her. There was a green lighter on the table. A motherfucking green lighter. "Let's go," I order, already running to the car.

"What the fuck is going on?" Pops asks, winded as he gets inside. He's barely settled before I'm gunning the engine to take off. I see Colton jump in the backseat as we peel out. Good instincts.

"That fucking kid who has been hanging around, Bree. Jeff something. I caught him handling her rough once. He set my alarm bells off then. He thought she was at Roxanne's for

Christmas." My hands grip the wheel tight, white knuckled.

"Fuck. Step on it boy," Pops says, but he doesn't need to. I'm already pushing the fucking thing as hard as it will go. I've got to get to Bree.

She's got to be alright. She has to.

Chapter 60

Bree

JAX HAS BEEN gone for an hour—maybe longer. He's going to be mad, but if I don't go into town then the pharmacy will be closed. My doctor called in my prescription for birth control. We haven't talked about it, but Jax hasn't been wearing a condom. I just started my period so it's not a concern yet, but if I don't get on birth control soon it will be too late. I wouldn't mind it. I would love to have Jax's child, but he's just starting the club, and he has a lot of work to do. Until we have time to discuss it, one of us has to take precautions and it appears that's me. It takes me just a few minutes to do a quick change, grab my keys and head out. Unfortunately, Keys heads me off. *Shit!* Are they back?

"Where do you think you're going?"

"I need to run into town to the pharmacy to pick up some medicine. Are Jax and Pops back too?" I ask, looking around at the other men who are just pulling in, and then driving around the compound to the garage there.

"Nah, they went to check in with the garage down the road. Wanted to see if the owner knew anything," he shares with me. Keys is Jax's right hand man so to speak. I still haven't completely gotten over all the shit he said that one day back at the apartment, but at the same time, I know he was looking out for his brother.

"Oh. Okay then. I won't be gone long. Thirty to forty minutes, tops."

"Whoa, I don't think so," he says, putting his hand around my waist to keep me from moving. I don't like any man other than my own touching me.

"Let go of me. You can't tell me when I can go somewhere and when I can't." I stomp my foot down on the toe of his boot and it doesn't even phase him. *Steel toed boots.*

His brows raise. "So, you're saying Jax said you could leave?"

"Not specifically, but we discussed it. You do realize I'm a grown woman, right?" I scowl.

"Not specifically," he says with a grin testing my patience.

"I really don't like you," I huff.

"I'm real broken up over that. Let's get going, and I'll take you to get your crap," he offers.

"I don't want you to take me into town." I snub him. He's the last person I want to go anywhere with.

He shrugs a shoulder. If he wasn't such an asshole then someday a girl, not me of course, might find him slightly attractive. He has that bossy vibe that only works when it comes from Jax. "Then you aren't going. Simple as that."

"Why don't you like me?" I genuinely want to know what this dude has against me. I haven't done anything for him to not like me. I'm pleasant to be around, pretty to look at, and I make his prez happy. What more could he want?

"Never said I didn't."

"You didn't say you did either." I sigh, he's exhausting.

"Them's the breaks."

"You're kind of a smartass," I tell him trying to weasel away without success.

"You ready to go or not?" he asks still gripping me by my arm. His hold isn't hurting me, but it doesn't feel too good either.

"I'm ready."

"Thank God, I was turning gray." He laughs.

I have no idea how Jax could be best friends with a man like this jerk. I really don't. I'm going to try my best to get along with him, but right now I'd like to punch him in the nut sack. That thought makes me smile a little bit and distracts me until Keys pulls me hard to a stop.

"What—"

"Get behind me. We have company," he barks.

I look around to see a red car pulling into the concrete parking area. The men have been working on the fences and most of them are out behind the main compound so it's wide open. I have a moment of fear, but then I relax.

"That's Roxy's car!" I cry, excited.

"Roxy?" Keys questions.

"Roxanne. She belongs to Pops," I enlighten him smiling at the sight of her car. I've been so worried about her.

He appears almost amused by this news. "I didn't know Pops had an old lady?"

"He doesn't fulltime." I shrug.

"So, she's a club whore?" he asks, and now I can't resist. I punch him in the nut sack. "*Jesus Christ woman*!"

"You deserved it." I growl, pleased that Keys is bent over and groping himself. He looks a little blue in the face when he's trying to talk to me, and I have to admit that makes me happy.

"Breezy!" I freeze, my smile dying as I turn around when I hear my nickname. It's not Roxanne's voice. No. It's Jeff's.

"Jeff? What are you doing here? Where's Roxy?" I'm so confused. Why is he driving her car?

"I need you to come with me, Breezy," he states coolly.

I make a pained face. "What? Why?"

"It's time, Breezy." He's being weird and it gives me that creeped out feeling.

"Time for what? And will you quit calling me that. Only my family calls me that."

"It's time you come where you belong. *With me.*" He takes a step forward.

"You have men all over the place don't you, princess?" Keys mutters, but his face is trained on Jeff. I have a bad feeling it should be.

I smack at him. "Shut up, Keys. I don't know what he's talking about. I barely know him. We hang around the same crowd at school."

"You might need a new crowd," he states the obvious.

"Tell me something I don't know," I smart off.

"*Breezy*!" Jeff calls, bringing my attention back to him.

"Jeff where's Roxanne? Is she with you?" I ask him, walking a few steps closer to him, only to have Keys pull me back.

"Don't go any closer," he growls, and that's when I notice Jeff is holding a gun.

"Jeff? What are you doing with a gun? You don't even shoot. Remember? We went to that rally asking for stiffer gun laws," I remind him.

"Jesus fucking Christ, does Shaft know that shit?" Keys yells at me.

"Can you shut it, we're in a little bit of a jam here in case you haven't noticed," I direct his focus back to Jeff, the crazy guy with the gun.

"We're not in a jam. Your friend here is about to die."

Jeff's voice comes out cocky and so sure, "That's big words for a man who has a gun on him."

"Not the first time. You just drove into the Saint's home turf. Do you really think you're going to get out of this alive? Put the gun down, and I might let you live," Keys warns.

"All I want is Aubree. She goes with me and it's done," Jeff attempts to negotiate.

"I would, but that would make my brother upset, so that's off the table," Keys refuses his demand sounding like the asshole he is.

"You really are an asshole," I mumble, trying to figure out what to do here.

"Just keep him talking till the other men come through. And remind me to rip your man a new one about not having more men."

"It's on his list!" I grumble, taking up for Jax.

"It might have come before taking down the fences."

"Those might have been up if a dead body hadn't been thrown…Wait…Jeff? Where *is* Roxy?"

"I had to take care of her," he grins at me. His eyes dark and hollow.

"Take care of her?" I ask, a sick feeling coming over me. What did you do?"

"She was a bad influence on you Breezy. She's one of the reasons you lied to me and thought it was okay to take up with *that* man."

Was. The body, earlier. Oh God. I nearly crumble to the ground, but Keys speaks to me.

"Keep him talking," he growls.

"*He killed Roxy*," I say the words out loud, but not really to Keys. I'm in shock.

"I had to. Come with me and I'll let your grandfather live," I hear Jeff say and anger floods me.

"You killed Roxy!" I scream, the truth of it hitting me. I want to go charging at him, and I try I get right to him, before Keys catches me.

"*Son of a bitch, woman*!" Keys grunts, yanking me hard. It's too late though…Jeff's gun goes off shooting Keys. He goes down, falling to the ground. I scream and that's when I feel the heated barrel of Jeff's gun push against the side of my head. *I freeze saying a silent prayer that this isn't how it ends.*

Chapter 61

Jax

"FUCK! WE'RE TOO late!" Pops growls, as we pull up a few feet from where that punk is holding a gun to Bree's head. My heart stops in my chest. I can't let something happen to her. *I can't.* This is my fault. I left my compound with a skeleton crew of mostly untrained men to guard not only it, but the only thing important in my life. *Motherfucker*! I just pushed forward without thinking like a club president. *This is all on me.*

"I'll distract him. When you get a clear shot, take it. Do you hear me? But you make sure Bree is safe," I order, my voice thick with emotion. Bree's my world.

"I've got it, but how the fuck do you plan on distracting him?" Pops questions.

"By giving him what he wants, old man. You just make sure Bree stays safe," I tell him getting out of the truck and walking towards the boy who is threatening my woman.

"Looks like you got yourself in a mess, baby doll," I call out, my voice gruff, but not betraying the stress I'm feeling. I don't want her to sense my worry. She needs to know I got this. I got her back, always.

"Jax," Bree gasps, she doesn't turn, but I can see a slight shake in her left leg and it kills me. She has to be scared to death. The fucker turns to look at me, pulling Bree with him. They're standing a little to the side so that he has both me and Keys in sight. His eyes are full of malice.

I look over at Keys. He's down on his stomach. It looks like he's dead, but I notice his hand is out against the concrete. He's pointing three fingers and tapping one of them. Skull had us all trained in old school Morse code. It's something that comes in handy on the battlefield, and most of us guys have served at one time or another. It's also something that comes in handy in the life we lead. Especially, in cases like now. I don't have time to watch him closely, but I get the gist of it. He's just grazed and biding his time. That means he and Pops can take on this asshole. I just need to get Bree clear. *Like that's going to be fucking easy.*

This fucking guy has his hand on my woman and his gun at her temple. He's a shit stain on the bottom of my boot, but that gun he holds is deadly. "Bree will be coming with me. Where she should have always been," he brags.

I keep one eye on him as I look to my woman. She isn't crying, but I can see that she wants to. Her bottom lip trembles, and I never want to see the pained expression painted on her face again. "She doesn't look like she wants to come with you," I tell him like we're discussing the weather.

He shakes his head, moving slightly, but not enough for a clear shot. "She did. She was always *mine*, until you came along and distracted her."

I need him angry, his attention needs to be more focused on me than Bree. "I didn't distract her. *I fucked her.*" I smirk at him.

"Jax, honey, I don't think now's the time," Bree calls outs, her voice calmer than I expected.

"She was a good girl until you came along!" Jeff shuffles and almost loses his grip on her. This will work, it has to.

"What are you most mad at man? That I beat you to that sweet pussy, or that you're not man enough to claim what you want?" I taunt him again.

"Jax, I think it's a good time to tell you that if we survive this, I'm going to *kill* you," Bree stresses the word kill at me. We get through this together and alive, she can do anything she wants to me.

I cock my head to the side with a grin. "It's a serious question, right *Greg*? Which is it?"

"*My name is Jeff!*" he screams at me.

"So, answer the question, Jeff." Just a little bit more, and I know he will take the bait.

"Bree was a good girl. A re-real man respects that, he…he nourishes it," he stutters, revealing that I'm getting to him with my words.

"*A woman like that*? Jeff I got to tell you, a real man sinks his dick so deep in that sweet pussy that he ruins her for other men. *That's what I did.*"

"Stop it! Stop it!" *He's losing it, he'll forget Bree and come straight for me.*

"She'll tell you. Ask her if you don't believe me. She'll tell you I ruined her for *any* other man. *Whatever* you got planned in that fucking head of yours is already over. She's not going to go from a *real man* to a *boy* who couldn't even close the deal."

"*I'll kill you*!"

"I bet you had to go home and nut yourself every day didn't you Jeff?"

"Stop it! Shut up!" he yells, starting to turn his gun my way, but not completely. I need Bree in the clear.

"You hear that baby? Ole' Jeff here was home spanking the monkey while you were begging for more." I grab my crotch and shake my dick to drive my point home.

"Jax—" Bree's eyes are wide as she says my name.

"Jeff? You want to know something about her? Bree, *fuck*

man, she *loves* cock." I laugh.

"I really am going to kill you," Bree says her voice still filled with tears, but she doesn't sound as terrified as she did before.

"She begs me for it. *Every fucking night man.* She begs for more. She can't get enough, and when she sucks my cock? *Jesus Christ*, she takes it—"

"You're lying!" he screams and then turns the gun fully on me. I hear Bree crying, and watch as Keys jumps up, pushing her to the ground, and shielding her with his body. I'm staring at the barrel of a gun, and I expect it to go off any minute. It's happening all at once, but somehow it seems like slow motion. I dive to the ground to give Pops a clear shot. I figure I'm probably going to die, but so will Jeff. *All that really matters is that Bree will be safe.*

In the next second, gunfire rings out. I have my head down, my eyes trained on Bree and Keys. He's lying over top of her, his body lifted up enough so that he can point his gun and he's shooting at Jeff. I hear Pops behind me, and I know he's shooting. I thank my maker that Keys and Bree are down on the ground, or fuck this would be bad, because I doubt Pops is being logical at all right now. That's his granddaughter, and he'll kill anyone who gets in his way. As I'm watching the mayhem, my eyes flash back to the first time I saw sweet Bree, God she was the most beautiful woman I'd ever seen. If this is the last breath I ever take, at least it's with her in my eyes.

The pain I'm waiting for doesn't come, I watch Jeff jerk with each shot he takes. He falls to his knees, then he smacks the concrete, head first. His life gone.

Jesus. I let out the breath I was holding.

"*You, asshole! I can't believe you did that! I thought you were going to die! You were so stupid!*" Bree cries. I've barely pulled myself up before *my woman* comes at me, throwing herself on me, so that we fall back on the ground. Her little hands are pummeling my chest, and she's sobbing. Her words are slurred from the tears and the way her breathing is coming out in gasps.

I let her beat on me for a few minutes, then I wrap my arms around her tight. That's all it takes for her to completely breakdown. She collapses against me, and I just keep holding her, letting my hand stroke against her hair trying to calm her down the best I can, loving that she's back in my arms, safe.

"Shh, baby I got you. You're safe now," I tell her, holding her captive.

"Don't you ever do that to me again," she cries, her entire body shaking, so much my body jerks with her.

"Okay sweetheart," I tell her still holding her close. I'm never letting her go, *not ever.*

"*Jesus*, I never want a woman," Keys mumbles walking over to us.

"Thanks brother," I tell him, searching his face.

"Keys! You're hurt!" Bree yells, as if she's just now realizing it. She gets up going to inspect his wound.

"It's just a scratch. He just grazed me," he shrugs at her.

"We better get you inside and clean it just the same. You don't want an infection," she mutters through her tears, trying to lead Keys toward the compound. That's my girl.

"Hey what about me?" I smother a smile.

"I can't talk to you right now," she mutters refusing to look at me.

"*Why the hell not?*" I growl, getting up.

She waves her hand at me as though I'm a nuisance. "Because you said horrible things about me! In front of everyone! Even my grandfather!"

"What I said wasn't horrible."

"It was!" Her eyes land on me for a brief second before she

turns her attention away.

"And it was not a lie!" I yell, trying to get her to dial her anger down a notch.

"I'm never doing that with you again!"

"Doing what?" I ask her, catching up to her and a reluctant Keys who looks like he's about to burst out laughing. *Hell,* Pops is standing just behind me and that fucker is laughing.

"You know! I'm never touching your cock again." Her eyes smolder, I know deep down she wants me.

"You're lying."

"I am not! You'll be the one to spank the monkey," she mutters giving up on pulling Keys with her and just walking off. I let her go, I'll deal with her attitude in a minute.

"Pops?"

"Yeah, boy?" He steps forward awaiting orders. *Fuck.* I really do like the bastard.

"See to the body."

He squints at me. "Reckon' I will. Too bad we don't have some of those gators Colton was wanting."

"Told you. Florida is where it's at," Colton says. *Shit,* I forgot all about him. I spare him a glance and he's holding a gun too. I wonder how many people Jeff had shooting holes in him? *Not enough, that's for damn sure.*

"Where you going to be while we're doing your dirty work?" Colton asks.

"Proving to my woman she can't live without my dick," I yell overtop of Bree's screaming as I pick her up, throwing her tight little body over my shoulder, then I stomp off toward our bedroom.

I guess being a president does have its perks.

Chapter 62

Bree

"HOW DOES IT feel to be kissing a high school graduate, honey?" I ask Jax as we break apart. I just attended my graduation ceremony, which was really just getting my diploma at the school board by the superintendent. It was even at his office, which is located by the bus garage. Not very fancy, and no big shindig for me. However, after all of the crap with Jeff, having to bury a woman who was like a surrogate mother, and just everything else, I needed simple. Besides, I have plans and this works right along with them.

"I don't know," he says and he's smiling, looking more relaxed than I've ever seen him. "It was pretty hot giving my dick to a schoolgirl." He grins wide showing his pearly whites.

"Pervert," I laugh, shaking my head at him. He joins in and gives me a squeeze while placing a kiss along the inside of my neck and shoulder.

"We better get going baby. Pops is planning a surprise party for you. Don't want to disappoint the old buzzard."

I look up at him, loving the smile he is giving me. "How's it going to be a surprise if you tell me?"

He shakes his head. "Like you didn't know. I swear that man doesn't know the meaning of the word secret."

"Well, last night, when he stood up in the bar and demanded everyone be there tomorrow at three to celebrate with his

Breezy, I did kind of get an idea." I wink.

"He's smooth, that grandfather of yours." He places a quick kiss to the top of my head.

"You like him," I tease.

"He's growing on me—kind of like a wart. Anyways, we better get going. You'll need to change before the party." He looks down at his watch. "It's almost time now."

"You don't like what I'm wearing?" I ask him, trying to hide my grin. We're weaving through the school buses.

"I'm sure what you have under that coat is great, baby. At least judging from those heels." He whistles. "But, I just figured you'd want to get comfortable for the club party."

"You mean you don't want me wearing a dress and showing my legs off."

"Those boys are some horny fuckers," he grumbles, rubbing his beard in irritation. He doesn't tell me not to wear my shorts or dresses, but it sure does aggravate him. Something I'm learning to use against him the last few days. I've learned the right outfit will get me carried to my room and definitely make Jax's commanding '*Daddy*' side come out. At first, that made me a little uncomfortable, but I can't lie. I find it hot as hell. It feels like power. I can make this big, bad alpha-male lose it—which only seems right since he does the same to me.

I shrug. "I think my outfit is fine for the party."

"If you say it is, I'll live with it. But, let's keep moving, or the party will be over before we get there," he urges, and I can tell by the way his face is tight, he's doing his best not to look at me. He wants to demand I wear something else. Probably sweats and no makeup. The thought makes me giggle. "I ought to spank your ass. I think you love torturing me."

"You're overreacting," I tell him—totally lying. "Here, I'll show you. Hold my diploma." I hand him the thick blue cover the diploma is encased in, and then undo a couple of buttons. I don't have many open. Just the top ones. I know when I unbutton those, all he is getting is glimpses of white from my shirt and cleavage.

"Let's just forget it. Show me when we get home." He attempts to hand my diploma back.

"But, I want to show you now, honey." I grin and then remove the belt which has the coat cinched around me. I let it fall to the ground, because after all, I don't really care about it.

"*Motherfucker*," Jax growls, the sound sending flutters of excitement through me. His throat bobs as he swallows hard, taking me in. Jax's eyes are dark and heated, full of desire. I'm pretty sure his mouth is watering.

"Does that mean you like?" I boldly ask, watching as his hand clenches in a fist.

I wonder if I can order a new diploma cause this one might not be holding up so well.

Chapter 63

Jax

BREE IS STANDING in the middle of a fucking parking lot full of buses wearing a barely-buttoned white top, with no bra, and the shortest plaid skirt I've ever seen in my life. I wondered this morning why she plaited her hair. She complains that it makes her look too young, but I've always loved it. I thought maybe she wore it that way for me. Now, I know she really did.

I just stare at her, unable to move. What else can a man do when he's given his hottest fucking fantasy in real life. Bree squirms, and despite what she's doing, and how bold she's had to be, there's a fine blush blooming on her face. It's cold outside, and I can see fine snowflakes flying through the air, even though there's nothing on the ground. I should be worried about Bree catching the flu. Instead, I find myself dropping her things to the ground and growling like the animal she turns me into. She turns around, the little skirt spinning up in the air giving me a glimpse of the barely-there white lace thong she's wearing. Even when the skirt falls back in place, her ass cheeks still hang out of the back of it. *Better than my dream.*

"Is it too short?" she asks, with a sassy little grin when she looks over her shoulder. I walk the two steps it takes to get to her. My hands instantly land on each of her ass cheeks, grabbing them and manipulating her thick globes. So fucking soft and sexy.

"You're trying to fuck with me, Bree?" I growl biting into her shoulder. I'm rewarded by her breathy gasp and the way her body shakes in reaction. Her ass pushes back against me. Always so fucking eager for me.

"I've been bad," she whispers, and *fuck,* I can feel my cock already dripping cum.

"Do you know what I do to bad girls, baby?"

"You punish them?" she gasps when I move one of my hands under her shirt and around her side, not stopping until I'm palming her tit. Her nipple is so hard it's stabbing into my hand, demanding attention. I'm being so rough with her, I know that I'm going to leave bruises on her body. *Fuck*, she'll be lucky if I don't draw blood. I tug on her nipple and twist it so hard my fingers push against her shirt, and I feel the material give.

"Do you need to be punished?" I ask against her ear, letting my beard scrape against the tender skin on her neck.

"Yes. Jax! Oh God," she whispers and the need in her voice is like barbed wire wrapping around me, cutting into my skin and leaving me defenseless.

I spank her ass in one swift slap, knowing the chill from the winter air and the heat of my touch is giving her a cold burn. "What is it baby?" I ask her, already knowing the answer. I snap the thin band of her thong, pushing the flimsy material out of the way, my fingers instantly find her pussy. Hot, wet, throbbing desire hits my fingers at first touch. "You're so wet, you little fucking tease. Were you wet when you were in class?" I demand, allowing the fantasy to take over as I thrust two fingers deep inside her pussy.

"Yes! I needed to come so bad. I even touched myself under the desk, wishing it was you touching me." *Jesus Christ.*

"I'm going to fuck you out here where anyone can see us, Bree and you're going to give me this pussy aren't you?"

"Yes! It's all yours... *Daddy.*" If it's possible for your brain to turn to mush in an instant, I'm there. My entire body feels like a livewire. I groan, taking my dick out. I'm so damned hard it's hard to get the zipper down. She's killing me. I wish like fuck I could last longer, but there's *no way*, and if someone else saw her like this I'd have to kill them. So, quick, hard, and fast it is.

I slide my cock against her pussy, the sweet juice there coating me, feeling so fucking good that I almost come right then. I use my hand to help guide the head right against her clit, sliding against it with pressure. I can feel her muscles tighten, trying to ride me and then spasm around my shaft. It feels so fucking good I mourn once again that there's no time to enjoy it.

"Brace yourself on the bus, baby girl. This is going to be hard and fast. I can't hold back," I warn her. I hear her hands slap against the bus at the exact moment I thrust home. She takes every inch of my dick, as I sink balls deep inside of her. For a minute, all I can do is stay deep inside of her and groan as her pussy welcomes me home. *Mine first and motherfucking last.* No one else will get this from her. *I'd kill them first.*

I grab her sides and then begin pulling out. I don't even manage half a stroke before I'm slamming back inside of her. She's right there with me though. Thrusting back against me and begging for more. Over and over I pound her body, too far gone to speak, too far gone for any of the words that I should give her. The only thing on my brain is one word and it's repeated over and over with each thrust.

Mine.

Her orgasm rips through her as she takes my cock. Her entire body tightening and then combusting with pleasure. She does her best to take me with her. I can't let her though. Not until she's finished. Not until she's endured all of the pleasure I can give her.

"Jax," she moans so loud it echoes around us. "Oh God, oh God, oh God. It's so good. It's never been so good," she whimpers and she's right. *So fucking right.* I keep stroking, following the signs of her body and slowing down as she rides out the last waves. The minute I can, I pull out of her and she cries out, begging me to come back inside of her.

"You stand right there and don't move," I growl, nothing gentle left inside of me. I hold the back of her tiny-as-fuck skirt up, exposing her ass. Then I use my free hand to stroke my cock. It doesn't take but two strokes, I'm that far gone. I aim as my cum jets across her ass, painting her with it. Painting her with my seed.

"Mine!" I growl as I come so hard my balls hurt.

"I'm all yours," she whispers. "I'm all yours, *Daddy.*"

I kiss the back of her neck in reward, not bothering to put my dick up because my hand is too busy rubbing my cum into her sweet ass.

"I need to get you in the car before you get cold," I whisper against her skin, wishing we could stay just like this.

"Take me home, Jax and love me" she tells me, her tone soft, dreamy. I reach down and zip up my still hard cock before grabbing her diploma and coat, and then I pull her up in my arms carrying her to the car.

"Always baby. Always," I tell her and that's a vow. There will never be a time when I won't love Bree.

She's my world.

Epilogue

Jax

One Year Later

I COME AWAKE with a start. I lie there for a minute trying to determine exactly what it was that disturbed me. I reach over to pull Bree into me, my arms are way too empty. I rise up when I discover she's not there. My eyes search around the room immediately, my heartrate accelerating. Everything settles back into place and calmness hits me when I see her in the pale light from the lamp on the dresser. She's in the corner of the room where we set up the baby's crib. Next week we move into our new home where the baby will have her own room. Bree has spent months making sure everything is perfect; doing the room in a mixture of daisies in pinks, whites, yellows, and greens.

"How's our little girl?" I ask, my voice hoarse with emotion.

"Hungry," Bree whispers, the largest smile on her face.

I thought I loved her a year ago. As I watched her grow round with my child, felt how deep she loves me, how deeply she loves our daughter…And now, since little Roxy's birth, I've watched her become a mother, that love I felt has grown into so much more than love, it's something much larger. There are no words for what I feel for her. I cross the room, joining the two of them. My finger brushes across the baby's cheek as she suckles at Bree's breast.

"I don't blame her. If that's where I got my food, I'd always be hungry," I tell her, and like always, she blushes deeply.

"Isn't she beautiful?" She smiles up at me, pride written all over her face.

"Gorgeous, just like her momma," I tell her and it's the simple truth. When she smiles that cute baby-smile, she looks just like Bree. She even has this beautiful cap full of soft blonde almost white baby hair. Every time I look at her, she takes my breath away—*just like her mom.*

"Smooth talker," she gushes, cooing at our daughter.

"Just honest." I lean down and kiss her forehead.

"You better go back to sleep, honey. You have a busy day tomorrow," she tells me while fixing her gown once the baby finishes eating.

"Let me rock her, baby. I want to spend time with our girl." I never thought I'd be a father. *Hell*, never thought I'd be much of anything, until Bree. She changed that. *She changed me.*

"But, you have to get up early. You and Pops have to be at the house at five in the morning to go over the final details of the swimming pool. The guy will be there and—"

"Shh, baby. I'll be fine. I just want to spend time with my beautiful daughter. You go get in bed, and I'll join you in a bit."

"Stubborn man. You hardly ever let me take care of you." She leans up slightly meeting my lips.

"You can take care of me when I get back in bed." I grin.

"She might hear us!"

"You can bite into the pillow." I wink as she hands me the baby, and I take her place in the rocking chair.

"You're horrible," she whispers, leaning down to kiss Roxy's head and then kisses me too. Her fingers brush through my hair. "Do you need anything?"

"No, baby. I got everything a man could want," I tell her and smile when she gets that dreamy look on her face.

It's the complete truth. There's not another thing in the world I could want more than what I have right here in this room.

The End.

Turn the page to read a bonus chapter featuring Beast…the main character in my next book:

Learning to Breathe.

Beast

I'M RUBBING MY hand under my neck. The scarred skin underneath is itching today. After all this time you would think that would stop, especially since the areas I'm burned the most are pretty much dead and little to no feeling is there. Cauterized. Burned and sealed closed. That's me. That's me to a fucking tee. I stare into the mirror. I used to have dark blonde hair, but after the burns they shaved my hair and when it came back, it's more deep brown. It looks like a damned jungle now. I can't remember the last time I had it cut and brushing it hasn't been on my fucking mind much. Showers that last over four minutes are rare. Get in. Get out. I don't want to see my body. See, touch or feel.

I've spent my whole life being unafraid, but since that one night when I lost everything I've been nothing but a fucking coward. The beard, the hair, the ink I keep adding over my body to hide the burns, all of it is a way to hide. Nothing helps. I thought once, I could live among my brothers in this tight circle and learn to be normal. The incident with Lucy is proof that it won't happen. The men liked to joke, thinking I was sweet on her. Maybe I was. She seemed the complete opposite of Jan. Why I thought she could see beyond what is now staring back at me is beyond me. That moment was a reminder. A reminder of what I am.

A monster.

And monsters do much better on their own. I haven't worn my club cut in a month. I wanted to make sure Bree was settled and the club was out of danger. Shaft will do good as the new President of the Chrome Saints and the bond with him and Skull will make things more secure for everyone. My debt to the brothers is done. It's been done for a long time. Personal loyalty kept me here. I've been here too fucking long.

"You're leaving," Skull says from my door. I jerk my gaze from the man in the mirror to the man who has been family. The man it hurts me to look at. The man whose war cost me the only thing I ever cared about.

"I'm leaving."

"This is your home, hermano."

"It's not." I want him to leave. I need him to be gone. I've kept everything hid from him, from everyone. But the temptation is there to kill him. To choke the life from this man. Would it make me feel better? Could anything?

"Lo entiendo," he says, leaning against the door. That's almost more than I can take. He understands? How the fuck could he understand? He understands nothing.

"You don't. Pray you never will. I'll be gone in the morning," I tell him and the anger bleeds through. I know he can hear it. Maybe he can even feel it. It's vibrating inside of me.

"We want you to stay. We're your family."

I don't answer that. He's not family. He's the reason I have no family.

"Beast…"

"You wake up every morning and see your children. You hold them, you touch them, you plan your days with them. I wake up every morning to nothing. I see you with your family. Torch with his and I hate you. I. Hate. You."

Can't get any plainer than that. Maybe he will understand now. When he was in war with his wife's family, they lashed out and their bomb robbed my child of life. My beautiful Annabelle is just a memory now. A memory that haunts me. A memory that cuts me from the inside out with every breath I take. The scars on my body are a reminder. A reminder of what I lost. A reminder that I failed. I didn't rescue her from the burning car. A reminder that I'm a monster…

"Where are you going?" Skull asks, resigned. Yeah. He gets it…finally.

"Don't know. Don't care." Just fucking away.

"The club owns property…"

"I'm not part of the club." Not anymore.

It's ten acres on top of Whittler's Mountain in North Carolina. There's no house there, but there is a barn at the base of mountain with a loft that could work to stay in. You could…"

"I'm not part of the club," I repeat, no matter how appealing it sounds. Ten acres would be enough to hide in. To let the animal that is devouring me find quiet.

"It would be yours free. The club would have no claim to it."

I turn to look at him, wondering what the catch is. There's something, because I can tell by his voice and the way he's looking at me, there's something he's not saying.

"What?" I ask, waiting.

"Pistol's sister…"

"No."

"She lives…close to there."

"Not my problem."

"Si. But you could satisfy my curiosity and make sure she's there."

"Why? I don't give a damn. Not sure why you do either."

"Not sure why I do to be honest, hermano. But if you satisfy the wanderings of an old man, then I'll give you the land. Free and outright," Skull says and the promise of that alone is enough to make me stop. Ten acres. Privacy. Alone.

"If I go. I'm not reporting in. I'll take a picture and tell you if she's breathing. That's it, and no one bothers me. I move to that mountain I shoot first and never ask questions, I don't care what cut they are or aren't wearing."

My voice cracks. Another reminder. The burns bothered my vocal chords, the burns on my neck run deep. This is why I don't talk. One of the reasons why. Skull is watching me and I don't know what he's looking for, but he finally nods his head in agreement. He finally leaves and I'm left standing in the room again with nothing but my mirror to stare back at me.

I punch my fist into it, knocking it from the wall. I watch it fall landing among pieces of shattered glass. It didn't make me feel any better but the blood on my fist at least calms me. Then I walk out the door, leaving my cut behind. Leaving everything and everyone behind.

Just…*leaving.*

Other Available Titles by Jordan

Savage Brothers MC:

Breaking Dragon

Saving Dancer

Loving Nicole

Claiming Crusher

Trusting Bull

Devil's Blaze MC **

Captured

Burned

Released

Shafted

Lucas Brothers Series

Perfect Stroke

Raging Heart On

Works Written Under the Pen Name
Baylee Rose

Unlawful Seizure

Unjustified Demands

** Only series available on all markets at this time.

Links

Want to keep up on all the latest happenings? Here's my social media links! Make sure you sign up for my newsletter. I give things away there and you get to see things before others!

Newsletter:
eepurl.com/barBKv

Facebook Page:
facebook.com/JordanMarieAuthor

Twitter:
twitter.com/Author_JordanM

Webpage:
jordanmarieromance.com

Made in the USA
Middletown, DE
08 August 2017